This Book is a Gift

MAKING THE
HOOK-UP

EDGY SEX WITH SOUL

EDITED BY
COLE RILEY

CLEIS
PRESS

Published in the United States by Cleis Press Inc., 2246 Sixth St., Berkeley, California 94710.

Printed in the United States.
Cover design: Scott Idleman
Cover photograph: Purestock
Text design: Frank Wiedemann
Cleis Press logo art: Juana Alicia
First Edition.
10 9 8 7 6 5 4 3 2 1

ISBN: 978-1-57344-383-8

A special acknowledgment for Peter Wolf and Dian Hanson, who ushered me into the world of erotica and temptation with the late **Oui** *Magazine long ago.*

Also, special props to the late Ray Locke, editor supreme, who published some of my earliest books when I was learning my craft.

Contents

I INTRODUCTION

M y quest to create this anthology stems from a conversation I had some years ago with Calvin Herndon, author of the bestselling *Sex and Racism in America,* who told me, shortly before I attempted my first erotic story: "When Black people are allowed to indulge the usual sins, the customary fetishes, and all the regular vices humans are permitted, then they will have achieved total sexual citizenship. Otherwise, they will remain trapped in the usual stale stereotypes and labels the world has assigned to us."

I never forgot that statement. With this collection, I sought to expand and broaden the psychological and sexual terrain of the Black community. The reflection of the Black sexual being, as Professor Herndon added, should be just as creative and innovative as the soulful simmer of singer Nina Simone, the barely concealed bite of bluesman John Lee Hooker or the electrified muted moans of jazz trumpeter Miles Davis. As sexual beings, our people should be able to reflect joy, pleasure and other blissful emotions in their lives besides rage and bitterness. It's there in our music, our walk, our sense of fashion, our art, our literature, everything: that hip element of sexy soul.

When I sent out the call for submissions, I noted that I was "looking for edgy, stereotype-busting erotic stories with sizzle and soul.... No baby daddies. No tireless studs with anacondas between their legs. No hotties or chickenheads with 'motor-driven coozes.'"

The stories poured in from all over the world, sexual yarns that were not about the Other or the Outsider, but people of color redefined and redeemed in sensual terms. Writers took risks, embracing themes of tolerance, acceptance and worth, as if the erotic world wanted to be rid of unpleasant generalizations and sexual bugaboos and just get on with the natural business of living and loving.

These stories feature lovers and partners on a wide range of emotional and sensual adventures. The characters retain their dignity while communicating with and even submitting to their partners' feelings and needs.

These stories show lovers and partners going for it all despite the reality that they may not get much in return, that circumstances may lead to separation. That's what I like about these tales. They insist that lovers and partners reach out again and again to move beyond the loneliness, isolation and boredom. As they take risks and make substantial changes in their lives, they sometimes find intimacy that promotes healing.

You will find both old friends and new faces in this tribute to the diversity of our fantasies and the potency of provocative sexuality in all of its many forms. Tenille Brown's "Lonnie's Licks," has playful fun with the concept of addictive behavior. Monica Elaine's "Got Milk?" combines both the erotic and screwball comedy. Preston Allen's "Three Kisses," features a casino setting and a pair of devious, horny individuals trying to outsmart each other with raw talk, big cash and a trio of sumptuous kisses. British writer Leone Ross pens a mellow yarn of fantasy and flesh in "When the River," where things have a way of going awry. A very real river is the focal point where the erotic past is reclaimed in the present in R. Gay's thoughtful "Strangers in the Water."

Zetta Brown tells of a juror named Number Nine with good reason in "Hung," in which a single woman alleviates the tedium of civic duty with steamy activity. In "For Nita," Jolie du Pre, editor of *Swing*, tracks the blossoming of a formerly meek woman who flees an abusive marriage and recaptures her sexual self through the ministrations of not one, but two horny men at once in a fantasy come true.

The nature of a fetish life is what concerns Shakir Rashaan in "Welcome Home," a story of a lusty Master embraced by two submissive women after being on the road. If it's potent romantic love you want, a trio of stories, Garnell Wallace's "Sex and Chocolate," Zaji's "Lights on a Cave Wall" and Asha French's "All Day" provide warm kisses, overflowing hearts and glowing embraces. Veteran erotic writer Shane Allison contributes a raunchy encounter between two previously unacquainted moviegoers facilitated by a convenient leather jacket in "Dangerous Comfort."

Any sexual experience expands our consciousness, especially when unrestricted by money, class or custom. Kweli Walker, Fiona Zedde, Deepbronze, Reginald Harris and Jolene Hui explore those areas outside of the classic themes of lust and desire with skill and imagination.

In *Making the Hook-Up,* you are invited to fantasize, dream, think and imagine yourself in each story. The stories tell some basic truths about us: how we live and how we love. Enjoy—and put your soul into it!

Cole Riley
New York City

THREE KISSES

Preston Allen

Docta Love had it bad for this little PR dealer he met up at the Indian casino, and when Docta Love had it bad, Docta Love hadda get his medicine.

Got up that morning, took his customized van to the Handy-Wash, had 'em do the Deluxe Super Duper Special on it—$89.99 plus another $39.99 for the buff and wax.

Motored up to the Indians, parked in the Self Park (another $15.99). Strolled inside. Solid gold swinging on his neck and blinking on his fingers. Looking big and fine in his trademark black Stetson, black polo to show off his tight biceps, and black droop-hip jeans that hung just right on his lean hips to show off his six-pack, his long, strong thighs.

Walked right up to the floor man and slid him fifty. "What she dealing tonight?"

The floor man laughed as the fifty disappeared. "Texas Hold 'em."

"Then that's what I'm playing."

"There's a long line ahead of you," the floor man informed him. Another fifty appeared, another fifty disappeared, as the floor man nodded. "But I'm sure I can fit you in."

The place was crowded tonight. Gamblers on top of gamblers crowding the machines for a chance to lose. Gamblers on top of gamblers waiting for seats at the poker tables.

Docta Love striding past all of them, passing through the velvet ropes as angry heads turned, angry comments hurled under and over angry breaths. Taking the one empty seat at her table, the seat right next to her luscious, lickable Thank-You-Jesus thighs.

Popping his gum at her in greeting. Giving her that Docta Love smile. Perfect white teeth. Handsome broad-nosed black man with a cleft chin and double dimples.

The PR dealer smiled back at him, nodding her head like, *You again? Shit, you can try as hard as you like, brother, you ain't getting none of this.*

But Docta Love had it bad, and Docta Love had a plan.

She dealt him 2-3. He smiled. Folded.

She dealt him 7-3. He smiled. Folded.

She dealt him 4-6. He smiled. Folded.

She dealt him 4-9. He smiled. Folded.

She snorted, "You ain't gonna play no cards tonight?"

She had that chiseled PR face, with sharp cheeks, the almost square jaw, and the raven black hair pulled back so tight on her head that her eyebrows lifted like McDonald's golden arches.

"I'll play..." he said deliberately slow, eyeing her swollen bosom, wondering fake or real, fake or real, fake or real, "...soon as you give me some cards, dealer lady."

She dealt him AK, big slick, suited. He smiled. Held it. Called it. Raised it. Reraised it. Raised it all in. Won the pot. A big pot. $190.99. Did the quick math. He was ahead for the night despite the car wash and the greased palms.

He gave her a nice tip. $190.

Kept the .99 for himself.

She liked that. You could see it from her smile. She liked that a lot. But she could also smell the trap. She closed up shop. Gave some kinda signal to her boss. Her shift, she suddenly announced, was over. She got transferred to another table.

He watched her sexy little walk as she carried her dealer's tray of chips and cards to the next table. Pretty little thing. Thick delicious lips. Her little button nose almost a white girl's nose, but for the small gentle wings that screamed Africa. Her skin, about two shades lighter than his, screaming Africa too. She couldn't be no older than twenty-three, twenty-four. Her booty singing *swish swish* as it swung in those tight dealer tuxedo pants with the velvet seams. Lord, it looked good. He watched until she looked back as he knew she would. Her eyes smiling like, *I told you you weren't gonna get none, brother. Thanks for the money. How you like them apples?*

He liked them apples a whole lot. Liked that ass, too.

He called the floor man over. Whispered in his ear, "Why can't my love and me be together?"

A hundred appeared, a hundred disappeared, as the floor man said, "I'm sure it can be arranged."

Three minutes later, Docta Love was transferred to her new table, smiling up into her pretty brown-skinned face, his seat right next to her lovely lovable Thank-You-Jesus thighs.

She dealt him 2-9. He smiled. Folded.

She dealt him 4-8. He smiled. Folded.

She dealt him A-A. He smiled. Held it. Called it. Raised it. Reraised it. Raised it all in. Won the pot. Another big pot. $294.43.

Gave her a nice tip. $294.

Kept the .43 for himself.

Oh, she liked that. You could see from her smile. She liked that a whole lot.

She fell into the trap.

An hour later, she was dealing and smiling and talking with him about things a virtuous woman with a good husband and happy children at home should not be talking about—bra size 44DD, all natural just like her mama's; virginity, lost it when she was fifteen, but regretted it ever since; orgasm, always from oral sex, almost never from the penis, unless it is a really big penis; swallowed, only once, didn't like it; anal, too painful, does it only to make her husband happy; cheated, no, never cheated on her husband, well, never with a man.

And he whispered, "I ain't kidding around. You do it for me, baby. I been loving you ever since I first laid eyes on you."

"But I have a husband."

"It's too late for that. I'm too far gone, girl. Look what you done did to me. I got a nice clean van waiting outside."

"It don't make no difference to me."

"Your husband don't make no difference to me."

"He does to me. I'm an honorable woman."

He sighed. Those tits were honorable. That ass—that ass was honorable. He laid his cards out on the table. Or at least he pretended to. "And I am an honorable man. My intentions are honorable. I think what happened was you misunderstood me. It ain't what you think it is. I don't want nothing from you, dealer lady, but a little kiss."

She replied, laughingly, "But I can't kiss you. I'm married."

Docta Love answered, "But what if it was a business transaction?"

"I ain't no ho," she rebuked him.

He put up his hands. "You misunderstanding me again. What

if the kiss was like part of an arrangement to fix something in your house? You and your husband so young. Young people always need money."

She shook her head. "We both have jobs. He is a police officer. We got enough money to fix whatever breaks in our house."

Docta Love splayed his fingers on the table so she could get a better look at his expensive golden rings. Compared to the cheap bauble she wore on her wedding finger. Hubby loved booty, but he was not, apparently, a wealthy man. "You tryin' to tell me there ain't nothing in your house need fixin'? So young. How many kids did you say you got?"

"Two."

"Two young people with two kids...ya'll live at home with your parents?"

"We have our own house."

"Two kids and a mortgage. My, my, my."

"And we can take care of it."

"I can too."

"Good for you."

"You know how much money I won last year?"

"How much?"

He leaned in and whispered the obscene sum into her ear. He was slain by the whiff of perfume. Her soft skin. He whispered it slow.

"Wow," she said. She was thoroughly impressed. Three hundred thousand dollars ain't no joke.

"You smell nice," he said.

"Thanks," she said.

"You look damned good too."

He leaned back in his seat, let her check him out real good. Long, strong, lean, and sexy. He looked damned good too.

She dealt a dozen more hands. Even when he got good cards,

he folded them. Just kept looking at her. Making his cheeks dimple. She was thinking it through.

A half hour later, he folded another hand, and she said. "To be perfectly honest, we have a bathroom that needs remodeling."

He said, "Done deal."

"But I haven't told you how much it costs."

He grinned, displaying those perfect, perfectly white teeth. "Money don't mean shit to me."

"Forty-five hundred."

"Whatever." He didn't even blink at the figure, but then he leaned close to her face. "Now let me tell you how we gon' do this. While you had me sittin' here, playin' me with this little waiting game, I been thinkin' it through. The kinda money I'm offering you is worth more than one kiss. One kiss ain't enough. I gotta have three."

The dealer nodded her head. Three kisses. Okay fine.

Then Docta Love added, "Three kisses across three nights."

Three nights? The dealer, missing the sly smile playing on Docta Love's lips, considered the expansion but another trivial amendment and she quickly agreed to it.

"Deal?" said Docta Love.

"Deal," the dealer answered. "Three kisses across three nights, and I want the money in cash."

Having sealed the deal, Docta Love laughed, folded a losing hand, and got up to leave. He flipped her $500 in chips as a parting tip and strode out of the noisy, crowded casino.

The dealer was thinking, *Well, it's not so bad. It's only kissing. And at least now we will get our bathroom remodeled the way we like.*

And Docta Love left the casino thinking, *44DD, my favorite size.*

Naturally, the kisses were to take place in the parking lot

of the casino in Docta Love's hooked-up customized van, out of sight of management because a dealer, of course, would be immediately fired if she got caught kissing gamblers on casino property.

On the night of the first kiss, the beautiful, top-heavy, and happily married dealer took her ten-minute break outside in the parking lot.

"To smoke a cigarette," she explained to her friends, though everyone knew she was a nonsmoker.

Docta Love, sitting behind the tinted windows of his van and watching her approach, felt his heart leap into his mouth. She was a Coca-Cola bottle with glorious hair and shapely legs. She adjusted her bowtie as she climbed into his van, after which she closed the door and sighing, turned to him with her lips in a fixed state of pucker.

Lord, they were juicy lips.

But Docta Love said, "No. The first kiss gotta be with you sittin' on my lap."

She shook her head vigorously. "I knew you were up to something. I knew this was a trick. I did not sign up to be groped and fondled, sir. I'm a happily married woman and my vows are sacred to me. Open this door and let me out of this van before I start screaming rape."

Docta Love fanned the thick wad of hundred-dollar bills in his hand, kissing it, waving it under her nose so she could smell it, resting the wad on her ample chest. "I promise I ain't gonna fondle you and I ain't gonna grope you, but for forty-five hundred dollars, I gotta at least be able to smell you when we kiss. I ain't no animal. I'm a sensitive man. So let's go in the back of this van so you can sit on my lap and kiss me as this kinda cash deserves. My money is honorable, too, girl. As honorable as a wedding ring."

The young dealer glanced down at the bills in his hand and then peered into the back of his customized van, which was set up like a bedroom.

Draperies on the walls. Velvet paintings over the draperies. Leopards and panthers. Supple, long-limbed black-skinned people in various poses of sexual suggestion. A velvet painting of the Last Supper—Jesus, Judas, Peter, the disciples, all of them, with brown skin, curly hair, and thick noses and lips. There was a long bed with satin sheets and satin covers for the big, soft pillows. Over the bed, a velvet sign that read "The Love Mobile."

She said, "Okay. I'll sit on your lap, but no more than that. And hurry up. I only have another five minutes of break."

With that, she went into the back of the van, the good Docta Love following behind.

She was thinking, *For a remodeled bathroom, it's worth it. Let's get it over with.*

And he was thinking, *That ass. Lord, you know I gotta tap that ass.*

And she did sit on his lap. And he did inhale her perfumed essence. Closed his eyes. Kissed her. Tongue to tongue. One of those real good kisses. Lips all slopping together. Teeth all crushed together. Tongues wrestling.

After that, her voice was breathy when she spoke—"All right. I did it. That's kiss number one. And if you were a fair man, you would call that number forty-three or forty-four, as much as you kissed me, but whatever, I see your little game. I see how you're going to play it. Fine. Just give me my money and let me get back to work."

She was heated, he noted, and seemed in a rush to leave the van. Her lipstick was all smeared.

Docta Love gave her that night's portion, fifteen hundred

dollars in cash, and watched her walk back to the casino. Her booty swayed when she walked, but she seemed groggy on her feet, rather than rushed. She stumbled twice.

He nodded his head.

Docta Love went to bed that night remembering that she didn't like anal, it hurt too much, but she did it from time to time to please her husband. Such a good wife. Docta Love went to bed smiling.

The next night when she got there, the dealer went straight into the back of the van where he was waiting.

She sat upon his lap, as she had done the night before, and he surprised her by placing his hand (the one that was not holding the hundred-dollar bills) upon her bosom.

She sprang up from his lap and cried, "No groping, sir! I'm not kidding about how sacred my vows are to me!"

Docta Love said to her, "For the second kiss, I need to feel you. What good is it to smell you if I can't feel? I promise I won't grope you or fondle you. I ain't no animal. I'm a sensitive man."

"But my marriage vows!" she roared

"I ain't no punk, and this is not negotiable!" he roared back. "Now all I'm gonna do is rest the palm of my hand and the tips of my fingers on your tiddies with such a light touch you ain't even gonna notice 'em there. When they get tireda being on one side, they gon' move to the next side, but I swear I ain't gonna fondle you because I was married once upon a time too, and I believe in marriage vows. I can tell you're a good wife. You believe in your vows and I respect that. But I believe in my money. And my money is sacred to me. I respect your beliefs if you respect my beliefs."

Sighing, the dealer sat herself down upon his lap, and Docta Love placed his hand on her bosom.

She puckered her lips for the kiss, but he was not ready to kiss yet, because his fingers and palm resting on the right tit had not yet grown weary of the acreage of that great mound.

Long minutes later, when his palm and his fingertips roamed at last to the other tit and began to fondle that new one, and his lips removed themselves from the sensitive part of her long, beautiful neck where they had been feasting, he kissed her mouth with his mouth, tongue against tongue. Fiercely.

When his hand grew weary of the other tit, it came back to the first tit, and she muttered somehow through the warm, wet clench of their twelve-minute kiss, "My break is over," and he released her.

Still seated upon his lap, the dealer gently pushed the large erect nipples back under the cups. Refastened her brassiere. Rebuttoned her shirt. Accepted his assistance in reattaching her snap-on bowtie. Checked her makeup in the mirror. Stumbled out of the van and began her groggy swishing, swaying walk across the parking lot. She got halfway to the doors of the casino before running back to the van to collect that night's portion of the money, which she in her drunken haste had forgotten.

"My bad," she told him.

"Your tiddies are incredible."

"I told you they were real."

"I could suck on them nipples all day."

"Bet you could."

"I want to make love to you."

"I'm a married woman."

"My dick is real big."

"I got to get back to work."

"You wear panties or thongs?'

She smiled wickedly. "Thongs."

"Ohmygod."

"I got to get back to work."

Their eyes locked in understanding, and they licked their lips to a great wetness in anticipation of the night to follow.

She raced back to the casino, running through excuses in her mind to tell her shift manager about why she was late getting back from break, and thinking, *He looks like he can keep a secret. Maybe I will let him hit it. At any rate, it's going to be a beautiful bathroom when this remodeling is finished.*

And he was thinking, *Wait a minute—she told me that night that she had never cheated on her husband with a man. Oh, I see what she sayin'. Oh, my god, honey girl is a freak. She kissed a girl? She ate pussy? She let some other girl eat her pussy? Hahaha. She's a straight-up freak. I'm gonna spank that ass. I swear to god, I'ma spank that ass.*

The third kiss on the third night did not occur in Docta Love's customized van because it was the dealer's night off, though that is not what she told her good husband.

The good husband was led to believe that she had been called in to work mandatory overtime.

The third kiss on the third night took place in an anonymous room of an anonymous hotel, and it was accompanied by good wine and digitalized song from the hotel's vast selection, which could be piped in for an additional $19.99 added to the bill.

Most importantly, there was the application of tongues to all the members of their bodies so that there might be taste.

He had told her, "How can there be smell and feel, but no taste? I ain't no animal. I am a sensitive man. I need to taste you. I need you to taste me. I know your wedding vows are sacred, girl, but my money is sacred too. What I'm saying is if you want this money for that bathroom you gon' have to let a brother get some satisfaction. Let me be frank with you. I need to see that pussy. I need to see that ass."

As he went through his little speech, she laughed, undressing.

She thought to herself, as she unsnapped her bra, releasing her enormous breasts, *I guess he has to say those things. I guess some men have to say things like that to convince themselves that they are in control. That they are making you do it. Oh, well, I'll play along with his little game as long as he has a big dick. As long as he knows how to work it. What a beautiful bathroom it is going to be. Large gothic mirrors. Italian tiles on the floor.*

He kept on talking—"I need to see that pussy. I need to see that ass"—as she stepped out of her tuxedo pants, releasing her luscious luscious Thank-You-Jesus thighs and her big brown-skinned booty. She wiggled in front of him, then turned around and bent over. The thong was lost deep down the crack of that enormous ass.

"Help me take this off," she said.

He reached out a hand to that bounteous booty.

She wiggled and jiggled it, and he heard her say, "Not with your hand. With your teeth."

The view from behind as he set about rescuing the thong. The twin honey brown loaves. Fresh-baked morning buns. The golden winking eye of her tightly puckered ass. The meaty lips from behind. Seashell red. Pouting, drooling lips. He plunged in with lips and tongue. He licked. He sucked. He bit and chewed. His mouth filled up and he drooled. It was so beautiful. She mewed with lust, and she fed him. Slapped his face with her delicious back end.

The dealer, Docta Love came to learn, tasted sweet in all of her parts.

The good Docta Love, the dealer came to learn, had a weakness for sweetness and a vigor that matched her own.

He ripped off his clothes. Flipped her over. Climbed over her.

Inverted. Placed his dick over her mouth. Placed his mouth over her dark patch of hair curling up her stomach. A golden-brown button of flesh sticking up out of it.

He put his mouth on her clit. He felt her inhale his dick into her mouth.

"Ohhhhh," he said.

"Uuuuuuhhh," she said.

"This is the best kiss ever," he said.

"Your dick tastes so good. It's so fucking big," she said. "Uuuuuuhhh."

"I told you it was big," he laughed. Lapping at her cunt. Her sweet-smelling cunt.

"Almost as big as my husband's," she laughed.

"Bitch," he said, lapping at her cunt with a fervor. Sliding a finger into that slippery hole. Sliding toward that special spot. Finding it. Rapid rubbing now. Expert licking now. Lap that clit. Rub the basement of that pussy. Rub faster. Two fingers now. Rub faster. Harder.

"Uh, uh, uh, uh, uh, uh shit, uh shit, like that, like that, uh shit, uh, uh watch out, watch out," she warned. Shaking her thighs. Trying to rub her thighs together. "I'm gonna cum. I cum wet. You better move your face. I cum wet."

Despite her warning, he rubbed. Rubbed faster. Pressured that clit. He felt her body clench. Knees came up. Stomach tightened. She gum-vised his dick.

"Uh, uh, uh, uh, there it is, there it is, baby, uh, uh, uh, I'm embarrassed. Uh, uh, uh. Uh, shit."

Her body convulsed. He pulled back and watched with delicious delight as her pussy gushed its river onto the satin sheets of the hotel bed.

She howled. She laughed.

She twisted and rolled. She crawled over him. Kissed his

chest. His muscular arms. His neck. His face. She grabbed his mouth with her lips.

He grabbed her ass. She grabbed his dick. Got on it.

Began to ride.

It was some kiss. It was some ride.

When he came, she said, "I want you on top."

She gave him a half hour to rest, then she positioned herself on the bed and he climbed over. It was another live fuck. He fucked her like a bull. She bucked like a bronco. He fucked her until she soaked the sheets again.

When he came, she said, "I want to do doggy-style."

"Hold on, baby," he laughed. "Gotta rest up."

"Well, hurry up," she laughed. "I have to get home soon. I have a husband, you know?"

After his rest was over, she got up on her hands and knees and pushed her delightful booty against him. His dick was having slight technical difficulties.

"Shit," she said, turning. "Give him here."

"I can do it," he said, jacking it like a long wet rope. "I can do it."

She laughed. "Give him here."

She took his dick into her mouth. Sucked. It helped. Somewhat. She shoved a finger up his ass. His eyes rolled.

She grinned. "See? I always get mine."

It was erect, and he got behind her and did his business, and he did it well.

Her pussy was slopping wet. He reached and grabbed a handful of her hair. He did that for about a hundred strokes. Then he reached and grabbed a handful of tiddy in each hand.

She screamed, "Uh, uh, uuuuuuuhhhh, you're the best, you're the best, I'm gonna cum, I'm gonna cum, you're making me cum," all the way through it.

When it was done, she said, "I know what you want."

"I want to rest."

She laughed. Reached down and grabbed his dick. She sang it now: "I know what you want."

He sang back, "I want to rest."

She jacked his long soft dick. "I know what you want. I know. I know."

"Baby, you are killing me. I'm only human."

"I know you want my ass. You want to fuck me in the ass. It is the curse of the woman with the big booty. Everybody wants to fuck her in the ass."

That ass. Docta Love felt a chill course through him.

She felt his dick grow rock hard in her hand.

"Well, I wasn't gonna ask you, but since you brought it up," he said.

She rolled over on her stomach. She still had his rock-hard dick in her hand. He got up on his knees. His hands were on her asscheeks, spreading them. Lubricating the hole with his hungry wet mouth. Probing, first, with a wet finger.

"Just be gentle," she said.

"Okay."

"Don't make it hurt too much."

"Okay."

"I trust you. I trust you."

"God, you gotta big ass."

"Oh, god."

"Big ass."

"Ouch. Ouch. Oh, god. Ouch. Ow. Ow. Ow. Oooohhhhh."

"Don't clinch up. Yeah, like that."

"Ooooohhhh."

"Like that. Relax."

"Okay. Okay. Okay. That's okay. That's good. That's okay."

"Yeah. Relax."

"Ooooohhhh. Mmmmmmm."

"Like that. See?"

"Mmmmmmmmmmmm."

At the end of the night, when the dealer came out of the shower and slipped back into her undergarments, all of her lips were quite worn out, so to speak, from "the kiss."

She dressed wordlessly as he watched her from the bed. His black Stetson rested on a pillow. One of his socks was on the other pillow. The rest of his clothes were all over the room.

She was at the door clutching the last of the money in her fist, fifteen hundred dollars. She looked down at the money as she stood there at the door. Docta Love was worn out, but he had enough sense to know that he had to get up and go to her.

He went to her and put his arms around her. She smelled nice. She felt so good. She was beautiful. Beautiful little PR. He lifted her face and kissed her.

"What are you thinking?" he said.

"I had a good time."

"Me too."

"You're a good kisser," she joked.

"You too."

"I need to get home now."

"Yes. To your family. To your man."

They kissed again. She was not moving, so he kept holding her. Kissing her.

"What are you thinking?" he said.

"Nothing," she said. "I guess I'll see you around the casino."

"Yeah," he said. "I'm a gambler. It's what I do."

She touched his face. "Kiss number three was a good kiss."

"The best kiss of all."

"I'm glad I did it."

"Yeah, me too."

He kissed her again.

Then he blew a kiss after her as she left the room.

As she left the room, she was thinking, *I should have told him the truth. He hit my spot. He rocked it. I think I could love him. I should have told him the truth: I have no children and I am not married. I have a boyfriend, sort of, but he does not count because I know he's still sleeping with his ex. I don't have my own house. I still live with my parents, but their bathroom is a mess, and I can't wait to see the looks on their faces after I remodel it. Gothic mirrors. Italian tile. I am going to hook it up for them.*

And as he went back to lie down on the mess they had made of the bed in the anonymous hotel room, Docta Love was thinking, *Jesus, what a beautiful girl. That had to be the livest pussy I ever had. If she wasn't married, I would be all over that. Why is it the good ones are always married? Her husband is one lucky dude, going to bed with her every night. I hope he appreciates what he's got. It's gonna be a while before I get this one outta my system. Lord, Jesus, it's gonna be a while.*

FOR NITA

Jolie du Pre

Janice glanced around. Touches of gold paint accented the white ceiling molding—a nice idea for her own apartment. If she could have stolen that framed Greek garden print bolted above the desk, she would. Who likes hotel room pictures? Nobody. But this one was lovely.

She looked down at Derek. Though still asleep, he stretched his body, causing his strong chest to rise a little and then lower. The sheet covered the bottom half of him. Janice wanted to pull it down and take another look.

She studied his face, dark brown, with the longest lashes she had ever seen. He looked peaceful sleeping next to her. That's how she would describe it, peaceful.

She positioned herself more comfortably against the headboard and tried to block out yet another image of her husband. Charles would kill her if he knew.

Nevertheless, a slight smile crept onto her face. She looked over at the mahogany desk that sat next to the plush baby blue chair. Those would look great in her apartment, too. Her own apartment, with her own pictures and her own furniture—and no Charles.

Janice placed her hand on Derek's chest, which was smooth, with barely any hair. He opened his eyes, which startled Janice and made her pull her hand back.

"Hey, girl!"

"Hey, yourself."

He turned toward her. She lowered herself down, facing him. There was no hesitation as she placed her arms around his frame. He pushed in closer to her and put his lips on her neck, kissing it. The scent she had splashed on her body last night now mixed with the lingering smell of sex and male musk.

Derek was built, every muscle developed. Yet his skin was as soft as the butter rolls she loved to bake. His cock, large and stiff, poked her leg. She reached down and grabbed it.

"Mmmm...you tryin' to start something?" he whispered.

"Maybe."

He put his lips on one of her large breasts, drawing the nipple into his mouth, then licking it slowly. Janice closed her eyes.

Another image of Charles invaded her thoughts, and his face was right there. But it faded as Derek's strong tongue traveled to her other breast.

Charles had grown fond of calling Janice lazy in the last couple of months. It was in addition to the other names he had for her: fat, stupid. "You're too stupid to leave me," he'd say.

It was no secret how unhappy she was. And there were many times when she could have made a break, but she didn't. She stayed and took it, like the victim of a schoolyard bully.

Charles would glare at her, the lines on his caramel-colored face deep with frustration. "Go get me a beer." "Get your ass in the kitchen and make my dinner." "Who are you talking to? Get off the damn phone."

Sometimes he called her "tired looking." But behind those steel gray eyes, she knew he really saw her as ugly and fat.

Fifteen months. That's how long it had been since she and Charles had had sex. And even before that, the spontaneity and freshness that they knew before was gone.

The ladies at the boutique convinced her to buy the red negligee. Charles liked red and the color worked well with her copper skin tone. They told her looking sexy helped a marriage.

When she put it on and joined Charles in bed, for a moment, there was sparkle in those gray eyes. But not even an hour later, it was gone.

Derek brought his face to Janice's. His long lashes framed big brown eyes that were full of lust and desire for her. He kissed her slowly at first, but Janice increased the speed, moving her lips faster and darting her tongue in and out of his mouth.

Janice had been friends with Nita as far back as first grade. She was her closest friend and they talked about everything. Consequently, Nita knew all about her relationship with Charles and the lack of sex. Nita had said fifteen months was too long. Way too long. And she had been right.

"You kiss good," Janice said.

"Derek is here to please, baby."

"Just keep doing what you're doing. Keep doing that."

"Ask for what you want," Nita had advised her. "It's your body."

It was her body. And right now her body felt damn good. Now Derek's tongue was firmly against her stomach, soon to explore even lower.

Janice closed her eyes again. Right now, right here, she was happy.

But it was not so long ago that it took everything in her power just to get out of bed in the morning. When she finally managed to lift herself out, it was only to avoid Charles's wrath, which usually came anyway.

"Get your ass in the kitchen and make my dinner."

Charles had insisted she quit her job once they married, better to be home with the children. But children never came.

She'd sit at the kitchen table and stare out of the window, for hours, like a mental patient.

Friends would call, but she rarely answered the phone. Only Nita was brazen enough to come over, unannounced, forcing Janice to let her in.

If there was ever anyone who knew what she wanted out of life, it was Nita. Married, with two grown children, Nita worked as a psychiatrist with a successful practice in the downtown area. She lived in a home suitable for the pages of *Better Homes and Gardens* and she was fond of the sunflowers that she had planted in her backyard. She was tall, dark and proud, and soon Janice leaned heavily on her for the support she so desperately needed. Sometimes Nita's advice was so good that Janice felt like she should be paying her, like one of her patients.

One day Nita brought books over. "These will help you get your shit together," she had said.

One book focused on gaining a positive attitude. Another book focused on diet and exercise. There was one on spirituality. Still another examined how to get rid of fear. *Do the One Thing You've Always Wanted to Do,* it was titled.

While she made Charles steak, fried potatoes and other high-fat foods that he ate every night in front of the television, she prepared separate meals of vegetables and lean meats for herself.

The diet books warned her that she'd have to exercise also. So in the mornings, after Charles went to work, she joined Nita as a guest at her health club.

Then, as the months went on, she enrolled in classes to obtain a degree as a court reporter, a job that had always intrigued her.

"Yeah!" Janice hollered as the first stirrings of an orgasm began to tickle her core. She pushed her thighs tight against Derek's head.

"I see you two have started without me," said the other man, who had been sleeping on her right side. His name was Junior, a name that she would never forget. Her first boyfriend was named Junior, only this Junior was cuter.

"You better come on then, man," Derek said. "We can't wait for you!"

Janice smiled just as big as she had in the bar the night before.

Charles had thrown the pan of meatloaf on the floor, angry that Janice had burned his dinner. Normally, Janice would have cowered in the bedroom. But this time she dressed and left, leaving Charles to scream, "Where the hell are you going?"

Weeks before, Nita had taken her to a club that catered to African Americans. So Janice had returned to the place, walked in, ordered a diet cola from the bar and then sat alone at an empty table.

Sometime that evening, the two most attractive and youthful men in the club whisked past all the much younger women and stood right next to Janice.

"You sitting here all by yourself?" Junior had asked. He was the tall one, skinny, built like a basketball player, wearing a black pin-striped suit. "Can we sit here, too?"

"Yes." Normally, she would have been too shy to speak. But that was before she had found enough courage to leave her house and go into a bar by herself. That was before Charles had reduced her to nothing.

Junior grabbed a stool and brought it close to the table. Derek did the same.

Derek was bigger, but still lean. Dressed in a blue business suit and dark Gucci shoes, it was obvious that the brother had money, or at least he looked like he did.

"Can I get you another rum and coke?" Derek had asked, looking at Janice with those big brown eyes.

"No rum, just diet please." Junior stared at the cleavage she had deliberately revealed once she was out of the house and her sweater was off. She had enough courage to walk out, but not enough courage to walk out with cleavage showing. Interesting.

"Are you two a set?" Janice had asked. "Where are the women?"

"I'm looking at the woman," Junior responded.

All Janice could do was smile.

Two or maybe three hours later, Derek and Junior were on either side of her. They sat close. Derek had even found her knee. And she imagined his fingers crawling up her thigh. She wore panties, but they were soaking wet.

They talked about a variety of topics. Derek and Junior listened to her. They asked her questions. Even if ultimately all they cared about was getting in her pants, they treated her like a Nubian queen. The attention was nice. She had missed it. She had opened up about her marriage and why she was in a club alone on a Friday night.

"From what I can see, it seems to me that your husband is crazy," Derek had said. "He doesn't deserve a fine-looking woman like you."

The men lived in her city, but on the other side of it, about an hour away. They had rented a hotel room for the business convention that was happening in her neighborhood.

Do the one thing you've always wanted to do.

"Take me to your hotel," Janice demanded

When those words came out, she barely recognized herself.

"You sure?" Derek asked.

"I'm sure. Take me to your room."

"We can do that," Junior had said.

She had excused herself to go to the restroom and while there she dialed Nita.

"Girl, they could rape you! Put you in a closet and leave you for dead! I'm coming to get you!"

"Nita, I'm fine. I drove, plus I've been drinking diet cola all night. They won't hurt me. This is something I've fantasized about."

"You're crazy!"

"I'm not crazy!"

"You just better call me when you're done with that shit. I need to know you're okay."

Why wasn't she afraid? Why didn't she excuse herself and leave the bar? Why didn't she screw up her happiness like she always did?

She thanked Nita for that. Every time she came to visit, Nita dropped off a new book. With each book, with each wise word, Janice had grown stronger.

And now it was morning and here she was, in bed with two of the finest black men in town. Janice screamed in pleasure as Derek and Junior worked on her body. The way she reacted to their touches seemed to turn the men on even more and further ignite their ferocious libidos.

Junior grabbed Janice's breast, his hold firmer than Derek's. Meanwhile, Derek continued to devour Janice's pussy. She opened her legs wider. Derek was working her hard, her juices flowing heavy on the sheet. She was so wet she could hear his every slurp.

Derek was on her clit, but soon Junior moved down and took

over. He did more than just lick and suck. His fingers moved deep inside, pulling her pussy lips apart as he stuck his tongue in as far as he could.

"I want you to fuck me, Junior!" Janice screamed. "Fuck me now!"

"Fuck her, man!" Derek breathed heavy at the sight of Junior planted between Janice's thighs.

Unopened condoms, and several used ones, were scattered all over the floor due to the previous night's tryst.

"Get a rubber!" Janice screamed. Obedient, Derek threw one to Junior. Junior ripped it open and slid the rubber over his swollen cock.

He plunged his dick deep into Janice, harder than he had done the night before. If Derek was large, Junior was obscene. His balls were the widest she had seen, bouncing and hitting her skin with every powerful thrust.

Ravished, Janice looked up at Derek. "Give me your cock, baby!"

He shoved it into her mouth and she held it steady with her hand, working her lips up and down his shaft. Then Derek moved his pelvis back and forth as Janice grabbed his ass and swallowed his cock.

Time seemed to stand still and the only sounds were the various moans that each of them made as Junior pushed into Janice, while Janice gave Derek a blow job.

But it wasn't Derek or Junior that came first; it was Janice, stronger and louder than she ever had come before.

Later that day, she drove home. Charles was there, but he refused to open the door or come outside. He had changed the locks and thrown a large amount of her clothes, shoes and other belongings on the front porch and even on the sidewalk. Had he discovered what she had done with the two black men she met in the club?

She called Nita. "Did you tell him?"

"Girl, you know I don't speak to Charles."

Janice lived with Nita after that and enjoyed the observation, watching the way Nita lived her life and carried on her days, so organized, so in control. Here was a woman who did have her shit together.

Charles didn't fight the divorce. In fact, soon after the papers were signed, and barely after the ink was dry, Janice learned that another woman had moved into his bed. He had been seeing her for the past year. As cruel as Charles had been, Janice never suspected.

She continued to go to school to study court reporting and before long her course work was complete. She was such a good student that an instructor hooked her up with a job immediately after graduation. It felt good to get out of the house and work. It felt good to make her own money.

But the relationship between Janice and Nita was changing. There was tension, unlike anything they had experienced before.

"I don't know why you keep seeing those men."

"Because they make me happy. I think it's time I was happy."

"But you're acting like a whore! Look at you. You've got a new job, a new body, but you're a whore."

"I am not a whore! Derek and Junior are my friends."

It was conversations like these that forced Janice to move out. She had always wanted her own place, and now was the time to go for it before her friendship with Nita deteriorated beyond repair. Nita had never spoken to her harshly before, and she didn't want to stick around for any more of it.

Janice made sure her new apartment was exactly the way

she wanted it. The gold on her bedspread matched the gold she had sprinkled on the molding. The mahogany desk included a mahogany chair.

Sometimes she fucked Junior and Derek at Junior's condo, across town on the north side of the city. Sometimes it was at Derek's fancy townhome on the lake front. But eventually, she convinced them to come to her place—her own place.

"I like this little crib," Junior said. They grew fond of the Jacuzzi bathtub, a feature that Janice was willing to pay a little extra rent for. Often, they all climbed into the tub and fucked there after having dinner at a local Italian restaurant or that little seafood place down the street.

Sometimes Derek bought ice cream, and they lay naked in the living room, eating vanilla or chocolate, topped with caramel.

"What kind of black men are they? Why are you sleeping with two gay guys?"

Janice tried to explain to Nita that Derek and Junior were not gay. She tried to explain that they were two black men who treated her well. But no matter how hard she tried, Nita's mind was made up. Janice was a whore. She might look good and have a job now, but she was still a whore.

One morning, after a particularly luscious evening with Derek and Junior, the sunlight woke Janice. She had stopped reading the books Nita had given her, had moved on to reading other things. But she thought about the last book Nita had brought over, one that said to make peace with those who can't forgive you.

Later that day, she walked into a grocery store and bought a sunflower. If there was one flower that Nita loved more than anything, it was the sunflower. She also bought yellow paper and bright markers.

At her kitchen table, she created a greeting card, while Junior and Derek munched on popcorn and watched the baseball game on her flat-screen TV.

When she was finished, she held up the card so that they could see. "Pretty?" she asked.

They nodded their heads in agreement.

Sunday night, after Junior and Derek headed home to get ready for another work week, Janice drove over to Nita's. She quietly left her car, carrying the sunflower in a vase, the card she had created taped to its side. She placed the vase on Nita's porch, then returned to her car and drove home.

It was a thank you for Nita, for showing her how to change her life. She might never have Nita's friendship again, but Nita would always be in her heart.

GOT MILK?

Monica Elaine

I woke up to the glaring whiteness of new-fallen snow peeking through the openings of my curtains and groaned. I hate snow. The pristine whiteness that delighted others simply signified discomfort, cold and wetness, not to mention the misery of driving in it, to me. But what the hell, it was Sunday morning, and I wasn't going anywhere. Glancing at the alarm clock, I realized it was an hour later than the time I usually got up. I yawned, stretched and fell back on the bed.

An emptiness gnawed inside me. I had been in this podunk Midwestern town for six months, and my life had degenerated into a routine of work, home and back to work again. I needed a man: a nice, big hard man. The thought immediately brought my dream man to mind and caused my hand to drift down in between my brown thighs. I stroked my warm moist cleft slowly, feeling the growing dampness at the thought of the dream man and the hard cock attached to him.

I imagined stroking its hot silky skin, feeling it grow and

harden beneath my fingers. I swirled my thumb over my wet clit and imagined my thumb moving over the hole in his red swollen cock head, wet with his precome. I wanted to taste it. I slid down his long hard body and hungrily took his cock between my generous lips, and my dark brown hair fell over my eyes, obscuring my features. I don't know exactly what my dream man looks like, only that he was fine. Soooo fine and all mine. My tongue swirled around the tip of his dick, and my hot mouth engulfed him. He tasted heavenly, sweet and salty, all man.

My fingers dipped deep into my pussy. A soft sigh escaped my lips. Now, his tongue was lashing my clit in a regular tireless rhythm. Ahhhh, it felt so good. I shoved my fingers as deep as they would go into my wet slickness, working my sex furiously. My hips bucked as I imagined his cock plunging...

The doorbell rang right before I rolled over the precipice of desire and came. I cursed with frustration. It rang a second time, insistently. I rolled out of bed in one smooth motion, grabbed my white terry cloth robe and drew it over my body, my pussy wet and dripping, my large brown nipples hard and tingling. If this was someone I didn't want to see, I'd be pissed. Hell, I was already pissed. Too bad I wasn't the type to ignore a demanding doorbell. It sounded again and I cast one last regretful glance at my rumpled bed, resentful that the man I had dreamed up wasn't it.

I pulled open the door, not bothering to rearrange my features into a mask of politeness. My neighbor stood there, and I frowned at him. He'd just moved in a few weeks before. He'd spoken to me once or twice and I had responded, but he was hardly my dream man. My dream man was at least six foot two, with rock-hard conditioned muscles. He possessed the type of face and body that made other women cast envious glances at me.

This was not my dream man. The white guy standing in

my doorway was an average height, probably around five ten, average build, not fat, not skinny, but hardly buff.

"I'm sorry to bother you," he was saying.

I raised an inquiring eyebrow at him. I usually made guys nervous. My brother once told me it was a combination of my looks, my brains, and my "don't give a damn" attitude. It was true. But I didn't give a damn about my looks. I rarely looked in a mirror, except when I brushed my teeth. I knew I looked all right: long, wild brown hair, smooth brown skin that only needed a touch of makeup, if any. I shopped for clothes only when necessary, and rarely got dressed up, wore jewelry and full makeup, or did all that other stuff all us women are supposed to not be able to live without doing. Perhaps once I met this dream man, I'd frill up a little, but until then it was simply too much trouble.

Now I always had time for sensual pleasures—hot scented baths, the exhilarated feel of my body after a good workout, and the wrung-out feeling after I came hard.

"I just wanted to know if you had some milk," he said. "I'm all out and I poured a bowl of my favorite cereal..." The guy stammered and shivered, and I decided to take pity on him.

I let a small smile play around my lips. "Just like the commercial."

"Yeah," he answered, a look of relief crossing his features.

"Come in out of the cold," I said, stepping aside. "I have some milk, I'll get you some." The hotness in my pussy was fading away, and I felt more charitable. I turned and walked into the kitchen, sensing him following me.

Without looking behind me, I opened the refrigerator, bending down to pick up the gallon container of milk. When I stood up and took a step backward, I bumped into him. I felt his hands linger on my behind.

"Steady there," he murmured.

Suddenly, warmth flowed back between my legs. I don't know if it was the deep maleness of his voice, or if I'd caught his scent, and his male pheromones excited a primal response within me. Whatever it was, he turned me on. The soft, nubby texture of the terry cloth robe felt good sliding on my bare nipples, as I set the milk on the counter. I felt the belt of the robe loosen. I didn't bother to tighten it.

I'd never exactly been sexually forward before, preferring to take my risks in the realm of imagination rather than reality. But I blamed it on my hormones when I didn't turn around, but instead took another tiny step back, then another, until I was full up against his body. God, I needed a fuck. It had been so long, and my pussy was on fire for the feel of real cock filling it.

He didn't move anything except his hands. They curved around my body and settled on my hips. I pushed my bottom against him and felt his thickness. His cock was lodged in the small of my back, since I'm not a tall woman. I moved sensuously against him, feeling the wetness gather like dew in between my legs. He made a small sound deep in his throat, almost like a moan. Yes.

I wanted him inside me, now! It wasn't thought but lust that compelled me as I turned around swiftly and leaned back against the counter. I pulled the end of my belt and let my robe fall open. The guy looked stunned, as if I'd just slapped him. His eyes narrowed and his face slightly reddened. I let my gaze drop to assess the effect below his belt. Satisfactory, very satisfactory.

"My girlfriend is back at my apartment waiting for the milk," he mumbled.

I felt my face burn as I drew my robe together and pulled the belt tight. *For once, I take the dive to boldly seduce a guy and see what happens.* So much for my brother's pronouncement of looks, brains and attitude; I felt ugly, stupid and ashamed.

"I'm sorry," he said, making it even worse. He just stood there.

"Go on," I said, anger surging within me. I gave him a little push.

The milk hit the linoleum with a soft thud, much softer than the sound of the liquid that erupted and splashed me from head to toe with a frigid shock of whiteness. I jumped in pure reflex and my feet slid out from under me. Scrambling gracelessly for a moment, I landed at his feet, my robe wide open, naked body exposed and legs splayed in a V.

I couldn't move, just lay there breathing hard, feeling the wet greasiness of the milk drip off my chin and nose and trickle into every crevice of my body. Tears of humiliation welled up in my eyes.

Then I heard a wimpy female voice call out from my front door. "Rick? Excuse me, is Rick there?"

"Shit," he said. "That's her." He ran a hand through his hair and straightened up.

Then I heard her step through the door. What was wrong with the bitch, just walking into somebody's house?

"Shit," Rick said again, and strode out of the kitchen. "Here I am," he called just as sweet as you please, as if a naked woman who'd tried to seduce him wasn't lying in a gallon of milk in the middle of her kitchen floor.

"I wondered what happened to you," she whined. Well, maybe she didn't exactly whine, but I hated her voice anyway. She sounded like one of those helpless flighty women, her voice light and whispery like she was pretending to be a child.

"I was helping this lady, she fell," he said.

"Oh, no, is she all right? You just left her there?"

I heard her walking toward me. I flopped over and raised

myself up on all fours. Lord, I was sore. I'd fallen hard.

"She's okay, let's go." I pictured him tugging her toward the door.

"Rick, how could you?"

I pulled myself up on the counter. At least, the girl seemed concerned.

"How could you leave without the milk?" she asked.

"She didn't have any." I heard him answer.

To my extreme relief, it seemed like they were going to get out of my apartment. I straightened up and pivoted—and hit the floor again in the spilled milk. I don't know what happened. One second I was on my feet, the next I was back on the floor wallowing in milk. I let out a squeak, but the thud of my body hitting the floor echoed through the apartment.

She came rushing in, Rick at her heels. She was blonde, petite and had a passing resemblance to Meg Ryan with curly hair. She gave a swift intake of breath as she took in my predicament, and my naked milk-covered body, my long dark hair plastered wetly to my breasts.

She turned to Rick with an incredulous look. "What did you do? Throw her on the floor and pour a galloon of milk over her? You make me sick!" The words erupted from her mouth. I flinched back from her sudden vehemence. But it wasn't me that she was screaming at; she stared at Rick, her baby blue eyes gone all hard and narrow. "All you think about is sex, sex, sex." Her voice had transformed from a breathy whisper to something coarse and harsh.

"I told you when we got married, we could do it every Saturday night, but no, you couldn't wait, could you? How long have you been screwing that slut?"

A look of sorrow crossed his face. "How could you believe I would cheat on you? I love you."

I wanted to puke.

She really went at him with total fury. "Why didn't you prove it, you rutting animal? Now I know why you didn't buy me that tennis bracelet. You were spending all your money on her, you lying dog."

I was weary of all of this. "Take it out of my home," I said. I would have stood up but didn't want to risk falling again in the slippery milk until they left. I didn't bother covering up, because what was the point now? Everybody had seen everything I had.

"You heard her," Rick said to his girlfriend. "Get out."

She looked at him, her eyes widening with disbelief. "What did you say to me?" Her voice had regained its baby tones.

"I told you to get out."

She gave a little shriek and stormed out of the apartment.

Rick turned to me. "Now, where were we?" he asked.

"You were rejecting me because of your girlfriend," I said angrily.

"I've changed my mind," he said.

He pulled his sweater over his head and threw it behind him to the dry carpet. He followed it with his T-shirt. Not bad; he wasn't bulked up but I could see the hint of strength in his arms. I liked his hairless chest; he was built like a swimmer. He slipped off his tennis shoes and his socks, and slid his jeans over his hips. He was a briefs, not boxers, type of guy.

The milk had warmed up by now and felt like wet silk against my skin. He pulled off his boxers and I gasped. Eight inches rose from him with the glory of Venus emerging from the ocean. Damn, I don't think even my dream man packed such an impressive load.

He straddled me and leaned down. His tongue delicately lapped milk from one nipple and then the other. His balls grazed my belly and his rock-hard tool pointed upward to my breasts. I couldn't stop the moan that emerged from my throat. My hips arched to him and I pulled my arms out of the sodden robe and reached for him, wanting him to sink his thick rod deep inside me.

"Not so fast, lady," he whispered.

Then he kissed me. That man sure could kiss. Slow, easy, yet draining me dry of every drop of passion I had. When he raised his head, I was breathless.

"What's your name?"

"Randy," I answered.

He chuckled. "Appropriate name."

Then he proceeded to show me how randy he could make me. He started at my throat. His tongue traced a milk trail, dipping into the hollows of my collarbone, tasting me in a lazy, teasing way. He swirled his tongue around my nipple, then sucked gently, pulling a sigh from deep within from me. My pussy was aching, needing, wanting. He moved slowly down to my belly button and sipped the milk that had welled within it.

My hips rotated and my pussy had a mind of its own; it began to slide up, up to those delicious lips of his. I groaned when he finally kissed it and his tongue found my clit. He teased it a little, then plunged his tongue inside me, rotating it inside my sex. *Oh, god.* His mouth worried my clit, then his tongue went in and out and around my moist opening. I felt my stomach clench with the pressure of the impending explosion.

Suddenly, he slid his body up mine in a smooth quick movement and impaled me with that glorious cock of his, pumping in and out of my hot slick tunnel. My knees gripped his hips, and I bucked wildly under him, my clit beating against the base of his cock while it slammed against my pussy. The explosion within me built beyond critical mass, and I imploded with a force I'd never experienced before, my cunt spasming against his rod in huge gulps. Shock waves crashed through me. My body went stiff, and I couldn't breathe. The world went black for a moment.

When it was over, I relaxed with a soft moan, feeling as if a giant had picked me up, wrung me out and left me limp. Rick drove into me again and again, abandoning himself to his own ecstasy. I felt him shudder and the hot spurts of him bathe me inside. So good. If that sorry-ass girlfriend of his had ever screwed him, I don't see how she could have walked away from him.

I must have said it aloud. My bad.

"But I came back," a feminine voice said from a few feet away.

Rick jerked his head up and I craned my neck. Girlfriend was sitting on the carpet right outside of the milk-soaked kitchen where we lay. Buck naked, she sat there, her fingers working her blonde cunt furiously. Her eyes were fixed on me, and her little pink-tipped breasts heaved with her panting.

"Get off of her," she said to Rick, not taking her eyes off me. He complied and she moved to me and put her pussy square in my face.

"You took my man. You owe me. Give it to me." Her voice was raspy, her breath coming in short gasps.

I nodded, everything clicking into place for me. I've always been the type to try anything once. I moved to her, grabbed her hips and flipped her over. Easing her ass into the milk, I noticed her body wasn't bad—not as good as mine, but not bad. Her pussy was surrounded by neatly trimmed blonde hair. I had never done this before, but it shouldn't be hard, I'd just give her what I liked.

I circled my tongue around her clit, and soon I had her gasping. She was clean, with a healthy womanly scent. She tasted slightly salty. I glanced up at Rick as he sat in the milk, his hand on his cock, watching us with rapt eyes.

I worked on her with my mouth for only a few minutes before I had her squirming as well as gasping. Making love to a woman was a piece of cake. I wondered why some people made such a big deal about how it was so hard to please a woman. A few flips of the tongue, and I had the blonde ready to be scraped off the ceiling.

While the woman-on-woman thing wasn't distasteful, it was boring. I took her to the edge, then not feeling exactly charitable toward her, I motioned for Rick to take my place. He dived in with much more enthusiasm than I had mustered. She moaned in a protesting way, but soon dropped back into the groove, her hips bucking up at his face. Suddenly, he plunged into her with his big cock. I love it like that, the feel of a man impaling me unannounced with his flesh.

I'd just slipped my hand into my own wet pussy when her eyes blinked wide open and she started pummeling his shoulders. Nope, it wasn't passion.

"Get off me, you ruined it, that hurts, dammit!" She raked her nails across his face.

He rolled off her, a look of sad shock on his face.

She twisted her body and glared at me. "You had it going on and then you let him come in…"

I turned to Rick and shook my head. Her problem wasn't that she had a bad case of the sushi syndrome. "She's not a cold fish who doesn't want sex. It's men she doesn't want," I told him. "Savvy?"

I had to give it to him, he wasn't dumb. His eyes narrowed and he stared at her and nodded slowly.

"You don't know me," she said to me, her voice coarse and heavy again. "Who do you think you are to say what I am or not—bitch."

She spit out her words with venom. She pulled on her clothes quickly, heedless of the wet splotches of milk dampening them. "Are you coming, Rick?"

Silence. She gave him a demanding glare, her face intense.

A mocking smile formed. "Apparently not with you," he said.

"Fuck you, then," she screamed and stormed out the door.

I stood up and held out my hand to him. "Shower?" I asked.

He took my hand. He was so hot that he could barely wait for the water to match his erotic heat. Once the water was spewing over our bodies, I dropped to my knees in front of his erect cock. I could barely get him all into my mouth. He tasted so good. I worked my mouth up his shaft slowly, rotating my tongue around the head of his cock. He was so much man. He grabbed my hair and groaned, thrusting into my open lips. I felt him grow so big. My pussy was on fire. I wanted him to explode. I wanted his come in my mouth. I sucked and licked him, grabbing him with both hands. He trembled throughout his entire body and stiffened. Then he came, big creamy spurts that I could barely swallow fast enough.

He had collapsed against the shower walls when I thought I heard someone else and pulled back the shower curtain. Sure enough, there she was, fully clothed this time. This heifer was hard to shake; she kept coming back like some sort of boomerang.

Rick looked at her and groaned. "Jesus, I thought you were gone."

She was staring at me again. "You were right," she said, ignoring Rick. "I do like women and I really like you. Maybe we can get together sometime. I'd do anything for you."

She looked so pitiful. I felt sorry for her. "I'll let you know," I said. "Tell you what, why don't you go and clean up that milk on the kitchen floor while I think about it?"

She nodded meekly and left the bathroom.

"Are you going to…?" Rick started to ask, looking shocked.

"I might do her a favor here and there if she works hard enough. Maybe I'll even order her to fuck you once in a while. Would you like that?"

He nodded, looking dazed.

I looked at his flaccid, thick cock and then at him. "Why don't you go and lie down on my bed? Take a little nap, regain your strength. God knows you're going to need it."

Like I said before, he wasn't dumb. "Good idea," he said, a little smile on his lips.

RAIN

Kweli Walker

Yanni? Don't you think it's time we meet?" His voice was ocean deep and butter soft, warm and wild with need.

"Yes."

Yes...after waking her at two in the morning with, "Sorry, I have the wrong number."

Yes...after months of long daily discussions about everything from the Challenger spacecraft explosion and Dogon Cosmology, to global warming and its effect on the migration of monarch butterflies. Together they had analyzed Toni Morrison's metaphors in *Love* and *A Mercy*, and contemplated Picasso's "borrowing" horned figures from the Afro-Cuban artist, Wilfredo Lam. Religion and politics were the flesh and bone of their most lengthy and heated debates. Art talks were dessert.

Yes...after months of her harsh rules:

1. No calling between the hours of 7:00 a.m. and 5:00 p.m., or after 11:00 p.m.

2. No personal questions.

3. No photo exchanges.

4. No requests to "upgrade" from platonic to committed *anything*.

5. No sex.

Yes...even after he broke every single rule in the last week alone. He called whenever he chose, brazenly asked whatever he wanted to know and, in open defiance, sent her a sepia-on-silver photo of himself: phone pinned between his shoulder and jaw, completely nude, stroking his thick gleaming penis arched high above his taut fist. From the time and date on the digital atomic clock, he had clearly been talking to her. The subtle beauty was that the photo had been taken during their first serious conversation about sex. The sight of his muscled body, slight love handles and all, sent her fingers fluttering wildly into the moist folds and hungry crevices of her body.

At the time of the photographed call, Aden had been describing a hand-carved bench he purchased from a Ghanaian artist who had lived in Japan. It had been expertly designed by a master carver to provide an exotic array of sexual pleasures—a long boat-shaped hole in the center for adventurous sucking and fucking of blood-engorged pussies and dicks.

It had been thundering and lightning for an hour. Finally, a powerful storm began pummeling the earth. Its ancient fragrance filled the air.

"I remember you saying how you hate the rain. I'd be happy to come to you. Would you like me to bring the bench?"

"Yes. Aden, I don't really hate rain. I just don't like driving in it and thunder and lightning makes me...well...a little nervous." Rain made her nervous, thunder and lightning terrified her, but nothing was coming between that gorgeous deep chocolate man in the photo and Yanni Roberts's pussy...but that hand-carved bench. Nothing!

"May I have the directions?"

"Yes."

Halfway to her house, he called her on his cell. "You nervous about meeting? We can do it another time if you're uncomfortable with this."

"I'm fine, Aden," she said with the splatter from the showerhead splashing her body behind the beautifully etched heron in the glass of her shower door. "I'm just..."

"Wondering?"

"Yeah, wondering."

"...if we're going to destroy something great by having sex?"

"That's always a possibility, Aden. What do *you* think?"

"I have the strongest feeling this is going to be the best decision either of us has ever made."

"What if I'm too...?"

He answered for her, "Too evil in the morning, or when you get interrupted?"

"Yeah," she chuckled, "I know I have a tendency to snap, when provoked."

"I can handle that, but do you think you can handle me being too..."

She said warmly, "Too smart? Too witty? Too sweet? Too kind? Too...fuckin' persistent?" He smiled. She had only seen part of his smile in the photo, but she had felt them hundreds of times, like a sightless person senses a red light, a crowd, or a curb.

"Well, what if you don't like the way I look in person? You haven't seen my whole face, you know."

"Please...let's not even entertain that kind of shallow bullshit, Aden. I've thought about this long and hard. I don't care what you look like."

"Well, what if my head is too big or I'm too short for you, or something?"

"I can't believe you're doing this. Do you eat pussy or is it against your religion?"

"Yes, I do! And you just might want to make sure that your drywall guy's number is handy."

"I want some of that 'encore sex' you bragged about last night. By the way, I have my own version of encore sex. And whatever you do, don't you dare forget that bench." *Click!*

As he slowly inched across The World's Largest Parking Lot—the notorious 405 freeway—he thought back to their first long conversation about flowers. She said that she never painted them, but she enjoyed having them near, while she painted. She inadvertently told him that the scents and colors excited her imagination, and that golden angel's trumpet was her favorite, even though it was deadly poison. She mentioned that it was still in bloom. He stopped by a nursery in Westwood and bought her a premium hybrid that would reach her roof in two seasons and spill bushels of humongous, bright yellow blossoms, emitting their heavenly scent from dusk to dawn.

She also mentioned that her favorite food was Japanese—but just the cooked stuff. He stopped and got them a tray of her favorite dishes—eel roll, spider crab roll, miso soup, tempura veggies, teriyaki chicken rolls, and baked dyn-o-mite mussels on a half shell. He bought seasonal fruit from Farm Boy Produce Market—blueberries for her, cantaloupes for himself...tangelos for her, Fuji apples for himself. He didn't just listen...he heard.

By the time he pulled up into her driveway, he was excited as a child on the first day of first grade. Finally, he'd have a face to go with *that* voice. When he pulled up in front of her house, he thought about how much it looked like she described: a periwinkle and white two-story Victorian, surrounded by a tall used brick fence. The melodic sound of her wind chimes and the compelling abstract design on her garage door screamed artist-in-residence.

The first thing he unloaded was the large paprika red, pit-fired pot of angel's trumpet. He lugged it up the steps to her porch with Mack, his new "mutt plus," half-Jack terrier, half-?, noisily darting in and out of his legs. While Mack ricocheted from one end of the unfamiliar yard to the other, he discovered a well-fed but bitchy calico, Diva, resting in a damp bed of cool moss, and made the unwise choice to sniff her. She gave him a stiff warning across the tender salmon-colored nose. He yelped and raced back to Aden, busy positioning the cumbersome flower pot beside the tall white porch column. With Mack close underfoot, he unloaded his luggage and grocery bags from the trunk of his car. He headed back toward the front door and from the corner of his eye, he noticed the curtains in the French doors sway. She had been peeking. Partly to calm himself and partly as a joke, he called her on the phone. Businesswoman that she was, he knew she'd answer.

"Hey." Her response was short but sweet and rich as fresh cream, and saturated with the smoky mezzo tone that had instantly captured his attention.

"Come down and let me take a good look at you, Ms. Peeker."

She opened the white wooden screen and leaned against the frame of her door. She was wearing a long white chenille robe. As plush as it was, it was plain for him to see that she was thick and shaped like a beautiful milk chocolate coke bottle. Her belt was cinched tightly around her waist, and from her waist, her robe fell like a waterfall from her wide hips and plump ass. Underneath, she was naked, except for ultrasheer hot pink tangas.

He raced up her steps, out of the thick cool mist that was threatening again to become rain, and set down the bags of food and groceries on the kitchen floor.

"I brought Mack," he apologized. "He found me a few weeks ago. He was too young to leave wandering, so I took him home until I find someone who'll care for him."

Yanni wasn't a dog person, but Mack was the kind of warm, fat-bellied wiggler and licker that defied anything that resembled dislike. She picked him up and blotted the blood droplet off from his harsh encounter with Diva.

"Looks like rain. I'm not much for animals in the house, but Mack can stay on my service porch, if he promises not to cut into my bench time. By the way, where's my bench?" She pouted playfully.

"I'll get it on my next trip to the car."

He had rehearsed a truckload of clever ways to break the ice, but when Yanni bent over to pick up a handful of junk mail, and her robe swung wide open at the top and the bottom, nothing clever came to mind. He stood transfixed, with his thick dick pulsing against his fly...begging for a long grinding hug.

"Oh, I'm sorry," she teased, half-closing the top of her robe, to the protest of her soft round breasts.

"May I hold you?"

Yanni didn't say yes or no but didn't budge as he moved in closer. They were contrasting shades of brown. Neither of them was thin, but they were both fit, which seemed strange, being that they enjoyed such different food. He had worried that he wouldn't be tall enough for her, but she was only about five five, in her bejeweled flip-flops. He was five eight and a half...five nine (or ten), on a good day. She had very thick curly mahogany brown hair that hung to the middle of her small but well-shaped breasts. Thick clusters of it danced in the wind. After enjoying their first physical contact, Aden's hands shot straight to the bejeweled side-ties that carved a perfect *T* across Yanni's wide curvaceous hips and down the split of her magnificent peach of an ass. Yanni went straight for his gorgeous dick. No need to beat around the bush, play nice girl, or pretend indifference—she was on fire and let him know.

"You're more beautiful than I ever imagined," he said, sliding his meaty arms tightly around her waist. "Let me know if I do anything that makes you uncomfortable, Ms. Roberts."

"So far, so good," she whispered. "Maybe we should take all this inside, *fo some'm catch on fire*. I don't think the fire department would appreciate being called in the rain." It was starting to come down in large drops.

"Movin' in?" she teased, wrinkling her nose and pointing at his two sizable pieces of luggage and his overnight case.

"Maybe...if things go as planned."

"I've never lived with a man before, Aden."

"From what you've told me, you never been thoroughly loved and fucked before either." Those words sent blood rushing.

"Tell me, Mr. Laws, how does a thorough fucking go?"

"Show me where to put my things away and I'll be glad to show you."

"You'll have to let go of me," she laughed nervously.

"I don't think I really want to move," he said, grabbing her even tighter. "Maybe, if you let me taste that sexy smile of yours, I could find the strength to let go."

She lifted her head and offered him the sweetness of her open mouth. He teased her, brushing her lips with his soft moustache, and circled her lips with a barrage of steamy kisses. When their lips finally met, he painted her tongue with his, sucking gently, to the rhythm of his stealthy fingertips, which had found their way to her stiff clit and begun cracking her code. As difficult as it was to end the firestorm between them, Aden eased to a stop. Both of them were breathing like wild animals after a flight-or-fight chase.

"Someone's done his homework."

"I wanted to be teacher's pet," he grinned.

She grabbed his small overnight case and led him upstairs to the master bedroom. She could barely walk, because of the profound swelling and pulse of pleasure still throbbing between her legs. She had braced herself to be able to accept Aden— no matter what, but to her good fortune, he was not only as polite and smart in person as he was on the phone, he was good looking—her style of good looking: thick forearms, wide meaty shoulders, medium height and a nice hard chunky dick. He was neat and well groomed but didn't give her the impression that they would engage in a daily competition for mirror space. His eyes were dark and tender, but he was quite manly.

He wasn't a flawless early thirties male model from an exclusive men's magazine, but he had nice white teeth, fresh breath, clean pressed clothes that fit and nice shoes. Nothing too faddish or conservative, he was right in stylish center. She was drawn to his small clear black shining eyes. He had a beautiful broad nose and fleshy well-shaped lips. She had imagined him to be a lighter, lankier, more disheveled, Afro-nerd type, mainly because he was so into technology and had such a strong command of business English. As she let her eyes wander up and down his fine frame, all she could think was that she had won the wrong number lotto. She had imagined him being taller, from the depth and strength of his voice, but was in no way disappointed. Things were off to a fiery start. She kept inventing ways to take peeks at him, as she moved about, showing him where to put his things.

"Please, go get that bench, before I lose my mind, Aden."

"Mack made a mess of your robe," he said, playfully, ignoring her, as he knelt before her and pretended to dust away a cluster of Mack's muddy paw prints. They were so deeply imbedded into the material, it was clear they weren't coming out until the dry cleaner's took them out. Aden stroked a little harder and in bolder strokes, until he had traveled up the right side of her body, up to her waist—stroking, rubbing and caressing. Finally he was standing and gazing directly into her eyes. He slowly slid his hands from the cool air of her room, to the inside of her robe, and onto her warm smooth naked body. With his chin resting between her neck and shoulder, and his nose planted in the middle of a fragrant cloud of her freshly washed hair, he surrounded her magnificent ass with his strong fingers, and slowly feathered them up and down the backs of her healthy thighs. He quickly reached down and freed his agonizingly hard dick from his pants. The sight of it and the sensation of its pressure and the stroke of his large hands made Yanni moan and reach out for him. She miraculously gathered enough strength to take control and reciprocate his sensual generosity. She turned up the heat by lavishing his dick with exotic caresses, premoistened with the sweet sticky juice from her body. She took a deep breath and guided him, by his shoulder, down to the carpet, and then she knelt. When they were facing each other again, she pulled the mauve satin tip of him into the slick curtains of flesh that surrounded her pussy. He closed his eyes and gasped. She encircled his muscular neck with her arms and gave him a few long hot kisses.

She didn't stop until they were both completely out of breath and in the royal blue velvet mood for a full-blown fuck-o-rama. They both said something unintelligible and almost by instinct, they stood and faced each other. The moment was so intense that she started to back away, but Aden grabbed both of her hands and pulled her back into him. He slid his hands through her arms and rested the knot of his clasped hands on the shelf of her firm ass, and sighed, "I'm sorry about your robe, Yanni. I'll have it cleaned for you, baby. Give it to me. I'll put it in my car when I go get the bench."

"My robe?"

"Yes...I want to see you—all of you."

Some of her hesitation was "first time" awkwardness, but most of it was masterful teasing. Yanni's robe had never come off more seductively. Aden enjoyed the slow lusty dance. Her skin gleamed from the herbal oil salt scrub she had used. When she was done, she extended her paw-printed robe to him and bowed. Suddenly, his hands shot out and gently trapped her breasts. Like fleshy reins, he guided her to him by them, and then kissed her more deeply than ever. Still holding one of her breasts captive, his warm moist inner lips trailed slowly as a bead of honey to her other breast, where he tongue-whipped her stiff nipple into a joyful buzz. He buried his other hand deep between her legs and slid it back and forth in her slippery warmth. With all the discipline she could muster, she asked him to stop.

He opened one eye. "You don't like it?"

"I adore it. I just want...to try that bench."

Aden sighed, slid his hand from between her legs, and calmly licked it clean. *Nothing quite like a man who looooooves the taste of hot pussy,* she thought.

He sulked. "I shouldn't even have told you about it. I should have kept it a surprise."

"Ha! That little bench is the reason you're here. You piqued my curiosity."

"Well, since you put it like that...I'll go get it. You're gettin' ready to experience a *fuck royale,* Yanni Roberts."

She seductively spread her legs, bent at the waist, gently grabbed her ankles, and then slowly ran both hands up her legs.

When they reached her pussy, she took up where Aden left off, only with more hungrily desperate moves. She trapped her clit and lips in a tight V of her fingers and fiercely smoothed them. She flipped her hips and hair from side to side, continuing to please her body, with her back against the wall—eyes closed.

Aden couldn't get down to his car fast enough. Yanni chuckled as she watched him slip and slide, like the long-lost fourth Black Stooge, down the grassy rain-slicked incline of her front lawn, hustling his way across the freshly muddied walkway, every now and then doing a little James Brown move, in his "way too nice for the rain" boots. He finally made it back to the porch.

Aden carried the bench with ease. When he returned, they shared a beautifully odd and silent moment, pregnant with possibility.

She was still giggling as they climbed the stairs to her artsy loft, but things turned serious once he revealed the unusual bench.

"The bench..." He winked.

"Ooh," she sighed, easing her smooth feet back into her fluffy feather-trimmed white high-heeled slippers.

The intricately inlaid legs of the bench were adjusted to have a slight incline and a space below that was just large enough to accommodate another body. Cut in the center, the top had a long boat-shaped hole the size of a generous piece of pie. It reminded Yanni of an ornately carved wooden tricycle with adjustable legs instead of wheels. The handlebar ends were padded with pastel blue-green velvet grips. Just imagining how it would be used made her sigh steam.

"I'm going to take you on ride, you'll *never* forget."

With Yanni's highly skilled assistance, Aden undressed. He walked to the window to enjoy the sight and sound of the rain, beating down much harder, joining a powerful wind that was bullying the leathery leaves and branches of a row of old eucalyptus nearby. Other than the flame of a single candle, the lavender-blue light from her window was the only light in the room. The candlelight enhanced each sweat bead, dip, and dimple on their bodies, polishing the dresser tops and hardwood floor with shimmering pale gold.

"Ready?" she clipped impatiently, straddling the low bench. He walked back to her.

"I was told by the artist that a woman can intensify the already powerful sensation by pulling back her lower lips, before she sits." Yanni pinned back her thick outer lips and squatted back down onto the bench, easing her burning cunt into the diamond-shaped cutout. The wood nearest the hole had been tooled and sanded to a surprising comfort.

"Ooh, that feels incredible," she purred. "So, now what?"

"Just hold on and enjoy, baby."

Aden opened his small dark green overnight case and pulled out a bottle of black cherry–flavored lubricant.

He said, "I'm going to start with my hands, so I can have the pleasure of seeing your face twist, and your body twitch, while I proceed to Fuck! You! Up!"

He began by delicately ice-skating with his fingertips, into and away from her clit. Every time she started to lose it, he'd slow down to a crawl, or distract her with other exotic toys—a naughty ivory silk scarf from Paris, decorated with a thousand black, maroon, and golden-brown dicks—a powerful miniature finger vibe from China that looked and waggled like a human tongue. Aden applied soft maddening strokes from a large antique bamboo calligraphy brush and gently kneaded her most sensitive flesh with an obsidian stone that he had warmed. He used his strong skillful tongue to give her an encore.

"Sssssssss…" she winced. "Aden?"

"Yes, ma'am?" He pulled his head out from under the bench and looked directly into her eyes, still busily attending her gulping pussy with his circling palm. She admired the tapestry of veins and the hard pulse of his penis, in the rapidly fading last light of the dreary day.

"Sharing pleasure makes me even hotter. Would you mind if I sucked your dick?"

"Oooh, I don't know," he teased, but stood as fast as he could and positioned his hard dick near her full, parted lips.

She leaned forward and pulled him into her mouth with her lips. He buried his fingers in her long rebellious curls until he had two secure fistfuls of her hair in his command. Sure he talked his macho shit, but it was clear to both of them that his hands were only along for the ride. Yanni knew, without being guided, the power and tempo he needed to be licked, sucked, and touched into retreat. She went berserk on his dick with her mouth and the cup of her upper throat. He had to pull away to keep from coming. Once he regrouped, she used the silky veined underbelly of her tongue to massage his balls and thighs with an uncommon tenderness—taunting him until he recaptured control.

"Can't take it, huh? What you gon' do when I whip this spasmin' pussy on you? Come back here! Where you trying to go? I ain't th'ough with you!"

He started rockin' it into her mouth, like he was unaffected, and in rebuttal, she started roughin' him up with powerful dick-length sucks.

"So, you want to play hardball, huh?" he finally moaned, pulling out of her mouth. "Ladies first! I like to ride my pussy while it's in the middle of orgasm spasm."

"Fine!" she giggled.

He knelt in front of her and while kissing her, reached beneath the bench and applied the most glorious ten-finger manipulation to everything within reach. It felt like she was being devoured by a ten-tongued clit-licking machine. He didn't just massage, he talked insanely sexy shit to her. He told her how he was going to pound the pink out her pussy. He told her that he was going to spring her like last year's Slinky and that this wasn't a one-time wonder.

He said, "You're mine now. And from now on..."

"And from now on...what?" she sneered, on the verge of convulsion. He had methodically filled her juicy cunt full of cherry tomato–sized stainless steel balls, knotted together with a silky silver cord.

"When we're together, you're mine, and you'll do as I request, understood?"

Ordinarily, she would have snapped, "Buuuuull...shit!" but she was feeling so beyond wonderful, from the inventiveness of his touch, she whimpered, "Maybe!"

They laughed so hard they almost had to start back at square one, but both of them were so heated from all the wild love play on the bench, that it didn't take much time to return to their earlier height of passion. Aden dived back under the bench and started a relentless onslaught of clit tricks.

As Yanni began to release, he slowly pulled the long steel beaded cord from her body, still suckling her stiff pulsing clit. Simultaneously, he massaged her hungry anus with a barrage of slithering strokes. It was the most body-wracking cum she had ever experienced. Aden continued devouring every nano-particle of her clit, vulva and vagina and all she could do was moan and receive his exquisite pleasures. When he added a chain of deeply penetrating kisses, Yanni's body began to throttle like she was being electrocuted. She helplessly blurted confessions of love. Inspired, Aden mined her clit with his talented tongue, for wave after wave of orgasm. Just when she started settling into a zone of Zenlike peace, he lifted her from the little bench and positioned her in a gaping *V* on top of her dresser. A single opalescent rivulet of love juice trailed from her voluptuous ass. He captured it, sensually circling her long thick nipples with it, and sternly circled the inside of her opening with what was left. He kissed her again and anxiously searched for her Good Spot with the stiff curl of two fingers. While exploring her fleshy lips with his tongue, he carefully pressed his satiny head into her damp, still clenching bowl and began a slow and methodical fucking that left no wall untouched.

The sight of him—eyes half open, mouth contorted in a sensual snarl, nostrils flared as he bent down and savored the scent of her neatly shaved bush—made her pussy reignite. As he pushed and pulled his thick hard meat in and out of her, the rhythmic sticky smacks began to sound off from her lower lips, causing her body to explode back into flame.

In a blaze of sexual madness, Aden snatched her legs up into the air and placed her ankles in the yoke of his shoulders. He tilted his head into her feet to enjoy the feathers of her slippers brushing against his hot skin. He took complete advantage of their new position and dug, deeper still, into her, bullying her slippery clit between his thumbs. She responded with asswhirling grinds and riotous animal-like cries and grunts. She met each of his thrusts with matching grinds and begged him to hold it right there, with his bold new strokes.

Suddenly, still deeply embedded, he moved them into the bedroom chair that faced the rain-streaked French doors, and swiveled her body, so that she faced the view.

Aden had used several Eastern techniques to keep from coming, but the sound of Yanni laughing through tears, begging and taunting with her magical voice, moved him dangerously near the edge. Suddenly a loud clap of thunder, followed by bright explosion of lightning, filled the room. Yanni yelped and broke for the bedroom door. She was running in air, even after Aden caught her.

At first it tickled him how frightened she was, but he never laughed. He could see that she was terrified. She begged him to let her go, but he wouldn't. He asked, "Go where, Yanni? Where could you ever be safer than here in my arms?"

He gently positioned her back onto his dick and held her there.

"You probably think I'm being a big stupid baby," she said, wiping her tears, shivering and jerking with every thunderclap or crackle of lightning.

"We all have our fears."

"What's yours?"

"Promise you won't laugh?"

She cut her eyes at him and sniffed, "I can't afford to laugh at anybody."

Yanni couldn't see it, because his face was buried in the trench of her spine, but Aden's face was twisted like he'd just sucked the sourest lime on earth. He shook his head vigorously in a contorted frown and confessed, "Mice."

"Mice? Mice are more afraid of you than you are of them," she chuckled in disbelief.

"Oooh, that's where you're wrong, baby. If you see a mouse in the house, don't say a word...just get my ass out quick and don't mind having everything in my path demolished on my way out."

"Whoa! That's bad. Not even a pet mouse?"

"Oxymoron...as far as I'm concerned."

She didn't laugh out loud, but the thought of a full-grown man falling apart at the sight of a mouse was funny to her. She had several pet mice as a young girl and thought nothing of Diva hopping in her lap to share a semiconscious little treasure she had literally "played with" to the brink of death. Yanni would wrestle its limp body from Diva's mouth, place it in a shoebox with a jar top of seed, grain and water, and when it had regained its strength, she would release it in a nearby field.

"Do you realize that you haven't flinched once, since we've been talking, Yanni?" He tightened his arms around her waist and slid his hands to the soft damp strip of mink between her legs, gently undulating her sopping-wet clit between his fingers.

"The lightning flashes scare me the most," she said, closing her eyes and rolling her head back into the fleshy nest of his shoulder.

"I bet if I make you cum while you're watching the storm, you'll never fear thunder or lightening as much again. Do you think you can watch, while I break you off again?"

"I'll try." Yanni nervously sat back in his lap and wriggled back onto Aden's pulsing dick. He moaned from her fear-induced tightness and rapidly bloomed to steely hardness.

He moaned in a whisper, "I don't think I've ever had a better fit."

Still rolling her clit in its own juices, he started leisurely plowing his dick into her body from the back. He stopped only once, to spread her legs more widely apart by draping them across the arms of the chair, but immediately resumed his rhythmic expedition into her depths. While he explored her body from behind with his mouth, hands and cock, he started a gentle pep talk to calm and distract her. "A coward dies a thousand deaths, Yanni. You're no coward, baby. You couldn't have done what you've done in your life if you were a scaredy cat. You left a career some people would kill for, to become an artist. That took courage. You have to remind yourself that all it is, is just nature taking its course. It's only a positively charged cloud and a negatively charged cloud bumping into each another. It's only precipitation."

If it hadn't been thundering and lightning, and if they hadn't been in the middle of the fuck of both their lives, Yanni would have undoubtedly let him have it for talking to her like a child. Between strokes, she chuckled to herself, *A guy who's terrified of mice, giving me a pep talk about thunder and lightning? How many people have been killed by a mouse bite? But, daaamn, this man can FUCK!*

Once again, he began to feel her hot inner flesh churning around his meat. She let go of all inhibitions and began a soulful, booty swirling bounce to counter his slow deep thrusts from down under. Now, oblivious to thunder, lightning or his endless chatter, Yanni crumbled under the skillful manipulation of his fingers and the slow rolling thrust of his hips. Aden, unable to hold out any longer, pulled her into him even tighter, and shuddered, rippling with several rounds of powerful spurts.

Together, they chased the final throes of bliss, until they lay powerless—Yanni, with her eyes closed, heart pounding, and a fuchsia meteor shower slashing the maroon curtain of her eyelids, enjoying the burning tingle of having been thoroughly fucked, enjoying the last soft pulses of Aden's penis, begrudgingly retreating from her, and Aden, collapsed beneath her, in the well-padded bedroom chair.

In spite of what she thought of his little lecture on "fear," Yanni came to consciousness feeling a cross between love and adoration for the man who had only been an intelligent friendly voice for the last year. She swiveled her body around to face him and lovingly kissed him awake.

His eyes slowly opened and he smiled. "Wheeeeeeew!"

"Wheeeeeeew is right," she whispered into his jaw, "but no more lectures on fear."

"When did you start writing my curriculum?" he snapped back with a laugh.

"Tonight, mouse boy," she quipped sternly. He cringed for a second, and then they laughed between kisses.

"And that bench stays here."

"Not without me."

"Oh, all right!" she sighed into his chest, still damp from the love they'd made. Love? Lust? Whatever it was, it was *on*.

STRANGERS IN THE WATER

R. Gay

I owe my existence to the frantic coupling of two strangers in 1937 in the shallow and bloody waters of the Massacre River that separates Haiti from the Dominican Republic. The story of this incident is told in hushed, awkward tones, on those rare occasions it is told at all, as if it is we who must bear shame for the indiscretion of my grandparents. My mother never speaks of it. She tries to distance herself from the geography of so much pain, and now, only travels to Haiti when absolutely necessary. It is not that she is ashamed of her mother, or the circumstances of her birth, but to imagine her mother and a stranger fleeing the Dominican Republic, hiding in the waters of the river while soldiers slaughtered people on both banks, only to seek solace in each other reminds her of a history she only wants to forget. Perhaps it is a history we all want to forget. But every morning when she stares in the mirror, or when she catches her reflection in a storefront, she is forced to remember.

I am fascinated by this story—this moment of desperation

and conception. I asked my grandmother about it once, when my husband Todd and I were in Haiti for a few weeks. I remember how she stared at me with milky eyes, her small hands, scarred from working in sugarcane fields in Dajabon, the first town across the Dominican border, and how she held her glass of rum and water so tightly I thought the glass would splinter in her hand. I took the glass from her, told her that she had almost hurt herself. She looked away and whispered, "Scars cannot bleed."

Todd and I have been married for three years, together for over six. My mother refers to him as "Mr. America," because in her mind, he represents the wholesome American image she has come to resent. We met at the University of Nebraska, but after our twins were born, I insisted we move to Washington, D.C. because if we stayed in that cold, remote place, our little brown babies would always be more mine than his. I try to explain to Todd what it means to be Haitian but it's hard for him to understand that there are places in the world where power outages are commonplace, and the majority of the population wallows in poverty—where no matter how rich or poor you are, you want the same thing: an end to the chaos, a breath of fresh air, a moment of peace. It is hard for him to understand why I would want to be in that place. But it is hard for me to understand why I would want to be anywhere else.

My husband and I have been to Haiti together twice. The first time, he brought a case of bottled water, and found it inexplicable that I wouldn't speak to him for a week, afterward. The second time, he brought ten bottles of mosquito spray. Every night, we would swelter beneath the mosquito netting of our bed, and when we tried to make love, he made me nauseous with the aerosol stench of insect repellant.

Then, upon our return, in the airport in Miami, he kissed the ground, and was subject to two weeks of the silent treatment.

For the sake of our relationship, we keep international travel to a minimum. But now, I have this need to go to Haiti, because it is the only place in the world that truly feels like home. My grandmother is getting older, the country is getting worse, and if I don't go now, the places I remember, the people that make it home, will no longer be there. My grandmother lives in Ouanaminthe, the first town on the Haitian side of the Massacre River. I don't understand why she chooses to live so close to a place of horror but sometimes I think that she can't bear to part with the memories, as if the farther away she gets from that place, the more she will forget. Her house is a small, cement affair. There are palm trees in the front yard and a small iron gate to ward off unwanted visitors. She often sits on her porch, staring toward the river, a distant look in her eyes. When she's like this, I can only watch her. A silence surrounds her that demands respect.

She and my grandfather worked on a plantation in Dajabon, cutting sugarcane. They didn't know each other, but they didn't need to. They shared the same condition. I have heard the stories of cane workers—days beneath a tormenting sun, cruel overseers, little pay, a life much like the slaves in America. I cannot imagine what it must have been like for my grandmother, a small woman in a big world that she could not hope to understand. When General Rafael Trujillo ordered all Haitians out of the Dominican Republic, she gathered her few belongings and wrapped them in her skirt. She ran from the overseers, and people throwing stones and marauding soldiers only to find more soldiers on both sides of the river. She found a shallow place and even beneath the moonlight, she could see that the water ran red with blood. The water was icy cold and as she waded in, a body floated past her. She waited, her heart stopping every time she saw the barrel of a soldier's rifle or heard the heavy footsteps of military boots plodding along damp soil. She heard the screams of men, women, and children being slaughtered, the thrashing of limbs in water, the silence of death.

She closed her eyes and thought about her childhood, the sound of her mother singing, the smell of fresh laundry, her father's paintings. She didn't notice when a large man slipped into the water. She couldn't scream when he tapped her shoulder. She wanted to tell him to go away—that two were easier to spot than one, but she looked into his eyes and saw her fear mirrored there. As she lay in the water shivering, the small part of her heart still remaining opened up, and she wrapped her arms around this stranger. For hours, but perhaps it was only minutes, they lay there holding each other until she could feel his heart beating against hers, every breath of his followed by one of hers until she was certain that they were breathing for each other.

She did not protest when she felt his cold lips pressed against hers. She opened her mouth and felt respite at the warmth she found in his. His large hands unbuttoned her blouse, covered her breasts. They lifted her skirt, and turned her onto her back and held her as he entered her swiftly. He buried his face in her neck. She buried her face in his shoulder. With each thrust, the coarse fabric of his shirt scraped her cheek. She felt a tightening between her thighs. His chest seemed to hollow as he sobbed silently. Even after they came, he remained inside her. He remained inside her until young shafts of morning light gave witness to the carnage around them. Only then, did he withdraw and steal home, as silently as he had crept into the water.

She saw him again, later that day. His name was Jean-Marc. He was neither handsome nor ugly but from his demeanor, she decided that he was a good man. At first, they pretended not to recognize each other, but then he smiled a sad little smile, and again, her heart opened up. He reached for her hand and she brushed his fingertips with hers. He took her to get warm clothing, a bit of food. She would have married him, my grandmother told me, but he was killed three weeks later as he snuck back into the Dominican Republic to find his younger sister. When she found out that my grandfather had died, she wanted to cry, she wanted to scream, throw herself in the river but instead, she found work as a maid with a well-to-do family. She gave birth to my mother. She finally did cry when she saw her daughter, an exact likeness of the man she knew but for a moment. And then, she hoped to never cry again. Instead, she lived as close to the river as her heart would allow, and talked to the waters as if they held the spirit of Jean-Marc.

There are no pictures of my grandfather. Sometimes, when I think of my grandmother's story, I imagine him, tall and strong, proud. I imagine the times he and my grandmother should have had, and when I do this, I cry the tears my grandmother cannot. There is no explanation for this. It is as if my grandmother's grief skipped a generation and now resides in me. And her grief is a burden I did not ask for, but one I bear. The tears I cry for her, for Jean-Marc are yet another thing Todd cannot understand. He knows the story, as he was there when my grandmother told us her saga and I believe that he truly mourns the tragedy, but he mourns it the way he mourns other atrocities—from a comfortable distance—a distance I cannot nor will not share.

My mother disapproves of my going back to Haiti. "Nothing good will come of it," she told me. "And it's not safe." But nothing good will come of not going, either. Just as Todd cannot understand certain parts of me, I cannot understand certain parts of my mother. I cannot understand her unwillingness to go home, but perhaps it is that her memories are stained with a different, more paralyzing brand of grief that holds her where she is. At the airport, she hugs me tightly, and I can feel wetness against my chest when she pulls away. She stuffs a thick envelope into my hand, orders me to give it to her mother, not to open it. I beg her to come with us, but she shakes her head, hides behind a dark pair of sunglasses, grips the handles of the twins' stroller, the veins in her hands pulsing. As we head into the airplane, I think I hear her calling after us.

After we make it through customs, Todd and I are standing in front of the airport waiting for a cab. I am already irritated with him and the expression on his face. The air is heavy, thick enough that it takes effort to breathe. In the distance, we can see black plumes of smoke filtering through the sky as political dissenters burn tires. Cab drivers lean against their cars, sucking their teeth, inspecting passengers as they try to deduce who will pay the most for their services. At once, things are silent and loud, still and frenetic. It is a scene that can only be found here on my island. Todd is sweating, his tie hanging loose around his neck. His nose is wrinkled, as if he can't quite place a distinct and unpleasant odor. I pinch the soft skin beneath his elbow and he winces.

"Why did you do that?"

"Stop looking like that."

"Like what?"

I bite my lower lip. "Never you mind."

A cabdriver finally decides we'll pay him enough and throws our bags into the trunk of his beaten Mercedes. Todd and I climb into the backseat, and as the car lurches toward downtown Port-Au-Prince, we hold each other's hands so tightly, I can no longer feel my fingers.

Driving in Haiti is a peculiar thing. There seems to be no reason nor rhyme as to how fast people drive, where in the road people drive, or any other traffic rules I am accustomed to in the States. By the time we arrive at the Hotel Montana, where we will be staying for a night before heading to Ouanaminthe, Todd looks peaked. I forgive him the heavy sigh of relief he exhales as he shoves a few dollars into the driver's hands.

Our room is rather bare, but well appointed. This hotel, it seems, is one of the nicer ones in town. But the towels, though clean, are worn. The cakes of soap in the bathroom are so thin, it's a wonder how anyone could properly bathe himself. The bed is old and small, and the air-conditioning coughs on our sweaty skin ever so faintly. Todd takes a shower, and I lie on the bed, naked and waiting for him. It has been a long day for both of us. I wish my mother were here. I don't like not having a clear understanding of why I am here. I'm hoping that I won't regret the decision to bring my husband along. But nonetheless, I am glad Todd is here, because he is home and Haiti is home and I want to savor the experience of these two homes together.

When he comes out of the bathroom, all the steam from the bathroom enters the room and the air thickens. I can literally feel sweat covering my skin. Todd smiles shyly, and my lingering irritation disappears as lightly as a whisper. He lets the towel around his waist fall to the floor and crawls into bed, atop me, his damp skin clinging to mine. His cock is hard, momentarily resting against my left thigh before he is inside me and we're struggling to move against each other but already, I feel sharp spirals of pleasure working their way up my legs. We make love so quickly that afterward I can hardly believe that we've even touched. Todd falls asleep first, but I lie awake, staring at the cracks in the ceiling, wondering about the sound of my grandfather's voice.

We wake early the next morning, and through the dirty window we can see that the sky is still dark with plumes of smoke. We take breakfast in our room—mangos, toast and cheese. And then we sit, bags packed as if we are afraid to move forward from this point. I call my mother, assure her that things are fine but I can hear the doubt in her voice. Perhaps, I hear the doubt in mine. Finally, Todd stands up.

"We'd best get going."

I smile. "Yes. My grandparents are waiting for us."

Todd looks confused, but he gets our bags and soon we are driving on what passes for roads, towards Ouanaminthe. We pass mile after mile of sugarcane fields and dark sweaty men stare at us as we pass by, sucking their lower lips, machetes paused in midair, and you can tell that they'd rather strike themselves than one more stalk of cane. And then, their machetes fall as if they are thinking, next time, next time I'll have the courage. Working in cane fields is brutal, bitter work. Men and even women spend twelve hours a day beneath the unforgiving island sun, as their skin is shredded by the brambles about. My grandmother has told me stories of how she used to tend to her friends' wounds as they lay on the dirt floor of the servant quarters late at night, using a poultice and strips of old clothing to hold back blood and infection. She would tell me of the guilt she felt when she was moved from the fields to the master's house, watching her friends from the comfort of a kitchen or sitting room window, and then the relief of no longer having to toil alongside them. It is strange—so many years later, very little has changed in the cane fields of this island.

When we arrive in Ouanaminthe, that sense of anticipation is gone. There is not much to see here. It is a small town that looks like most towns in this part of the country, in every part of the country. The houses are worn cement blocks, all the windows open. There is a small market with a sad array of wares, a few bars, and other shops. And on a small dirt road so close to the water that I can taste the Massacre River in my mouth, there is my grandmother's house surrounded by a black iron fence. For some reason, I expect to see her standing in the dust of her front yard, but her lot is empty, save for the coconut trees, standing naked, skeletons of fertility.

As we park in the small driveway and close the gate behind us, my grandmother appears in the doorway and I gasp, gripping Todd's hand. As his fingers curl around mine, it feels like they are wrapping around my heart, holding it safe. Looking at my grandmother reminds me of the trees in her yard; she looks like a ghost of the woman I knew growing up, of the woman I saw in the black-and-white photos in my mother's albums. But her eyes, a deep blue, shine as she drinks me in, cautiously steps toward us. When she opens her arms, I know exactly what she looked like as a younger woman; what she looked like before grief formed a home in her features.

She leads us into the house and we sit at a small table, Formica, cracked and wobbly. In the center of the table is a pitcher of lemonade and three clean glasses. She pours for Todd first, then me, and finally herself before sitting down. I remove my mother's envelope from my backpack and slide it across the table to my grandmother whose eyes water as she traces the edges of the envelope with one knotted finger.

"Your mother couldn't come?"

It is less of a question, more a statement of fact. I shake my head and gently cover my grandmother's hand with mine. "She stayed behind to watch the twins." Beneath the table, I nudge Todd's knee with mine, and he pulls their pictures from his wallet, smiling proudly as he lays them on the table.

"Miriam," my grandmother whispers.

I smile, but there are tears streaming down my cheeks and I don't quite understand why. "Jean-Marc and Sebastien; we named them Jean-Marc and Sebastien."

She nods slowly; swollen arcs of tears rest on her lower

eyelids. "They look like your grandfather." She turns her head to the side, toward the river, and rests the palm of her hand against her breastbone. "Yes. They look like your grandfather."

I can only take her word for this. The only images of this man in my mind are pieced together from years of my grandmother's stories—the same stories repeated over and over as if to tell a few stories many times will take the place of the life she and my grandfather did not have, stories she should have had. I study the pictures of my children and all of a sudden I miss them. I've been so wrapped up in being home and not understanding why I'm here that I haven't had time to miss their sweet and sour breath, their coos, their chubby hands and feet. I want to bring them here, when the time is right, when we can look at the Port-au-Prince skyline and not see smoke, when we can walk down the street and not worry about the children being kidnapped for ransom. Everyone here thinks Americans are rich. In many ways, they are right. But I don't want my children to be victims of that fact. I want that perfect time to be sooner than later. And I want my mother here as well, so that we will be four generations of my family standing on our native soil. I want a lot of things. It is the nature of my people to want things we do not know how to have.

Until Todd and I started visiting Haiti, I hadn't been here since I was ten years old. Back then, we came to Haiti every summer but that last visit was special, almost idyllic. We were sheltered from the island's truths. My father shinnied up coconut trees, his pants rolled up his thin calves, and threw down coconuts that my mother cracked open with a machete. We ate *douce,* a kind of Haitian fudge until our lips shriveled in protest. My brothers and I swam and stared at each other under water, marveling that there was water on this earth clearer than anything we had ever seen. One day, while my mother shopped in the city, my dad took us away to La Citadel, a fort, and as we climbed and climbed and climbed, my father told us stories of warriors and freedom and I knew that this was the happiest I would ever see him. I remember thinking how much cooler my parents were in Haiti than back in the States.

And then, they took us to Ouanaminthe, and as we approached the town, all the smiles and laughter disappeared and in a far too brief moment, I thought I might never remember what my parents looked like when they were happy. My mother fidgeted in her seat, my father gripped the steering wheel so tightly his knuckles turned white, and my brothers and I sat nervous and knobby kneed, trying to understand why all of a sudden, things were so different.

There was my grandmother, who smelled like lavender and rum and spoiled us rotten with sweets and attention and long walks. But then she and my mother would disappear for hours at a time. We were under strict orders not to follow them. We'd pester my father for an explanation, but he would brush us off, look toward the river, then distract us by carving puppets or telling us more stories. Finally on the second to last day of our visit, my father lay down with my brothers for a nap, and left to my own devices, I was determined to find my mother. I set out through the gate and followed the trickling sound of water until I reached the banks of the Massacre River. I knew nothing about the river, then, but I saw a bridge in the distance, and I saw soldiers and rifles. It was just like something in a movie. And there, maybe twenty feet from where I was standing were my mother and grandmother, kneeling as they ran their fingers through the water. Their lips were moving but I couldn't hear them. I walked toward them, but they didn't notice me until I was standing next to them, and even then, I had to clear my throat. When they looked up, at the same time, I remember thinking that they looked like paper dolls because their profiles were so alike. And I remember that they were crying—their eyes were red like blood—their eyes were so red that I could not recognize them as women who gave me life, women who loved me. The sight of them scared me so much that I ran back to my grandmother's house and crawled into bed with my father, resting my head against his chest so I could smell his cologne and hear the beating of his heart. We never spoke of that moment, and the next day as we drove away, I stared at my grandmother's figure through the rear window and she had that same look in her eyes—hollow, desperate, lonely.

The first few days of my visit with my grandmother pass without event. We talk about the children and my parents and my brothers and my job. When Todd is exploring the town, mixing with the natives, as he calls it, we talk about him. My grandmother likes him, his simplicity, the tenderness he shows me. She says you can trust a man who looks at a woman the way he looks at me. She says my grandfather looked at her that way. When I ask her what way, she sucks her teeth and looks at me with disgust. "You," she tells me. "You are in many ways like your mother. You take the things around you for granted."

At night, Todd and I lie beneath mosquito netting, our bodies damp and heavy. "Is it always like this?" he asks.

"It's an island."

"Seriously."

I sigh. "Haiti has always been hot, will always be hot. I don't question it and thinking hard right now would just make me hotter."

Todd chuckles. "I can think of a more enjoyable way to make you hotter." He traces a line from my chin to my navel, and gently nibbles my earlobe, but I push him away.

"It's too hot for that sort of thing."

"It's never too hot."

"Then this will teach you a lesson about never saying never." I can feel him pull away in the darkness. I don't need to see his face to know that he is pouting. I thought I would feel closer to him, being here with him, but mostly I am annoyed by his presence. He is keeping me from what I should really be doing, whatever that is.

"Maybe it was a mistake for me to come," he says.

"I wanted you to be here," I whisper. I know I don't sound convincing.

"What you wanted and what really is are two different things. I feel like you're expecting something of me without telling me what that something is."

I turn away from him, wrapping my arms around myself. "I'm tired. Go to sleep."

I lie perfectly still and pretend to fall asleep until I hear his snoring. My slumber is punctuated by a torment of slain bodies and cruel soldiers with white, freakishly large teeth and the husks of small children floating in massacred water.

The next morning, Todd wakes up before me, and when I stumble into the kitchen, he and my grandmother are sitting at the table drinking coffee. He refuses to look at me, but I kiss him on the forehead and sit down, rubbing my eyes.

"You look like you had a terrible sleep," my grandmother says.

"Bad dreams."

"There are no other kinds in this place."

To hear the resignation in her voice only saddens me. I am overwhelmed by her hopelessness, by the hopelessness I see in the faces of the men and women and children all around me. I spend the day with my grandmother. When she goes to the river to talk to my grandfather, I go with her and she doesn't protest. Instead, we walk together and we are silent, but again her lips are moving, as if she is filling him in on our visit, his great-grandchildren, the details of her life. In my mind, I talk to him too. I ask him if he ever found his sister, if it was worth all this pain to go back for her. I ask him to send my grandmother some sign that he actually hears her. The river is much smaller now than it was then; it is more a stream than anything else. The soldiers are still there, but they hardly pay attention to anything other than their gossip and the cigarettes they smoke. The river is still shallow and dark and when I run my fingers through the water, it is a frightening kind of cold that demands escape. I can hardly imagine it, the people fleeing, thrashing through midnight waters, dead bodies floating to the surface, the water running red. But I can hear echoes of their screams as the water runs around rocks and a child splashes about in the water under the watchful eye of her mother. When my grandmother and I finally look at each other, I wonder if I look the way my mother did when I stumbled upon them so many years ago.

I leave my grandmother there with her memories. It is clear she needs to be alone. Todd is nowhere to be found so I crawl into bed and wait for the cool of night. Later, when it seems that the entire world is asleep, I awake and Todd is beside me, wrapped around the edge of the bed. I shake his shoulder and he turns to me.

"Is something wrong?" he asks, groggily.

I press my finger against his lips, hand him his shorts, and motion for him to follow me. It is an eerily quiet night. It is darker than a night ever could be back in America.

"Where are we going?" he asks.

I shake my head and we keep walking until we are at the river. I step into the water and look up at my husband. "My grandfather died here. Thousands of people died here. But my mother was also conceived here. Strange, isn't it, that this river is both a place of death and life?"

"Yes," Todd says. "It's such a small river."

"I thought the same thing this morning."

He nods, rubbing his eyes. "Why are we here?"

I pull my T-shirt up and over my head, tossing it onto the riverbank before stepping out of my shorts. I stand naked before him. Then I lower myself into the water, and gasp.

"What are you doing?" Todd whispers, loudly.

"Come here."

He looks around nervously and in the pause I feel terribly alone. I now understand why my grandparents did what they did, anchoring themselves to each other.

"Please."

He wades into the water. I can feel the silt of the riverbed beneath my body. It has a life of it's own as it works its way around my elbows and into the small of my back.

"Take your clothes off."

"I don't know about this, Miriam. What if we get caught?"

"We won't," I promise.

There is doubt in his eyes, but he strips quickly and squats, shivering. I lie back and giggle as the water tickles me. I can feel my hair fanning out. Suddenly, it is as if Todd realizes what I need him to do. He crawls atop me and I sink lower into the river, until only the tips of my breasts and my nipples are above water. The muscles in my neck are aching slightly as I hold my head up. He brushes his lips along the sharp of my collarbone and I look at him, once again marveling at how pale he is compared to me. Shadows from nearby trees cast across our bodies. The night is ever so still. I don't really feel like I'm here. In my mind, it is 1937 and I am cold, afraid, and hungry for this man atop me to commit the act of touch. I clasp the back of Todd's neck with my hand and press my lips against his, so hard that they become numb. He forces his tongue between my lips—he tastes salty and there is rum on his breath. His fingers press into my shoulders. There will be bruises in the morning. I wrap one leg around his waist and wince as small rocks cut into my back. The water is colder now. I close my eyes for a moment and when I open them, the water is red, almost as warm as blood. I hear screams in the near distance. At once I am alone and with Todd and surrounded by ghosts. He covers my mouth with his other hand and my head sinks into the water. My eyes burn. The water tastes sanguine.

My husband makes love to me in a slow steady rhythm, and I pull him deeper and deeper into me until I'm certain that our bodies will remain forever joined like this. Cool water and soft silt slide beneath me and I begin moving my hips, forcing myself against Todd, urging him to fuck me harder. I want this to hurt. I want to remember him like this, fucking me in the river, tomorrow when I am sitting. He nestles his chin in the space between my shoulder and my neck.

"I don't understand what's happening," he says, hoarsely.

I don't have any answers for him.

I can't stop crying. I cry enough tears to fill this Massacre River—tears for my grandmother who cannot forget, who will never feel what I am feeling in this moment and in every moment after; for my mother who pretends she has forgotten; for myself, and the burden of this country's grief. I scream into his hand. I hate that this feels so good but I don't want to stop. The sound of his body splashing against mine overwhelms me. When I look at him, I hardly recognize him. His jaw is set with determination, his eyes, almost vacant. I let my head fall underwater and then he looks hazy, like an apparition. My chest tightens but I remain submerged. I allow myself to drown. In this moment, the ghosts of these waters will breathe for me.

Todd is saying something to me, but I cannot hear him. My ears are filled with water and memory. I begin to shake and as I rise for air, my hair plastered against my face, I throw my arms back, and the upper half of my body floats. I look up and see the moon. My body shudders violently until I feel so much pain and pleasure at once that it is unbearable. I have to push him away from me. We stare at each other and for a moment, we too are strangers in these waters. And then, his arms are wrapped around me, and he is leading me onto land. I know why I needed to be here.

KEEPING UP WITH THE JONESES

Reginald Harris

Once you get married and you get busy trying to build a life together, ecstasy gives way to common sense. Working, raising kids and getting them out of the house and off to college, cars that break down, bills to pay, doctors and insurance to worry about, clothes that get grown out of too soon, broken ankles and busted pipes—*life*, you know what I'm saying, just life. All the things your parents used to worry about are suddenly dropped on you, and you have to deal with them. It makes you realize what an amazing job they did, making it seem like they knew what they were doing when, in fact, they were probably just as lost and confused as you. But you keep going, because, well, that's what you do, right? And even though you really do still love your wife, what can I say? Inevitably, the passion cools, you're too busy for sex, or too tired to do anything but cuddle—if that. All those gay people you see on TV now, marching up and down, talking about same-sex marriage? Little do they know that the comedians are right: after about a year or two it turns into a *no*-sex marriage. I'm positive the inventors of all those porn websites and high-speed Internet access are married. Not that I know anything about that, mind you. I'm just sayin'…get married and your life changes.

Lynn and I do it once a month now—maybe. Most of the time we have to make an appointment, which I hate. I mean, yeah, sure, it's great to have her look over at me on Friday evening after we've both come home from work and suddenly reach over, squeeze my dick, and say, "I'll see you tomorrow night," and know I'm going to get some. But I miss being spontaneous. Like when we first moved into our townhouse and were hitting it right and left because we wanted to "christen" every room: doing it on the carpet in the living room during yet another "Law and Order" rerun, playing Jack Nicholson and Jessica Lange in *The Postman Always Rings Twice* on the kitchen table, getting between her luscious brown legs and eating her pussy on the stairs, or doing our own version of *Jason's Lyric* out in the backyard in the middle of the night, hoping none of the neighbors were watching. Now that was fun. But you know…life happens and things change. Suddenly you're both older, thicker, and you're not kids anymore. That's just the way it is. You seem to forget that a finger slowly run up her inner thigh always gets rewarded with a shudder and wetness between her legs. Somehow you put away the fact that it is her *left* nipple and not the right one that is more sensitive for that fuck-filled tomorrow that doesn't come as often as it did. She no longer scratches you behind the ear like a pet, causing the skin on your arms—and your dick—to stand at attention. All these things get lost as Life Happens, and a quick trip around the Internet becomes the easiest way to get rid of a morning hard-on. Not that I know anything about that, of course…

Sometimes you need something to remind you of what's what.

"Have you met the new guys next door yet?" Lynn asked me one night.

I put down the remote and called out to her in the next room. "What was that? What did you say?"

"I said," she repeated, wiping her hands as she came into the room, "have you met our new neighbors yet?"

"No, not really. I mean I saw them when they moved in, we both did, you know, with all their boxes and furniture. Brian and...uh...Joe, right? I might have seen one of them a few times as I was on the way in to work, but I can't say I've met them yet, no. Why?"

"You know they're gay, right?"

I looked at her. "Gay? What do you mean 'gay'?"

"You know. I mean 'gay.' They're, like, homosexuals."

I shook my head. "Get outta here—those guys? Come on." Brian, light-skinned, bald and thick, and Joe, the shorter, darker of the two with longish dreads, seemed like just average brothas to me. I thought they were two young guys who'd maybe been friends or roommates in college and were sharing a house to save on expenses until they could get places of their own. "How do you know?"

"I was running a little late today leaving the house, and they were leaving too. And I saw them kissing each other in the doorway, and then they both left together. I don't think they saw me until they got to the end of the walkway and waved to me as I started to drive off."

"Kissing? Like out in public? In the open? On the porch or what?"

"Not completely in the open, no, in the doorway. There wasn't anyone else out on the street, but even if there were I don't know if anyone else could have seen them."

I shook my head. "I'm not sure that this neighborhood is

ready for two men kissing on the front porch."

"I thought it was sweet."

"Yeah, well, you would. All that running around with your brother and his friend and your cousin Derrick… You're used to that kind of thing."

"See, I always knew you were homophobic."

"I am not homophobic! I just…I'm not sure how safe it would be for them to be doing that in public around here, that's all."

"What do you think? That somebody's going to do something to them? A mid-morning mid-kiss drive-by or something."

"No, no, of course not, this isn't that kind of neighborhood. Most people don't care. I don't care. I mean, look at those two lesbians down in the next block—everyone's fine with them."

"Everyone calls Lisa whenever their drains clog."

"Well, she does advertise herself as 'Ms. Fix-It.' She's a terrific plumber, what can I say?"

"I'm surprised this bothers you so much."

"I'm not bothered. I'm just…I don't know."

"Homophobic."

"Stop saying that!" I slapped the couch. "I'm not no homophobe. I'd just…I just rather not see them doing anything that's all. I'm sure they're cool guys and all, but they need to keep it inside." I picked up the remote and turned up the volume on Sports Center. Lynn looked at me for a while and then went back into the kitchen.

And that should have been the end of it, right? We had new neighbors. They were quiet and kept to themselves—no problem, right? Gay? No big deal, I couldn't care less. But then, later on that week, Lynn and I were upstairs in the bedroom. I was just about to fall asleep when she poked me in the side.

"Did you hear that?"

"What? Hear what? I don't hear anything."

"Listen."

I listened. "I still don't hear anything."

"Wait for it…"

And then, yes I heard it. Squeaking. But not like a mouse or a floorboard. Squeaking springs. Rhythmically squeaking springs. And then an occasional knock or tap on the wall of the bedroom opposite our bed. There was no mistaking it: the guys next door were having sex.

"Oh, man, I *don't* want to listen to this," I said, moving to get out of bed.

"Wait a minute, Roy, where are you going? What are you going to do?"

"I…I don't know. Knock on the wall or something. Let them know we can hear them and that they need to keep it down."

"You can't do that!"

"And why the hell not?"

"It would embarrass them."

"Embarrass them? What the fuck do I care if I embarrass them? I don't want to listen to buttfucking in my own bedroom!"

Lynn harrumphed. "You didn't object to that the time you asked *me* to do it."

"That…that was different. That's you and me, a man and a woman. I don't want to hear two guys going at it."

The rhythm got faster and the tapping became a knocking. A muffled, husky "Uh, uh, uh, ooh…" drifted through the wall.

"Oh, shit, here we go…"

Lynn sighed. "I remember when we used to knock headboards against the walls."

"Yeah, well…it's been a while."

"I know. I hope we didn't wake our neighbors when we did it."

"There's nobody on this side," Lynn said, reaching back

and touching the wall behind the bed. "So no one would have noticed. Truth is, you just like it quiet."

"And you don't?"

Lynn shifted a little in the bed, the strap of her nightgown falling off her bare shoulder. "Loud can be fun, sometimes. But quiet is fine... You remember that time in New York? In the rain, after that horrible trip up?"

"And the cheap-ass hotel..." I laughed and moved closer to her. "Yeah, that was wonderful. Who knew? Maybe we should check into no-tell motels more often."

"That would be great. 'Mr. and Mrs. Jones' like a couple cheating on their spouses." Lynn laughed and moved into my arms. I held her tightly and kissed her on her forehead.

"You know, that was..." I cleared my throat. My skin began to tingle and flush.

"That was what?"

"Well...that was when I knew I loved you. I mean I guess I knew it before that night but...I think that was the first time we actually made love. We'd had sex before, but that was really making love."

"There *was* something special, you're right. We were both tired, pissed off, glad to get somewhere to lay our heads. We didn't care about what the place looked like, or that it was so small you really couldn't move without bumping into furniture."

Lynn paused and looked up at me, running a finger along the back of my hand. "Are you serious about that? That was when you knew?"

"Yes it was. Why?"

"Just...I think that weekend convinced me that I should marry you. I knew you didn't really want to go, couldn't care less about seeing some Broadway show, and only went because I asked you to. It was really sweet."

"Yep, that was some night."

"I don't think we've ever been so quiet like that, either. That was part of what made it so amazing; being with you and not saying anything, just making love to you in total silence...that was just...wow..."

Lynn's hand reached down to my suddenly erect member. "So I see. I don't know how you did it, but I think this guy actually got bigger that night, if that's possible." She waggled my dick around a little.

"He wouldn't go away either, if you remember."

"Oh, yes I remember. I could feel you all the next day, walking around the city. You can be a greedy bastard sometimes," she said, smiling.

I smiled right back. "I don't remember hearing any objections that night."

"Yeah, well, I would have but..."

"But...it was too good for you too, wasn't it?" Even in the moonlight I could see her blush. "Thought so."

Casually running my fingers up and down Lynn's arm, I looked at the wall separating us and our neighbors. "Seems to have quieted down over there."

"Mmm," Lynn said, her hand still wrapped around my erection. I leaned in and kissed her. The residue of the cherry flavor of her lipstick still lingered on her lips. Both were delicious.

Suddenly all the long days and weeks without sex came back in a flood of raw hunger. I wanted her desperately, wanted not to make love as we'd been talking about, but to just fuck my wife, hard and fast, to see her hair tossing and her eyes roll into the back of her head, to have her under me, begging me to keep going, to push myself deeper into her, her long legs wrapped around my waist. I wanted to turn us away from the dull married couple and back into not our former, younger selves, but into the raw rutting animals that still lived deep in the oldest parts of our brain, that we usually try to hide. A quick flash of concern in her brown eyes showed Lynn could see what I was thinking, what kind of fire was about to be directed toward her. Her lower lip trembled and a thin line of sweat slowly meandered its way between her breasts. Her breathing began to quicken, and she pulled me on top of her. She had an animal inside she wanted to let out, too.

In the middle of our passion, I had a brief flash of Joe banging Brian's 'high yella' back out. It stopped me and almost made me lose my erection.

"What's wrong?" Lynn asked, running her fingers down my back.

"Nothing, nothing at all," I said, flipping her over to have her straddle me. My dick grew hard again, a vine curling into the latticework of her pussy hairs, and I slipped back into her warm wetness.

"They're at it *again*?" I asked Lynn two nights later.

She listened. "I guess so. Young people…I vaguely remember back when we were like that…."

I shot her a glance. Listening more closely, thinking I heard a repeated, hissing, "Shit, shit, oh, shit," I said, "You know, that's not sex. I think that's a blow job."

"You can tell?"

"Yeah." Lynn looked at me oddly. "What can I say? It sounds different from fucking… Stop staring at me! It's a guy thing, okay? Kinda sick though, to think…I mean, I don't care that they're gay and all. They can be as gay as they want to. I just don't want to hear it, that's all. It's upsetting."

"It doesn't upset me."

"You're not a man, you don't have to imagine having a dick stuck in…I mean, having to suck another guy's dick or something."

"I suck your dick."

"Not lately."

"What?"

"Sorry, sorry, I didn't mean to say that...I mean, you know, yeah, like I know you're not all that crazy about it and that's okay. But I can still miss it, you know."

"You don't seem to be in no hurry to take care of business with your mouth down there for me either, buddy, let's get that straight, too."

"Yeah, yeah, well okay, so we're both..." I glanced at her and saw the weather on her face change and made an instant course correction. "I mean I'm wrong so...anyway what I was *trying* to say was, I don't like hearing them having sex. It's just creepy to me."

Lynn put her hands on her hips. "You didn't mind it when that other couple was next door."

"That's different. That was a guy and a girl. And they really didn't do it all that often."

"Not in the bedroom they didn't, no."

I smiled. "Yeah, that was funny, to be standing in the kitchen and hearing her that night...."

Lynn tilted her head back, and fluttered her eyes. "Oh, Michael!" she made her voice high and fluttery. "Oh—oh-ho, Mi-mi-*mike-all!*" We both laughed. "It seemed to inspire you, too. I'm still not sure you weren't thinking about her when we were together."

"Come on, baby, I told you I wasn't."

"Right. Tell me you weren't thinking about wanting a little somethin' somethin' every time that hoochie stepped out of the house. Those shorts she used to wear would've shamed Daisy Duke."

I opened my mouth, and then closed it quickly. Over the

years I've learned that there are times when it's better to just let things drop.

"I think you're really a…well, I don't know what to call it. It's not a voyeur, 'cause you can't see them, but I think you like hearing sex."

I shook my head.

"Oh, yeah?" Lynn nodded down at me. "Where did that tent in your sweats come from? Looks like you wish you were next door."

"No, no, not at all. It's just that sound. No way am I letting some guy suck my dick," I said, trying to push my jumping jimmy down. Damned thing really did have no conscience or sense of timing. In truth, wave the prospect of a wet mouth in front of him and he's up and ready, pretty much no matter what gender it's attached to.

"The lady doth protest too much me thinks."

"What's that, some kind of saying your brother and his gay friends came up with?"

"No, I'm just saying…" She stroked the fabric barely restraining my raging dick. She looked up at me and licked her lips. "I'm just saying," she said again.

I didn't have to be asked twice. I broke some kind of land speed record to get my sweat pants off. Lynn, too, moved quickly dropping her head down into my crotch while I still had one leg in the sweats.

It really had been a long time since she'd given me head, and I'd forgotten how extraordinary it was to have a pair of warm lips wrapped around your member. And guys do sound different when they're getting a blow job. There's the growl deep in the back of the throat, the jagged, irregular breathing. I nearly shouted when Lynn's lips first touched the flared head of my dick. Sighing loudly, I put a hand over my mouth, not wanting the guys next door to hear. But then I thought *fuck 'em!* Those two seemed to have no problem giving us an aural show with their sexual gymnastics, it was about time we held up our end for the straight community. And besides, I doubt that Lynn's head would have been bobbing up and down between my legs if not for them. Maybe what I really needed to do was to thank them one day, I thought, before looking down to meet Lynn's eyes staring at me.

She smiled slightly and licked up and down my dark brown shaft. I leaned my head back. "Oh, baby, yes," I said as Lynn inhaled my entire thickness into her mouth. She even surprised me at the end, not pulling away when I blurted out that I was getting close. There were tears in my eyes and it almost made me come again to see my cream splash across the plump ripeness of her lips.

Once, the two of them even woke me up. Brian and Joe had left the house one Saturday night, around eleven, just as Lynn and I were nodding on the couch. Not thinking we could make it through the new Tyler Perry DVD before passing out, we headed up to bed. Sometime around 3:30 a.m. I opened my eyes slowly to the sound of moaning and knocking behind the wall. But something else had woken me, too. I noticed that our bed was shaking. Moving my head slightly, I looked over. I could tell that Lynn's fingers were moving quickly under the covers. Her eyes were closed, her head back, pushing into the pillow. I wondered if she was imagining being in the room with Brian and Joe, getting serviced by two men. Or if she was just fantasizing about one of them digging her out the way one guy was digging out the other next door. She looked so beautiful it nearly took my breath away. Her pebbled nipples were hard and pointing at the ceiling through her nightgown, a thin veil of sweat covering her mocha-colored skin. She was irresistible, and my mouth watered, jealous of her searching fingers.

I slowly pulled down the sheet, trying not to make my movements too sudden to break the spell the neighbors had put her in. After uncovering her, I discovered that her nightgown was pulled up. Both her hands were at play, exploring the wet cavern of her vagina. My dick sprang to life, but that night I wanted to help her out more than to help myself, wanted to give *her* pleasure more than worrying about pleasing myself. I slid down the bed slowly, kneeling on the floor beside it and placing my head at the level of her V, watching my wife in search of an orgasm. Then I began, first gently caressing then licking at her fingers, lapping up her tart juices.

Lynn jumped and shook when my tongue began to lick at her lower lips. She moaned as I lapped my way around her snatch, and then stuck myself inside her. She grabbed my head, forcing my tongue deeper into her, pointing me toward her clit. I licked and sucked gladly, once again eating my favorite candy, as she held me to her with both hands. My hips involuntarily pushed against the side of the bed, my dick wanting to replace my hungry mouth, but I continued to work at eating her out. I wanted this to be completely about her. Lynn held my head tightly with her hands, wrapping her legs around my shoulders as she bucked and writhed against my searching tongue. Her legs slammed tightly against my head as she undulated when she came; I could barely breathe but didn't stop eating her hot and dripping pussy, busting my own nut against the side of the bed like a horny teenager. Through the wall behind me I thought I could hear someone say, "Oh, shit!" as they came too, right along with the two of us.

We'd been kept up at least once a week, sometimes twice, by some feral noise coming through the wall into our bedroom for more than a month. They even woke us up one Saturday morning with a sound that could have been someone repeatedly tossing a large rubber ball against the wall. But I don't think it was a rubber ball that was getting tossed. To make matters even worse, later that day the four of us found ourselves on our front porches at the same time, Lynn and I going in, Brian and Joe heading out.

They seemed nice enough guys, and Lynn started discussing the tomato plants the two of them planned on putting in next season. But it was hard for me not to think about the noises coming through the wall as we stood there talking. *Which one is doing what to whom?* I kept thinking the whole time. I couldn't tell which one…"pitched" and which one was the "catcher." I suppose that's kind of, well…not homophobic, mind you, but old fashioned, to think about gay men that way, but I couldn't help it. I don't think I would have known they were gay if Lynn hadn't told me about the kiss and I hadn't heard what was going on in their bedroom. They both were in good shape and probably worked out the way a lot of gay guys do now, Joe a bit more developed in the chest, perhaps, Brian with the bigger guns. I didn't want to look too closely at them as they talked to us, out of fear of thinking of where their mouths had been on each other.

Since Lynn had more experience around gay men—she quickly brought up the times she'd gone to bars and clubs with her brother and his partner, she quickly put them at ease, and they were soon laughing and joking with each other.

"What do you guys call yourselves?"

"What do you mean?" Brian asked

"I mean your relationship. What do you call yourselves? Are you lovers, partners, what?"

"Lynn!"

"It's fine," Brian said, waving his hand. "Thanks for asking."

"I think he has a preference for '*He who must be obeyed,*'" Joe said pointing at Brian.

"*Your Highness* seems to work for this one," Brian shot back.

Lynn laughed.

"So how do you like the neighborhood?" I asked

"It's nice, pretty quiet," Joe said as Brian nodded. "Most people seem friendly. A few have been a little chilly, but I don't know if that's because they're like that or it's because of who we are."

"The house is nice, too," Brian continued. "Might need a little work. You put some extra into yours, I think."

"Yes, we put the deck in out back, some other things. These buildings are pretty sound, though. You may have to worry about the pipes; they can be kind of old, original plumbing, you know. But otherwise they're fine."

And then it just slipped out. "The walls can be kind of thin, though...especially upstairs, in the bedrooms."

I swear, I didn't mean to say it, I really didn't. It just slipped out. Lynn shot me a look like a tazer. Joe seemed oblivious, but Brian, I noticed, blushed slightly. *He must be the one getting banged out every night,* I thought. *Damn, a big guy like that... amazing. And despite his size, Joe had to be packing pretty good to be giving it to him like that too. Wow...*

"Did you hear me, Roy?"

"Huh, what? I'm sorry."

"I said I think we should let the guys leave."

"Oh, oh, okay, sorry my mind must have been miles away somewhere. Let's get together sometime."

"That would be great," Brian said. "Maybe you can come over for dinner some night?"

"Let's do that," Lynn said. "That would be lovely."

We said our good-byes, and the two men left the porch and headed for their car. I was still wondering about the cryptic smile Brian gave me before they left when Lynn turned on me after we'd entered our house.

"You really couldn't resist saying something, could you?"

"I'm sorry, baby, it just slipped out. I didn't mean to."

"Yeah, right."

"And before you start in with the usual mess, let's get this straight right now—I am not no homophobic. I mean come on, you know how much I like your brother and Mark."

"You like Mark because you all can talk sports together. You like to have someone to lose money with in the March Madness pool."

"And what's wrong with that? And what do you mean lose; I made forty dollars last year, so there."

"Still, you really shouldn't have said anything. It's embarrassing."

"My saying something was embarrassing? What about listening to them going at it? Now that's embarrassing." I paused for a second. "And another thing, since I know you're going to wind up their good girlfriend now, or whatever, but don't get any...ideas when you start talking to those guys, okay?"

"Ideas? What kinds of ideas"

"You know...I mean I...I don't want any...toys or anything in this house."

"Toys?"

"Yeah, don't play dumb. You know what I mean. I know you've got your 'little friend' over there in your bedside table for when Walsh sends me out of town for some meeting. That's cool. I just don't want...well." My voice went down to a harsh whisper. "You're not going to be sticking nothing up in *me*; you know what I'm saying?"

Lynn rolled her eyes. "Negro, please! I don't know where you come up with these things sometimes. I really don't. Just because I'm friendly with the guys next door doesn't mean that I'm suddenly going to go out and buy a strap-on or something. You really need to stop being so paranoid."

"Paranoid or not, I'm just sayin'."

Lynn sighed. "Don't worry about it." She reached around and grabbed me. "Your precious ass is safe with me."

Later that night, through the walls, we could hear Brian and Joe moving around, talking, the thump of shoes as they got ready for bed. They giggled like schoolboys at some shared joke.

Lynn and I looked at each other. "Are you thinking what I'm thinking," she asked, scratching me behind the ear.

"I hope so," I said, grinning.

Lynn smiled. "Let's be clear now. This is not some kind of competition."

I shook my head. "This isn't about competing; this is about holding up our end on behalf of heterosexuals everywhere. We can't let these gays think they can get the better of us when it comes to sex, that's all. I don't want to be responsible for some kind of, you know, 'Fucking Gap' or something."

Lynn giggled. "You are crazy, you know that? Just crazy."

"Like you didn't know that when you married me."

"Whatever... We need to move the bed. Won't work without the whole headboard-against-the-wall thing."

"Really? 'Cause I was thinking maybe we could do it standing up, you know, leaning against...the...wall...." I stopped talking because Lynn was staring at me like I was crazy.

"We *who* up against the wall, kemosabe?"

I sighed. "Okay, we'll move the bed. You want to do it now, or move it later?"

"Yes." Lynn's hands ran under my shirt, lightly brushing

the hair on my chest. She put an index finger into her mouth, wetting it suggestively, and then ran it around the areola of her own left nipple. "Do it now *and* move the bed later."

I pulled Lynn to me, holding her tightly in my arms, and kissed her. Putting my mouth over my wife's ear, I whispered, "Let's show these young boys how to fuck."

DANGEROUS COMFORT

Shane Allison

Luckily, I've never been so much as five minutes late to a movie.

Hell, it's better to be an hour or two early I always say. Tonight I was tickled fucking pink I didn't have to stand in some long-ass line. I came around the corner to find that both box offices had lines that formed along Garfield's Bar and Grill, and damn near out of the double glass doors of the mall. I jetted past couples, teenagers and families of screaming babies, straight up to the boy tearing tickets. I had found an admissions ticket in my wallet folded between my tattered voter's registration card and two unpaid carbon-copy traffic citations that were so kindly given to me by Tallahassee's finest for running a red light and making an illegal U-turn. *Need to pay these fuckin' things*, I thought as I fished out my untorn ticket for *Constantine*.

"First theater to your left," he said. This was one of the smaller theaters with pathetic sound and hard seats. Not like the bigger theaters with THX sound and enough foot room to spread a sleeping bag in.

"Is this the only theater this movie's showing in?" I asked.

"Yeah, sorry," he replied. I walked in to check if I needed to get a seat right away or if I had enough time to get something to eat. The place was sparse, but filling up fast. I had ten minutes to spare before the coming attractions. There were four people ahead of me: a heavy, big duke of a dude who looked as if he was ordering everything off the menu that hung above the refreshment stand. From popcorn to jumbo pretzels, this man's hands were full of movie food. The skater boy in front of him with ratty, bleached-blond dreads was growing impatient, and so was I. The previews are the best part. I looked at my watch to find that I had five minutes left. Fat-ass stuffed his change in his plus-size pants, grabbed his feast off the counter and started down the lobby.

Finally, damn, I thought. Skater boy was up next. He ordered a strawberry slushee and a box of Jujyfruits, which I hate. I'm more of a Raisinette man myself. There were two young honeys going on about who's the finest, Usher or Ray J. Up in here looking like something right out of *King* magazine. Fine as hell too. They bought a box of Sour Patch Kids and switched them fine asses around the corner to their respective theater.

Before the concession operator could ask if she could help me, I blurted out, "Small popcorn, no butter!" I gave her four bucks and told her to keep the change. When I walked in, there were only a few seats left. Some people were holding spots for friends while you had evil bitches who would sit their pocketbooks in the seats next to them to keep people like me from asking if they were taken. I thought, *What is this, a movie theater or a school bus?* I didn't want to sit in the back only to be bothered by patrons still trying to squeeze into an already packed movie.

Didn't want to end my ass up in the front and risk suffering whiplash and burning eyes from sitting too close. I was going to wait until the next showing when I noticed a few empty seats in the middle row.

There were these two dudes sitting in the first two seats near the aisle. I think they were punks 'cause they were sitting way too close to be "boyz." "Are those seats down there taken?" I said. I never thought I would be asking that shit. Not me, Mr. Johnny Come Fuckin' Early.

"No," they said. I stepped over them saying excuse and pardon me. I took the last seat next to the wall. I hadn't yet made myself comfortable enough before the lights started to dim. Theater patrons were steadily rolling in, making their way down the aisle. As I munched on salty popcorn, this couple was standing at the edge of the row that the gay dudes and I shared. It was continuing to fill up except for two empty seats down by where I was sitting. I looked over and watched the shorty whisper something to one of them sitting on the end. I don't much like people I don't know sitting next to me. I usually have a female on my arm, but I decided to take a break from the shorties tonight. This female was fine though. It was so dark; I couldn't really see how she looked face-wise except for the thick mane of weave that draped along her back.

I staked my claim by securing my spot on the armrest. As they grew closer to my end of the row, she started to come in clearer. She was a brown-skin honey wearing a leather jacket stretched over a set of titties that were nice I'm sure. She had on one of them leather skirts that was hugging her junk tight. I didn't much care about her man. I was too busy watching this leather-clad honey dip. She sat her fine self next to me. The scent of leather was strong, mixing in with popcorn. I moved in closer to her to take a whiff of what that jacket was giving off. Just to smell it made me feel fifty feet tall. The texture of the leather glowed in the glare from the Fanta commercial.

I sat the salty popcorn on the floor next to my feet and wiped my fingers on my jeans as the movie started. She began peeling off her jacket to get more comfortable. She worked them cute arms one at a time out of leathered sleeves. The intoxicating aroma filled my lungs.

Yep, I thought. *Nice tits.*

When she leaned over in my direction and whispered, "Would you mind at all if I lay this 'cross our laps?" I swear to god, I got a hard-on right then and there. The girl spoke country, a Georgia gal, a sweet peach right here in the sunshine state. Her breath was like watermelon bubble gum as she whispered them words in my ears I inherited from Granddaddy.

"No problem."

"Thank you," she said. "I just don't want to get it messed up."

Her jacket covered us like an electric blanket. The heat beneath us was beginning to circle with my twitching dick misbehaving in the cotton tomb of my underwear. People were starting to simmer and settle with nothing but the sound of popcorn being crunched on and sodas being slurped. Things were quiet with just the sound of Keanu Reeves kicking demon ass in wide-screen mayhem. As the movie went on, the soft arm of this hot, black-haired beauty started grazing up against me. She pulled away each time she felt skin on skin, but a split second later her knee touched mine. I watched her from the corner of my eye not knowing whether these moves she was making were accidental or intentional. Even though I'm adamant about the armrest, I made an exception for her and moved over slightly, allowing her a bit of room to rest her arm, keep her from having to lull such a pretty limb in her lap. I watched her closely. She took in what I had to offer.

My palms started to sweat as the heat from the leather swirled beneath in our laps. The flesh of my elbow kissed the flesh of hers. She moved her arm steadily away; I veered in with a knee against her knee. She slid one of them long legs across the floor sticky with soda. This lady was hard to get, but I always get what I want. I'd missed the whole plot of the movie because of her, but who cared? I'd catch it again at Cinema Twin where the seats literally come loose from the floor, where you're lucky to catch the ending before the projectors falter.

I pulled one hand from beneath her jacket that smelled of perfume, and set it on the black hide. I only had my left hand now, using my pinkie finger to caress mahogany skin. I was scared as hell she'd turn and yell rape, break my bones with barbwire words. She smelled like angels oughta smell: the perfect woman, soft under the lap of leather. I moved with a steady pace across the bridge of her arm, careful not to get the attention of her man sitting next to her. One wrong move, if the jacket slipped, there'd be a reckoning. I moved my hand between her legs, gliding it up silken thighs. I watched her nervously, examining her reaction. Nothing except for the one going on in my jeans. This had never happened to me before. Not with any female. Her middle grew hotter to the touch as I stirred under the leather tent of her skirt, getting closer to her cunt.

I moved my right hand under the jacket to work my dick. The belt around my waist wasn't tight and I slid my hand past the waistband of my underwear, over rough pubic hair. My dick was stiff and sweaty. My other hand struggled with her stockings, tore easily through them to get to her, hoping that no one heard the rip but me and this angel. I pulled back panties and I was in. She was wet as fuck down there. Sloppy and Southern. The leather's scent steeped with sweat and perfume, making a toxic, musky mixture that worked itself through our skin, through a lightening bolt of veins, a flood of hot blood.

My hand was caught in her web of silk and nylon. Fingers skimmed along supple pussy lips and a tough dick in a simultaneous dance of masturbation with only the black jacket to hide my nasty act. I glanced peripherally into her blouse. The glare from the screen bounced off her sugar-brown breasts. I wanted to reach down into the satin of sleeves and seams and cop a feel, my tongue exploring dark nipples. I noticed her left hand bracing against the armrest as I pushed deep within her cunt. Pearls of sweat trickled along my face and down my chin as I moved my two middle fingers in and out again. As I fingered her through, I steadily jacked off under her jacket, thinking of this dick in her stuff. It didn't take me long to come. I burned and tensed in my britches.

I could feel semen coming as Keanu went head to head with the devil dressed to the teeth in a white suit. I wiped my hand on my jeans as I fingered her slow, careful to remember that I was in a public place and not the El Camino Motel with some stripper. I liked the feeling of her lips constricting around my fingers like her pussy had a mind of its own. I watched her with peripheral vision, saw her shut her eyes, each muscle in her Nubian face tensing, that hand of hers bracing on the armrest as I fucked her with these fingers. She was about ready to pop and I didn't stop till she came. Felt like she was having twenty orgasms down there. Good pussy.

I eased to a crawl, finishing her off. I slid my fingers out of her spent cunt, from beneath her leather skirt, gliding her sweet scent under my nose. My fingers coasted along my lips, slipping into my mouth for a taste. I stared down at her as she adjusted herself beneath the leather. The movie ended. Good kicked evil's ass again. The credits rolled, the lights came up and people started to file out of the sardine-sized theater.

Without so much as a glance back at me, she stood and followed her man out the row, the two of them descending hand in hand down carpeted steps.

"That was good," I heard him say.

Sho' was, I said to myself. What we did was better than any Hollywood blockbuster.

PHARAOH'S PHALLIC

Deepbronze

You just never know. I used to hear her talk about this dude all the time. *King Tut.* I knew that couldn't be his real name. She never actually *said* it, but I think she enjoyed him more than me. Deidre always talked about how this dude made her cum and did things to her that she had only *imagined* were possible. No, she never actually told *me* about him, but I would hear her on the phone whispering and giggling with her girlfriends about his ass. At first I used to trip, but then I thought about it. She wasn't fuckin' *him*, she was fuckin' me. And hell, every now and then I still thought about Pearl. Pearl was the woman who turned my ass out. Some of the older cats said she had been a prostitute in N'awlins before she came to San Diego. But then again, military guys always got a story about some woman. The truth is, everybody has that one good fuck that they never forget so I figured *he* was hers. But I never knew what was really up until one day I came home early from work and that's when I really found out about *King Tut.*

It had been a few weeks since Deidre and I had made love. I was worried about my job. There had been a lot of layoffs at the firm and rumors that more were coming by early February. It was December and the thought of not having a job in another eight weeks worried me. And then one day I just *couldn't*. I mean I tried, but nothing was happening. A couple of nights I got home from work before Deidre and decided to watch some videos to get in the mood: *Chocolate Cream, Joy Cums* and *Fantapussy*. There I was in the den watching beautiful black women with supermodel good looks, perfectly round tits and phat asses, and I couldn't get it up. And *Chocolate Cream* was my favorite too! It had one girl in there who had to be the baddest ass freak I had ever seen in a video. Her name was *Chocolate* and she was the bomb! She was givin' this dude head and hell, I felt it! But my dick wouldn't stay hard. So then I tried watching something else—*Fantapussy,* a ménage à trois. Hell, every man's dream—two women suckin' and fuckin' him to near unconsciousness. But no matter what I watched I just couldn't get real hard. At first I thought there was something wrong with my dick, but I went to the doctor and he told me it was just stress. So I figured that until I stopped stressin' on my job Deidre would just have to take care of herself. And you know, that's one thing I liked about my lady, she didn't mind touching herself. Hell, I think she would have eaten her own pussy if she could have reached it. Deidre was comfortable with her own sexuality and *that turned me on*. So I figured that this little lockdown time would be all right. I had no idea just what Deidre would do in a little sex drought...no idea.

So as I was saying... I came home early one day. I didn't even know Deidre was home. I came in through the garage and went straight to the den. After a half hour or so I went upstairs to take a shower. As I got closer to the bedroom I could hear Deidre moaning. Hell, she sounded like I was fuckin' her brains out only *I* was standing in the hall. I didn't know what to do. All kinds of shit ran through my head...maybe I should pretend to be Mr. Big and get my cane...or a pissed-off pimp and get my knife...or just a jealous lover and get my 45....

Only my cane, my knife *and* my gun were all in the room, under the night table that Deidre was obviously kicking with her foot each time she screamed *"Oh, damn!"*

I stood there paralyzed and hurt. I knew that I hadn't waxed that ass in a few weeks, but Deidre didn't have to go out and fuck another man and damn sho' not in the house—in *my* bed. Tears filled my eyes. Yeah, real men *do* cry. I loved Deidre and no matter what, I could never see myself fuckin' around on her.

Deidre and I had just celebrated five years together. We weren't *married* and we didn't have any children, but we had been together for nearly four years when she moved into my house a year earlier. No, she wasn't my wife in the *legal* way, but in my heart she was every bit *my wife* and I had the papers to prove it! Her name was on the house and insurance policies; she had stocks and every other financial asset that I could provide. I took care of her, brought my check home to her and treated her with more respect than most men do their *real* wives. But most importantly, I gave her my honor—I was completely faithful to her. I didn't give out my number and I didn't take numbers. So what was happening in that room between my lady and this mutha was fucked up. I was about to catch a case.

I stood there for a few minutes that felt like hours, and I still didn't know what to do. I was mesmerized and enraged all at the same time by my lover's orgasmic cries. The panting in her voice and the shrill sound she made each time he hit her spot turned me on. I was confused. I stood in the hall sexually aroused from hearing another man please my woman. Maybe it was all those damn porn movies. Maybe somewhere deep in my mind I wanted to have an orgy with my lady and some other dude. Yet I was angry that she would play me like a fool. Mad that the only time in my life I had ever been faithful I would end up with my woman fuckin' around on me. I was hurt because I had given this woman everything and she had turned out to be just like the rest. I was blind with rage. But the truth is, I wasn't about to catch a case at all—I was hard. I didn't know what was happening to me exactly or *why*, but I stood in that hallway with my dick about to bust a hole through my pants. I pulled it out. It was wet. I stroked it. I couldn't bring myself to move, but I wanted to *see*. I *wanted* to watch. Deidre's screams grew louder. The louder she screamed the more she talked: "King... oh, fuck me...ooh wee damn...my pu..pu..pussy...oh, oh, oh, I'm coming...oh, damn...Tu...Tu...Tut..."

I opened the door. I had never seen the shit I saw that day. Deidre was lying on her back, her right foot propped up on the night table, her left foot on the bed, knee raised. She was rubbin' her nipples with her left hand and holding on to her *love-maker* with her right. She squeezed tightly. The big, dark and obviously strong dick was between her legs.

Deidre didn't see me standing in the doorway. She was still being pleased while I stood, dick in hand, watching. Her ass was slightly raised off the bed and she was being fucked good. What looked to be an eight-inch rock-hard dick was pumping in and out of Deidre's wet pussy. She moaned. I couldn't believe my eyes. Slightly crooked, it moved *counterclockwise* inside her pussy. I didn't know how to do that shit without moving my entire lower body. But I knew I would have to learn 'cause Deidre was really getting off on that. And I guess that's what *really turned me on*—Deidre getting off. Yeah, I wished I was making her holler *my* name, but that day, I was only a voyeur and my lady was the star of the show.

Still near the door, I sat down. My pants dropped to the floor. I sat in the chair spreading my legs, allowing my own well-hung dick to grow more with excitement. I wrapped my large hands around my own organ, squeezing it while finding pleasure in watching Deidre's thighs shake uncontrollably as her clit was being stimulated. As the strong dick pushed harder and deeper into her pussy, her clit was being tickled and teased in a way that only a *professional pussy pleaser* could master. Her hips jerked from the sensation. I came. It was a small squirt, the first in weeks; and it came from seeing my woman have sexual convulsions from the deliberate strokes of this, her old lover.

Deidre was in another place. She still hadn't opened her eyes to see me getting off on this erotic fantasy. Deidre was beautiful. She licked her lips and I imagined them wrapped around my dick. Her face, contorted, strained from the intense pleasure of multiple orgasms. Overcome with passion from within the deep well of her pussy, Deidre continued to moan. She was almost at her peak.

The massive dick seemed to pump harder and push deeper as Deidre's legs spread wider and she consumed all of the pleasure inside of her. Her back arched. Making slow circular motions, the big dick continued to enter my woman's pussy. With every moan the rhythm increased—faster and faster until finally Deidre's waist and hips gyrated with the same rhythmic melody. Her breathing grew heavier and I was about to cum. My lady released a huge scream. And again, I came. For weeks I had been stressed out and in one erotic afternoon, I was a man again. With her lover lying next to her, still rock hard, Deidre rubbed the moist flesh between her legs that had just flooded like a dam breaking under intense pressure.

Slowly, I walked over to the bed. Deidre, still unaware of my presence, lay there nearly exhausted from the awesome experience she had just had. Crawling into bed, I caressed her inner thigh with my tongue. Startled, Deidre sat up and stared into my eyes. We held each other's gaze while her partner lay lifelessly next to her. As I worked my way from her thighs into her wet pussy, Deidre lay back on the bed. I forced my tongue deeper and deeper into her heaven, my paradise.

I moved my tongue in and out of her liquid pussy savoring every ounce of her love. I loved the way Deidre tasted. I wanted to make her scream just like she had minutes earlier.

Deidre pulled me to her. She kissed me deeply. Darting her tongue in and out of my mouth she held me firmly with her arms and I felt her love—something her exhausted partner could never experience. Rising up onto my knees, I pulled her toward me. Lifting her hips around my waist I entered her. Deeper, harder, I thrust my strong, hard dick into her pussy and she took all of me. Deidre swallowed me up inside of her and we made love.

Moving together we became one and I loved every part of her. I kissed her lips, cheeks, ears and neck.

"I love you, Derek."

Deidre caressed my head and kissed my neck.

"Be my wife."

I couldn't believe I had just said that. It didn't come with debate, but rather it was the thing in my heart at that moment. Deidre looked deep into my eyes. She pulled me closer to her, held on to me tightly and we came together.

I made love to my friend, lover and future wife. She didn't scream and gyrate like she had done that afternoon, but I knew that I had just given Deidre something that *King Tut* never could. I knew that I was the better man. I moved to the bathroom for a shower.

As I turned on the water Deidre brought her lover into the bathroom. She turned on the faucet; I stepped into the shower.

Deidre gently cleansed the strong dick that had just given her so much pleasure. Deidre shook the water off her still-erect partner and moved toward the special place she made just for him.

Opening the shower door, I took my future wife's hand. I knew that I had her love and her honor; and I would have that even when *King Tut* didn't have batteries.

LONNIE'S LICKS

Tenille Brown

It was what they called addictive personality. Lonnie diagnosed me with it himself, him being a psych major and all. For instance, I always ordered the same takeout and I was finicky about the type of movie I wanted to watch, and I had a favorite candy bar and a favorite sandwich and I had a preferred side of the bed.

I might have passed his judgment off as simply the perception of a shallow onlooker, except Lonnie was a friend, sort of. Well, maybe not as much of a friend as this tall, beautiful man who lived across the street and occasionally came over to fuck me.

"Addictive," Lonnie said. "You start something and you stick to it. You don't care to try something new."

If this were true, I suppose one could say I had become addicted to his dick. And it was only his dick. His kisses were nice and he knew what to do with his hands, but he knew as well as I did that I put up with those other things just to get to the prize, that glorious, mahogany dick of his.

I blamed it all on him, told him he should have never shown

it to me. If he had wanted us to remain friends, if he had wanted me to show interest in any other part of him, he should have never disrobed with his curtain wide open, knowing I was directly across the street and that I did my writing in front of my window, and I tended to look directly in front of me when I was deep in thought.

So, I confronted him about it, told him how he and his penis had distracted me so much I couldn't write another word for the rest of the day and how, when I was supposed to be thinking about irony and symbolism, I was thinking about his package and how it might feel inside of me.

Being the good and gracious neighbor that he was, Lonnie had apologized.

I, of course, had accepted, but I was sure to let him know that there was the unsettled matter of him flashing me and costing me a full day's work.

So, Lonnie agreed to a bargain.

The agreement was that we would fuck once, just get all that sexual tension out of the way and get on with our lives so that we could carry on like civilized people and be sensible neighbors, waving from across the street and borrowing cups of sugar and such.

And silly me, I figured he would be a mediocre fuck at best— most beautiful people were. I had run across enough of them in my twenty-three years and I had learned to expect to be disappointed.

But I wasn't disappointed with Lonnie. I wasn't disappointed at all.

In fact, I was in love, head over heels in love with his dick. It was gorgeous, solid and smooth. It was the perfect length and girth. He knew how to move. He knew when to give and when to take and he always came last, always.

Lonnie's dick made me forget he had hands or lips or even a face. He was the only man who could make me come using his dick alone, no fingers, no tongue, no dildo.

Of course, that type of pleasure always came at a price.

His dick was terribly distracting.

It made me wish he had fucked me badly. It made me wish he had been awful so that our relationship would become awkward and one of us would have to move. Then I wouldn't think about it so much. It wouldn't take up so much of my time and energy.

But instead, I searched for reasons to fuck him. Reasons like...I hadn't burned enough calories that day and it was too late to go to the gym...or I had this scratch in this really weird place, and if he could let me borrow his dick for just a minute I was sure I could take care of it.

Instead, I was calling him over to look at a sink that wasn't broken, or to taste my spaghetti with the special kielbasa sauce, or to read over a sample chapter, a sexy chapter, one that would have him all hot and bothered.

But, in true Lonnie fashion, he was soon on to me.

He mentioned it one morning after he had licked his way down my tummy, and I had viciously flipped him over and mounted him.

Instead of giving in, he said, "You know what you're doing, don't you, Stacey?"

"What do you mean, Lonnie?" I asked.

He said, "You're forming a habit."

I shrugged and said nonchalantly, "Well, everybody has 'em."

Lonnie nodded. "True. Then you should know what it is I'm doing, right?"

I leaned in, winked, played with the sleeve of his shirt because I knew what it was he *wasn't* doing. Then I said, "No, tell me, what?"

"I'm enabling you."

I crossed my arms. "Damn, Lonnie, it's your dick for fuck sake. It's not like it's crack or anything."

And Lonnie propped himself up on his elbows, cocked his head and looked straight at me. "Isn't it?"

And I couldn't argue, so I just gave in. I said, "Well, fine, Dr. Lonnie. What do you think we should do about it?"

"I think I should stop you. I think I should just take my dick away, cold turkey."

That hurt. It hurt more than I thought it would.

I guess some would call it dramatic. But his dick really was that magnificent.

Luckily for me, along with an addictive personality, I had a penchant for playing with fire.

So, I said, "Okay, so take it away then."

And suddenly there was a shiver in my stomach and a lump in my throat that made it hard to breathe when I thought Lonnie might call my bluff. I looked at him and waited.

He seemed to think it over for a moment.

"Not so fast," he said. "We're going over something right now in my psych class. It's called aversion therapy."

I leaned in. "Tell me more."

"Well, the trick is, when you have those addictive thoughts, say, thoughts about beer for an alcoholic, you need to redirect your feelings."

I nodded. "Okay."

"Can you imagine if every time you got the craving for some of my goods, you got this little shock, sort of like you stuck your finger in a socket or something?"

I scoffed. "I don't really want to imagine that, Lonnie."

"Of course, but what if every time you had an urge for my dick, you got a sound smack on your ass?"

I shrugged. "I don't know, Lonnie. I guess I'd have to experience it."

He eased me off of him, stood up and said, "Then bend over."

"Bend over?"

Lonnie was a spontaneous fellow, always creative and interesting in his fucking, but this threw me for a loop.

"Yes, right here, over the sofa."

I did as I was instructed. I walked behind the sofa and leaned over. I poked my ass out and gave it a little shake in case he'd want to throw this whole spanking thing out the window and fuck me instead.

But Lonnie was nothing if not determined.

He pulled his hand back and brought it forward in a matter of seconds. I lost my footing, taken aback by the feel of his large palm on my bare ass. I quickly regained my composure and awaited his next move.

The second strike was playful. It barely even stung. The third made me grit my teeth. Then his licks became firmer, more forceful, until I felt a burning in my cheeks. By the time he gave me the last lick, I was biting my bottom lip, and...

Coming.

I came so intensely that my legs tensed and my stomach cramped.

Hoping that he hadn't noticed, I hurried Lonnie away, feigning a deadline. I crawled up under my covers, my ass tender and my cunt wet, and slept for what seemed like a hundred years.

The next day, Lonnie called.

I was curled up on the sofa, twisting the telephone cord in my fingers.

He asked, "So, what did you think?"

I couldn't let him know the truth. So I said, "Frankly, Lonnie, I don't really see the appeal. I mean, you'd have to be really screwed up to enjoy something like that."

"You think so? So, that means you didn't enjoy it?"

"Well, I found it sort of degrading, and it hurt like a son-of-a-bitch."

I believe Lonnie's psych professor would have called this reverse psychology.

"We don't have to do it anymore." Lonnie sounded almost apologetic.

And I could see my newfound pleasure slipping right through my fingers. So I said, "Well, it wasn't *that* bad. Professionally speaking, I respect your methods, and I appreciate that you want to, you know, *help* me with my problem. I mean, I've barely written a word since I started fucking you. Clearly, I need help."

"So I'll help you, then."

But I didn't wait for Lonnie to decide when our next session would be. I showed up at his door two days later in my favorite jeans and most flattering top, bearing a gift.

When he pulled the brown leather belt out of the box, he half smiled, flipped it over in his hands and said, "This is really nice, Stacey, but I don't really need a belt."

I frowned. "That wasn't really the point. The thing is, I have a confession. I thought about your dick today. I tried not to, but I got sort of bored this afternoon and it just crept in. And I do have integrity and I can take my punishment like a woman."

So he spread me across his bed. It was good for a different kind of sensation, he said.

It was a different kind of sensation indeed. I tensed at every lick. I clenched my thighs and arched my back so that my pussy pressed into his crumpled sheets.

I grabbed one of his pillows and held it to my mouth to stifle my moans. I gripped a handful of his sheets and pulled them to me. I felt the lashes all over my ass, on the backs of my thighs and in the small of my back.

"Are you still thinking of my dick?" Lonnie inquired between lickings.

I shook my head. It was true. I wasn't thinking of his dick at all. I was thinking of his spanking. I was thinking of the many painfully sweet licks he was giving me as I lay naked across his bed.

He ceased shortly after I came, slowly and silently.

A satisfied smile on his face, he folded the belt in his hand, left me shivering on his bed and walked out of the room.

I felt Lonnie's last licks for three days after. I began to long for the pain. I loved how tender my ass felt when my hand brushed against it.

In the mirror, I admired my purple ass. Throughout the day, I thought of Lonnie's licks and became warm all over.

So it was a pleasant surprise when one afternoon Lonnie showed up at my door.

"How's the recovery coming?" he asked. "Thinking about my dick much?"

I saw the suspicion in his eyes, but I gave it a go anyway. "I fantasized about it today in the coffee shop, as a matter of fact," I said.

Lonnie cocked his head and held his bearded chin in his hand. "Really?"

"Yes, really. I was having a double latte and out of nowhere, all I could think about was kneeling down in front of you, and taking you in my mouth."

Lonnie dropped his hands at his side. "So, why don't you?"

And then he unzipped his jeans and whipped it out. I looked down at his dick, in all of its solid, dark glory.

And there was nothing.

No spontaneous shivers.

No sudden gush of wetness between my legs.

Lonnie chuckled and shook his head. "This isn't exactly what you're after anymore, is it, Stacey?"

I hung my head because he was right. His dick was no longer the focus of my attention.

I said, "Damn it, Lonnie, it's all your fault. You and those sweet fucking licks of yours."

Lonnie shrugged. "I suppose it *is* my fault. It was good while it lasted, though."

He turned to leave. He reached for the doorknob.

I grabbed his arm. "Before you go, Lonnie, would you mind, I mean, if it's not too much trouble, could you...just a little?" I brought his hands around to cup my still-tender ass.

Lonnie seemed to ponder the unspoken request. Then he shook his head. "No, Stacey. I don't think that would be wise."

I threw my hands up. "Well, why not? It could sort of be like 'one for the road,' you know?"

Lonnie nodded. "I know. But don't all addicts say that? It's like, 'I'm gonna smoke this last cigarette and then I'll quit' or, 'Just one more hit and I'll go clean.' Well, you know what the trick is?"

I didn't really want to know, but I obliged him. "What's the trick?"

"The trick is, you never have that last cigarette, you don't take that last hit."

And Lonnie turned the knob and walked out of my apartment. I stood at my sliding doors and watched him walk across the street to his own place. He wasn't even inside his door before I felt the cold sweat, and the tremors began to take over my body.

HUNG

Zetta Brown

*N*umber Nine is mighty fine.

Nola Vernier couldn't stop her mind from wandering. After sitting around the huge conference table for the last five hours, her large backside was almost as numb as her mind. She couldn't take her eyes off of him. They'd been sequestered for three days and he was the only member of the jury still bothering to wear a suit—or at least dress pants and a collar shirt.

He still took the task seriously. Not that everybody else didn't, they just couldn't be bothered with dressing any more uncomfortably than the situation warranted. She relished her choice of a lightweight summer dress that clung to her curvaceous frame, but the matching overshirt added the right amount of professionalism. Unfortunately, no neckline, however modest, would prevent her ample bosom from looking anything less than inviting.

Taking in what she could see of him, she noted that Number Nine's crisp, white shirt accented his dark chocolate skin while containing the firm muscles of his arms and chest. His close-cut hair complemented the shape of his head the same way his neatly trimmed moustache and goatee framed his square jaw.

For eight weeks, she had been observing Number Nine and she knew he had been watching her, too. Nola couldn't help but stand out. Standing just less than six feet tall, she was stacked and packed, and her plump, creamy toffee-colored skin made her a tempting treat. Men who saw Nola Vernier couldn't help but want to eat her up.

Tyrell couldn't wait. He grabbed both of her ankles and hoisted them up toward her head and from there, he commenced to pile drive into her.

Nola raised her hips and gritted her teeth. If she hadn't known better, she could've sworn he'd busted through to her cervix. She didn't care. He could fuck a tunnel to her brain stem and she'd still grasp on to his ass, to urge him deeper as she was doing now. He leaned forward and put his lips next to her ear.

"I'm gonna fill you up and drink you dry," he growled.

"Pussy tickler," she murmured.

"What was that?" asked Number Ten. He'd been elected foreperson on day one. He was possibly the oldest member of the jury but the only one who appeared comfortable enough to mingle with everyone else without suffering from the awkwardness that comes with getting to know a person.

Nola blinked. "Wha—? Sorry. I didn't say anything."

"Oh. Forgive me, I thought you did."

"It doesn't matter what was administered, when it was administered, or by whom. The outcome remains the same. Madison Daytona is dead."

Nola let out a pent-up breath when everyone took their eyes

off her to look at Number Three, who had just spoken. She was an attractive woman who Nola thought resembled a den mother, but she didn't know of many den mothers with a Celtic band tattoo going around their wrist. Nola couldn't decide if the woman had gotten the tattoo as a result of her true personality, or if it was a manifestation of midlife crisis or a desperate attempt for a spot on some boy's MILF list. Perhaps it was all of the above.

Nola didn't like judging people, yet that was the specific task before her. For eight weeks, she and eleven others had listened to evidence in the mysterious and sudden death of mega A-list actress Madison Daytona, who had dropped dead on the set of her latest film, *Death of a Comeback Queen.*

Never had a film been more aptly named, in Nola's opinion. Personally, she hadn't thought much of the deceased and she was still unimpressed. In a career that spanned thirty of her thirty-four years, Madison Daytona had more ups and down than a crack-house whore—and if any of the rumors were to be believed, Madison wasn't any better except for the fact that she had a staff who could get her whatever she wanted whenever she wanted. You didn't say no to Madison Daytona.

Now it was the job of Nola and eleven others to decide if Madison's personal physician, Dr. Paul Birger, was the person behind her death. His medical credentials were questionable, at best, and his character and lifestyle made him an easy prime suspect.

Serving on this jury was forcing Nola to confront her stereotypes and prejudices while at the same time, trying to dismiss them.

"Isn't that the point of our being here?" asked Number Seven. "We have to determine these things in order to decide if Birger is guilty or innocent." Seven was also Nola's roommate.

Nola liked Seven. She reminded Nola of her first-grade teacher: a plump, white woman who always wore her hair in a bun and had a melodious voice. Seven had told some pretty bawdy stories in their hotel room even though she never said anything stronger than "darn" or "fudge."

Rooming with Seven was fun, and convenient considering Seven slept like a log, eye mask and earplugs included. "Forty years of marriage to a man with a deviated septum," she explained.

The city had them staying in a nice, high-rise hotel consisting almost entirely of suites. The rooms were large and comfortably furnished. Each person had his own walk-in closet. That first night, Nola discovered their room had an adjoining door to the next room inside her closet. She debated whether or not to bring it to the attention of the court representative. Surely they had vetted these rooms before picking the hotel or assigning the rooms.

It wasn't until after dinner that first night, when the jurors were being escorted to their rooms as an entire group that she found out who one of her neighbors would be.

Perhaps the adjoining doors didn't matter after all.

"No soul is innocent," said Number Eleven.

"Oh, dear god, please keep religion out of this!" Number Eight slammed her pen on the table in disgust.

Despite the attempt for neutrality, there seemed to be enough religious fervor in the room to make Nola wonder if separation of church and state would be possible in this case. In the previous year, Madison Daytona's messy divorce revealed that the marriage was a sham to cover her lesbianism, and it was rumored that Dr. Birger had a preference for young men.

And the trial taking place in a state where the idea of gay marriage was an open, bitter dispute, just added more powder to the keg.

* * *

"Tyrell, if the court really wanted to protect us, our names would be sealed and not available for any hack to come knocking on our door for an 'exclusive' story. We wouldn't have to worry about some deranged Madison Daytona fan stalking us because he didn't like our verdict."

"That's a pretty cynical attitude coming from a woman like you, Nola."

"What do you mean by that?"

"Do you teach your Sunday School class to be so distrustful of people?"

To prove her point, she suddenly trapped as much of his cock inside her mouth as she could and sucked hard before letting it slide out with a wet *pop!*

"I'm sure there are things you wouldn't tell your buddies at the office."

He forced his cock back between her glistening lips and began to thrust. She closed her eyes and moaned.

"I don't know, girl. The world deserves to know about your mouth...."

Too fine, she thought, and resumed sucking on the straw from her now-empty juice box. But the straw was a sad substitute compared to the firm, juicy piece of manmeat she had in her mouth the night before.

Nola suppressed a smile as best as she could. The court tried to come up with the most diverse and nonbiased jury possible. The jury consisted of six men and six women, and while half of the jury was white, the other was comprised of two Hispanics, one Asian, one Native-American, and two blacks—herself and Number Nine.

It wasn't like Nola didn't know the names of her fellow jurors.

But it wasn't until halfway through the first day of deliberations that names were revealed, and by that time, Nola already had faces assigned to numbers and they stuck. She preferred to keep it that way, at least in her mind. Everyone deserved a right to privacy, and if she couldn't maintain that belief in her head where no one had access, there was no hope for the world.

Besides, she liked to pretend she was part of a collective. In this case, she was Four of Twelve.

This whole trial was making Nola sick. Eight weeks in court, three days sequestered. At first, her digestion turned against her until she thought she would become addicted to antacids. Now, her head constantly throbbed. It was from all the built-up tension and frustration. It needed an outlet. She needed an outlet.

And she wasn't the only one.

Nola rolled over and let Tyrell mount her from behind.

"Ride me, motherfucker...ride me!"

Tyrell soon found his pace and proceeded to split her from a new angle. His strong fingers clasped her hip bones, holding her in position. She pushed herself up onto her hands and knees and looked over her shoulder. She saw his feet digging into the high-traffic carpeting of the hotel room floor and anchored for purchase the same way a runner's foot was anchored in starting blocks. His efforts had the desired effect as Nola sensed his cock pounding harder, deeper.

The sound of a mattress creaking and a gentle snore made her lover stop only briefly.

Number Seven had rolled over on her back, still asleep.

"You would think that after fucking up—sorry—*screwing* up so many high-profile cases, the prosecution in this city would finally get their act together," said Number Two.

"Come on, everybody," the jury foreman said. "It's getting late. Let's vote. Those who think Paul Birger is guilty…?"

Hands rose. Eight to four in favor. Some groaned and others rocked their heads on the table.

"Okay," he sighed. "I think it's time we all take a break."

They lay sprawled on the floor. Nola smirked. Whoever assigned them their numbers must have seen Tyrell coming. Otherwise, how could they have known his size? She didn't make a habit of sleeping with men, considering the only men she encountered were at work or at church. But that didn't mean she was ignorant of a good fuck.

Outside in the hallway, the jurors wandered aimlessly, stretching their legs or their bodies. No one thought twice when Number One and Number Eight started doing wind sprints up and down the hall. They just got out of their way. All the jurors had found a way of letting off steam without resorting to snide remarks and insults…at least so far. But the politeness was getting more strained and starting to feel more forced.

Nola watched Number Nine insert coins into the vending machine, enjoying how his long, thick fingers punched the number of his choice and how he stood and waited for the machine to disperse his selection.

She walked over and stood beside him. Their eyes met in their reflection of the machine's glass. If she could, she would have said something.

Number Nine moved aside but not without giving her the tiniest wink she had even seen in her life. In fact, she didn't know if it was a wink; it was just the slightest dip of one eyelid.

After another hour, Number Ten stood.

"Vote. Those in favor?"

Ten to two.

"I can't say I'm entirely convinced the charge suits the crime," said Number Five. "That's the right thing, 'charge,' isn't it? We're supposed to determine Birger's guilt for the crime of murder. Why not manslaughter or culpable homicide or...or something?"

This question was met by groans.

"Listen," Number Eight began, "this ain't 'Law & Order,' or 'Perry-freaking-Mason.' No one is gonna jump up and say they're guilty. We were asked to determine if Birger is guilty of murder. Period. If we're in doubt we either need to ask some questions to get *out* of doubt or this may never end."

"Well, I think that there may have been some hanky panky going on and people have been talking where they shouldn't of!" Number Eleven looked around the table.

I know you're not gonna look at me in that tone of voice, Nola thought. When his eyes finally came to meet hers, he quickly looked away.

"That's a pretty heavy accusation you're making," Number Nine said calmly. Nola and the others looked his way only to see him looking at the notepad in front of him. "What makes him say such a thing?" And with that, he raised his head to look straight into the eyes of his roommate.

"I just want this to end. I've made up my mind."

"We can't discuss the case, Nola."

"So who's discussing it? I'm just saying..."

"Shh..."

Tyrell's lips covered hers and Nola luxuriated in their moist softness. His tongue, velvety smooth inside her mouth, tasted slightly of Drambuie. She reached up from her position on the floor to grab at the obligatory notepad and pen.

Breaking the kiss, Nola wrote her full name out on a piece of paper, folded it, and handed it over to him. "Here. Call me. I'm in the phone book."

He smiled.

"Maybe 'hanky panky' is the wrong choice of words," Number Eleven conceded and leaned back in his seat. "But whatever the case, the longer we stew over this, the less convinced I am that we're all gonna agree on a verdict."

"That wouldn't be our fault," Nola said. "We've been deliberating and going over evidence, visiting crime scenes, getting exhibits sent forward... If we, as a group, cannot come to a unanimous decision, then either the prosecution has failed or the defense has succeeded."

"And frankly," she said, and crossed her arms over her chest, "I'm not about to go against my convictions judging from what I have seen."

Number Ten sighed and looked at the clock. It was nearing six o'clock. Dinnertime was approaching. Either they would reach a decision tonight, or—

A knock on the door made all the jurors jump.

The hotel catered a lavish, rich dinner. Due to her cynical nature, Nola couldn't help suspecting that the increase in quality and choice of meals corresponded with the hopes of spurring the jury to reach a decision. They were tired but they didn't want to give up on something that had eaten away at their lives for over two months. Despite their wariness, the jury ate well and was given an additional half hour to unwind before resuming their work. They had until ten o'clock before the hotel van went back to the courthouse.

During this time, Nola wondered if she would really hear

from Tyrell again. Not that it really mattered or bothered her. From what little conversation was allowed between them, he was a nice guy and had a good job. He was unattached and said so, not just to her but to the rest of the group during casual conversation.

Whether or not their encounter last night was a letting off of steam, the venting of heat or simply in response to genuine lust, their time together was coming to an end.

Nola, even though she didn't like to judge, considered herself a good judge of people. She believed that several of them would stay in touch after the trial ended. They had created friendships in spite of their need to remain aloof. They were bound together by jury duty.

But nothing in life is ever certain.

"Okay, everybody...one more vote. Those in favor?"

The next morning, twelve jurors filed into the courtroom and took their seats. The jury foreman, Number Ten, passed over a note to the bailiff who passed it on to the judge who opened it and read it. Sighing, she took off her glasses and faced the jury.

"Are you absolutely positive, Mr. Foreman, that no consensus can be reached?"

"Yes I am, your Honor. This jury is well and truly hung."

IRRESISTIBLE

Cole Riley

Lightning crackled in long twisted bolts of illumination across the endless stretches of fertile, flat land in the distance. This was Kansas, the fabled territory of Oz, Dorothy and her little dog, Toto.

She kept her bloodshot eyes on the winding asphalt road ahead of her, trying to beat the rain that the dark clouds promised would come. On both sides of the old Dodge, there were golden lakes of grain as far as one could see, with an occasional farmhouse or silo dotting the line on the horizon. The car coughed, rattled and spat as she pushed it to the limits of its endurance, attempting to get to some lodging before nightfall.

Nowadays, she spent much of her time spreading the Gospel of the Lord, zigzagging across states, teaching the Holy Word wherever anyone would allow her to use their vacant field or building. Kansas was the fourth state on her current tour across the Midwest. It was a grueling business. Sometimes a good neighbor, one of her newly converted lambs, would take mercy on her and invite her to take a spare room rather than travel on the road in the dark. Sometimes she was not so lucky and would have to sleep in her car. Since she left Chicago three weeks ago, she'd worked most of the towns around Kansas City, everywhere from Lawrence, Overland City, Topeka, all the way to Emporia. Tonight, with luck, she'd stop in Iola, a small place in the middle of nowhere.

Before God, there was her addiction to men. Always men, of all shapes and sizes. She was brought to New York City more than ten years ago to audition at a modeling agency after a scout had seen her photo in one of the local papers in Detroit, a cheesy shot of her standing next to a new Ford. Her mother watched her like a hawk during that first stay in the big city, never letting her daughter out of her sight. The older woman lectured her endlessly about the perils of being seventeen in a metropolis like New York City without anybody to protect or guide her. Oh, the temptations and sins that awaited her. Everybody that saw her told her how beautiful she was, a combination of Cindy Crawford, Iman, and Veronica Webb. Something exotic, something original. She had no idea how obsessed with beauty the entire society was until she listened to her handlers and her mother discuss how much her face and body would bring doing runway and print work in Europe.

Often she wondered what her engineer father would have thought if he'd lived to see her on her way to fame and fortune. On her tenth birthday, he'd been killed instantly when a car driven by a teenager, hopped up on three 40s of chilled malt liquor, lost control of his vehicle. It jumped the curb and ran him down. It was a loss that left a void in her that would never be filled. And yes, she was tall, pretty, clever and healthy, but was she worth the thousands of dollars they paid her hourly to walk up and down in front of gawking people. Her mother continually cautioned her that looks didn't last. *Take advantage of them while you can. Nothing lasts forever. That's our only guarantee in life.* Her mother always concluded her beauty speech with this little pearl of wisdom.

Beauty carries such a heavy price. Nobody would have imagined that she spent so many weekends alone in a darkened room in front of a television. Nobody would have imagined she'd been dumped more than once by men intimidated by her looks or dreams. Nobody would have imagined how often guys had wooed her with lofty promises of fidelity only to flee at the first note of commitment or real intimacy. No, she'd learned that it was all so fleeting, the magazine covers, the chic nightlife, the fancy vacations, the high life. At nineteen, she was a has-been, burned out, with a serious cocaine habit and memories of an Italian boyfriend, Mario, who overdosed on heroin. The good times were behind her. When things got bad, her mother deserted her, just like she knew she would.

Life in the fast lane was too fast. Before Mario died, there was one night that damaged her trust of men forever. She came home from a photo shoot to a living room where her boyfriend sat with another girl, Laura, a model he'd been working with for a session for *Elle* Magazine. The shock on her face intensified when she saw the yellow girl was totally nude, except for the pale imprints where her bikini had once been. Her man was dressed in his boxer-briefs. They were smoking joints on the bed, twisted around each other and giggling. When she entered the room, they didn't stop what they were doing. Following five deep puffs of the potent ganja, she felt completely buzzed and let them undress her, and soon Laura's head was between her legs, her big, yellow behind up in the air. After a while, they changed places and for her, it was like a dream, fuzzy and disjointed. It seemed as if she was watching herself in a strange porno movie. From that day forward, it was all downhill, ending with Mario stretched on the bathroom floor, dead and bone white, with his crystal blue eyes rolled up in his head and a spike in his arm.

Ten years later, all of her big dreams of becoming a hotshot actress with a big-time movie career had evaporated, because the drugs had left their mark on her looks. The little cutie-pie girl from Detroit, who had been transformed into a super-model by a brigade of agents, stylists and photographers, was long gone. In her place was an older, wiser and sober woman determined to redeem herself, to find redemption in this world before going on to the next one. Turning her life around was not easy. It took the near-death experience of an overdose at an after party in the back room at Cosmos, a trendy Soho night-club, to bring her to the Lord. That autumn night, she'd been snorting coke for more that six hours straight when her nose started to bleed, and her heart began racing as if she had just finished the New York Marathon. Disoriented, she tried to get to the ladies' room, thinking she'd splash water on her beau-tiful face, when everything went black, and the floor came up to smack her in the mouth. A short time later, she was loaded in the back of an ambulance and rushed to St. Vincent's Hospital where doctors twice shocked her back to life after her heart shut down.

While she was fighting for her life, she saw herself stretched out on the gurney, with the doctors and nurses battling to bring her back. Nothing they did seemed to work. Her father, dressed in his usual splendor, gave her an orchid from his suit lapel and whispered to her that it was now her choice.

"Elizabeth, you can live or you can die," her father said. There was a sly smile on his long, narrow face that she would never forget. "Your choice." Dead or alive? That night, she chose

life. That night, she found the Lord. And she'd been working for
Him every day since.

On the highway headed for the next town, she plowed ahead
as the sky grew darker, letting memories of the past play quickly
and quietly across the screen of her mind. She reached for a can
of soda on the front seat, taking her eyes off the road for only a
second. A slender figure suddenly popped up in front of her car
just as she glanced up. The car's brakes screamed loudly, and she
lurched to a stop scant inches from the man, who leaped back
from harm's way.

He stuck his head in the window of her car. "Lady, can you
give me a lift to the gas station? My car's up ahead about two
miles, out of gas. It looks like it's about to rain, and you're the
first car I've seen in about an hour."

She looked him over carefully. A woman alone had to be
cautious about picking up a hitchhiker or supposedly stranded
motorist on the road. Still, covered with dust, he appeared not to
be the type that would cause any problems. Tall and slim, the man
was dressed in a dark suit, shirt and tie, but wore sneakers. That
worried her. His head was bald, and his body appeared to be quite
solid under the cloak of the suit. It was his face that captivated
her, unwrinkled and without any sign of the ravages of time. He
wore the face of a child, open, innocent and pleasant to look at.
She calculated his age to be somewhere in his early twenties.

"Redding, someplace, not even on the map." He stuck his
hand into his shirt for a cigarette, but left it there when he saw
the scowl on her face.

"Are you from there, this Redding?" she asked, keeping him
in her line of sight.

"No, I'm just driving back from Kansas City from a job inter-
view," he said almost cheerily. "A salesman job. I don't know if I
got it. The guy said he'd call me in four days."

"I was just in Kansas City a few days ago," she said flatly, watching an airplane dust a field far off in the distance, swooping down out of the clouds to release its load of insecticide.

"That's why the bees are disappearing, the insecticides," he said to her. "Bug sprays. It's killing them. Maybe mites, mobile phones, even the loss of their hives."

"What?"

"Did you know bees in this country pollinate more than fourteen billion dollars' worth of seeds and crops yearly?" He stood looking in her face, waiting for her response.

"What crops?"

"Mainly vegetables, fruit and nuts."

"How do you know so much about bees?" She still didn't trust him.

"I raise them on my place," he replied. "I have a few hives there."

She motioned for him to get in, which he did after swatting some of the dust from his clothes. "I didn't know bees were so important."

"Yes, they are," he said, smiling. "Bees keep the reproduction of plants going and keep them surviving. If the bees vanished off the earth, some say man would only have four years left. With no more bees, there would be no more man."

"Or woman, for that matter," she said.

"What do you do?" the man asked, reaching absently for the cigarettes again. "Do you live in Kansas City?"

She laughed and swerved to avoid something on the road, then straightened out the wheel. "I'm an evangelist. I travel around the country, teaching the Word of God."

"That must be pretty tough on your family, with you on the road all the time," he said. "What does your husband say about you driving all around preaching?"

"I'm not married," she answered. "I'm too busy for that kind of thing."

"That's odd. I thought all women wanted a husband, a family and a home. It seems like the normal thing to do. Surely God wouldn't mind if you took yourself a man. It doesn't seem right for a person to go through this world alone. Without love."

"Well, my personal life takes second place to the work of God," she said, thinking about what he had just said. "Sometimes it's not about what you want, but what He wants. He wants me to serve Him, taking his Word to sinners wherever I find them."

He laughed and said he'd been rude. "My name is Ray. Ray Draper, originally of Abilene and now of Redding. What's yours, lady?"

"Reverend Elizabeth Little," she replied. "Pleased to meet you."

"Reverend Liz, answer me this," Ray began, choosing his words with great care. "Do you miss men? Do you ever miss being loved and adored by a man?"

Sure she missed it. Not that she'd ever tell him what it was like, sleeping in a different bed every night, with your body throbbing and aching from the lack of touch. It had been so long since she'd been with a man. Maybe six years. Maybe she'd forgotten what to do if the opportunity ever arose. And then there was the matter of her Calling, her ministry, that Divine business that left no room for indulging the flesh. If she strayed from the path and took herself a lover, how could she say that she was a true disciple of the Lord? He'd saved her once, and she owed Him. Maybe this young man was a test of her faith, of her resolve, and she couldn't let herself be swayed by temptation.

"I've lived a full life and tasted every fruit," she said. "But that was all before I found the Lord. That's all behind me now."

"It's sad." He said it like he pitied her. "Your God won't let you be a woman. I know people who worship or preach the Bible, and they live a good, normal life without denying themselves anything. I don't think they're evil people or anything."

"Everyone has their way of serving the Master," she said, pulling into the gas station, which seemed to suddenly appear out of nowhere. "This is my way of serving Him. I don't question Him."

"How do you know this is what He wants you to do?" he asked her, watching the man at the gas pump take a fistful of cash from another man in a truck. "You might have it all wrong. It sounds to me like you're punishing yourself for something."

She wanted to answer the man but he jumped out of the car and walked over to the gas station attendant, who appeared to know him. As she watched him, they started quarreling and the attendant took a swing at her passenger, who quickly knocked the guy down with a punch to the face. Then he went through the man's pockets before taking the money from his hand. She revved up the engine to pull away but Ray ran in front of her car, waving his hands. There was a gun in one of them. He pointed it at her, and she lifted her foot off the gas pedal. He walked around to her side of the car and got in, pushing her into the passenger side.

"Why did you do that?" she asked, fighting down her hysteria. "Why did you hit him like that?"

"He owned me some money. Also, my wife and kids ran off with him. He's lucky I didn't kill him. That's what I came up here to do, kill him. He got off easy, I think."

"Where are you taking me?" she asked as he pulled back onto the road.

He didn't answer her. The car sped over the road for almost

two miles before he turned into an alley behind an old road-house. They barely made it inside before it started to rain, a downpour. She watched his hand with the gun and wondered whether she could make a run for it. Her mouth tasted like copper, full of fear. At that moment, she remembered that there had been no deserted car on their way to the gas station. What a fool she had been!

No sooner had he settled in the room than he found a bottle of Scotch in one of the cupboards. It was almost full. He brought out two glasses and offered her one. She shook her head but he still held out the glass. His request that she join him in a drink was not polite; it was an order. Her body shook while she stared at him pouring her drink. This was a moment she'd feared for much of her time on the road. Many nights she'd pass a tavern or roadhouse during her travels, and it took every bit of inner strength to keep going. Now she had no choice.

"You must have some past to be so scared of everything," he said, motioning for her to drink up. "What are you afraid of?"

"Myself. You wouldn't understand that. I've seen your kind of man before."

"What kind of man is that?" he asked, gulping the last of his spirits.

"The kind of man who no longer believes in anything, not even in himself," she said. "The kind of man who wants to corrupt and poison everything he touches. Am I right?"

"Maybe," he muttered and covered his face with his hands.

He said nothing else and continued to drink until he became sleepy. She drank one last drink with him and went to the bath-room where she stripped down to her blouse and panties, show-ered and washed her hair. At first, she wondered what he might do to her, but then he dismissed her fear and surrendered to the gentle spray of water. God was with her. No harm could come to her, not with Him by her side. When she returned, he said she could have the bed, and the sofa would be his for the night. He promised her there would be no funny stuff. It didn't take long for her to fall asleep. He got up and walked to the bedroom door and stood there, listening to her soft breathing, watching her lying on her side.

He could see that Elizabeth was truly a splendid woman for a beauty nearing thirty-five, with a pleasing face, great legs and a magnificent, mature set of breasts. The temptation to satisfy his curiosity was so intense that he turned to leave but did not.

Instead he knelt by her bed and moved his hand lightly along the length of her exposed leg. He continued his explorations of her warm flesh until she sighed in her slumber and flipped on her other side, turning her rear to him. Carefully, he slid under the sheets next to her, still in his underwear, and as soon as his skin touched hers, he felt himself get hard. She was now awake, pretending to be deep in sleep, but every inch of her body was sensitized to his presence. There was no doubt that she wanted him, the first man she'd laid in bed with for longer than she could remember. Far too long.

Somewhere in the room was the solitary glow of a burning candle. Fortunately, he was not the manner of man who approached lovemaking as a chore to be finished as quickly as possible. His fingers hoisted the back of her blouse, gently unsnapped her bra, then massaged the softness of her shoulders, back and the nape of her neck. It was growing more difficult for her to continue her Sleeping Beauty act, especially when she felt his patient kisses blaze along her spine, on the rise and ebb of her hips and the satin mounds of her rear. His intrusive fingers, his kissing and cuddling, fueled the pitched battle between her desire and virtue. He smiled to himself because her body responded although she fought every impulse to make his task of seduction any easier. For a moment, she barely opened her eyes to drink in his body in shadow, hunched over her with his distended spear of skin in hand. Once inside her, he moved his hips up and down slowly, building her passion skillfully like a campfire, and when he almost slipped out, she twisted under him to hold him fast within her. She swallowed hard with each penetration, shivering but never withdrawing from the power of his thrusts. Something happened inside her. All of her inhibitions in her life no longer mattered. This was a real man, not fantasy but real. The blood roared within his veins, his sex puffed up to a size where it hurt him to be in her, but he couldn't help himself with the background music of her moaning and talking filthy to him. He felt his seed rise yet he could not come, and she bucked and rolled in frustration on the bed after he withdrew from her without warning.

With a graceful motion, he lifted her from the bed and carried her kicking to the bathroom where he placed her against the sink, facing away from him. Now he climbed on her, gripping her around the waist as if frightened of being thrown, and danced into her with gyrating hips. There was a touch of something urgent and hysterical in their second coupling. Now at last she felt like a real woman, no longer a prisoner of her past. This unsuspecting man, she knew at that moment, had resurrected all of the emotions pent up by layers of deception, disillusionment and disappointment. He shouted and sagged into the wall behind her, his sex sputtering. Afterward, relishing the wonderful feeling of intimacy between them, they stayed in their individual poses, in the tiny cell of the bathroom, waiting for their hearts to quiet.

He smiled wickedly. "Was that all right?"

She laughed and wiped the sweat from her forehead. How could she answer him? Sure, she was grateful for what he had given her but there was no future between them. His face wore an odd hurt expression. She flinched when he took her hand gallantly, kissed it and begged her to stay with him. No answer existed for his questions. In her heart, she felt a tenderness for this stranger who had revived her sensuality, but she fought down an urge to surrender to him and submit to his every wish and command. She answered his probing eyes and questions by putting her arms around his neck, kissing his serious face and crying as she never had for any other man.

They talked for hours in the darkness, side by side on the bed. Sleep finally came to them both. The sound of a car pulling up outside awoke them and soon there was a hard knock at the door. Ray slid on a shirt, hopped into his jeans and padded barefoot toward the living room. She sat up on the bed, grabbing for her clothing to cover her nakedness. Two beefy white policemen stood in the doorway, quizzing Ray about his whereabouts the previous day, ultimately informing him that he was under arrest. Ray protested but to no avail. She sighed at the terrifying vision of her lover handcuffed by the officers, his massive muscular chest gleaming with sweat.

One of the officers found her purse on the sofa and fished around inside it. "You don't care who you screw, do you, Miss Little?"

Almost instantly, she was stuck by the compulsion to laugh. With the eyes of all the men fixed on her shapely frame, she faced them with a wild look in her stare, while she opened her blouse and adjusted her bra over her full breasts. Still laughing, she sat down and pulled her dress over her legs. They fidgeted, uneasy with the tantalizing spectacle of the woman.

"Boys," she said in a sultry voice, "take your prisoner and go. Bye, Ray. Thank you for a really wonderful evening."

"What did I tell you, Reverend Liz," Ray said as the men

marched him down the path to the police car. "I screw up every-thing, tarnish everybody and everything around me. That's what I do best. Screw up. I'm sorry for all this."

Just the roughneck sound of his manly voice caressed some-thing in her. "Ray, you're much too hard on yourself," she said. They were the last words she would ever say to her miracle lover bound for jail.

She remained in the doorway until the car was just a dot on the highway. "You don't care who you screw, do you, Miss Little?" That nonsense remark by the cracker officer only made her want to laugh again, only made her want to return to the tousled bed and think once more about the coupling of the previous night. Ray really sparked something inside her. One thing was for sure, she would never deny herself again, not in this life. And to tell the truth, the woman in her was alive, awake. Armed with this glorious knowledge, Elizabeth Little started laughing again, laughing until her entire body shook from the force of it. Certainly the Lord wouldn't deny her this small moment of bliss.

ALL DAY

Asha French

Take your panties off."

They were the first words Darius said when I answered the door. Shocked, I paused to eye the length of him, his usual shirt and tie replaced by an oversized tee and athletic shorts, his baseball cap turned backward like it always was when we were growing up. "I can't even get a hello?"

"Hey, babe. You look beautiful. Take your panties off." Darius took his hat off and placed it on the coffee table in my living room, brushing past me to do so. My knees felt weak. It was literally getting harder to stand my ground. I wasn't used to this side of Darius, my old friend who had only recently become a little more than that. I was usually the one barking orders—he preferred it that way—but today was different.

It started with his phone call around ten. When I picked up on the third ring, Darius's voice was on the other end. "Good morning, beautiful."

"Whassup, Darius?"

"Shit… I wanted to ask you something about Alicia's barbecue today."

"Okay. Did your plans change?" I was doing my best to keep my tone neutral, my voice perky. I could usually share any feeling I had with Darius, but I was a little afraid that the recent turn of events had complicated our relationship. Now that we were having sex, I was afraid I'd have to do a little more to guard my heart—something I'd never had to do before with Darius. Sex complicates things.

"You know better. Do I ever just pull out on you like that?"

I giggled. I couldn't help but remember his "pull out" the night before when I wrapped my legs around him and tightened myself around his dick the way I'd been practicing. I think I caught him off guard—or at least his eyes were telling me that much as he kissed my belly button and said, "What are you trying to do to me, girl?"

"Where's your mind at?" Darius's laughed, bringing me back to the phone call. "I was just calling to tell you to wear a dress."

"Tell me?"

"Ask you to please, pretty please, wear a dress to the barbecue today."

"Wear a dress? Is this some bougie, Jack-and-Jill-ass party where I have to wear the right thing? Should I press my hair out too, just for good measure? You want me to wear makeup? I got a lighter shade…"

"You forget who you're talking to all the time, Janae. But it's aight though. The dress is for me, you look better without makeup because you never get the shade right. No wonder you got a lighter shade. And Alicia thinks Jack and Jill is a Mother Goose rhyme, so it's good. Now, you gonna wear a dress for me? Please?"

"Yes." I laughed, thinking about how having sex with Darius had really only complicated things for me. Before we had sex a few days ago, I'd been convinced that he was a nice guy—just not for me. Now that we'd taken it there, I was treating him like any other dude who was pressed for panties. I'd become a lot more guarded and was afraid about what it would do to our friendship. "Darius, my bad…"

"No apology necessary. I was being allusive. I deserved all, well most, of that. I get it, although it does hurt my feelings when you forget how not lame I am."

"I know you're not lame."

"And you'll wear a dress for me?"

"I guess I can make that happen for you."

"Good. See you in a few."

Those few hours felt like days as I toiled over the choices of dresses. I wanted to look casual, but not clumsy—put together, but not contrived. When I finally decided on a plain white, knee-length sundress with skinny straps, the doorbell rang. So now I was in an unzipped sundress with Darius demanding that I take off my panties.

Darius moved behind me to zip my dress. He always knew exactly what I needed before I told him. When I felt his warm fingers against my back, then the nape of my neck, I felt my panties grow damp, clinging to me. Darius brushed his right hand across my nipple, holding it for a moment between his finger and thumb before dropping it lower and lower, until he'd reached the spot where my own wetness had begun to pool.

"Need some help?"

"Yeah. You can take them off yourself."

Darius turned me around so I could feel his hardness press against me through his shorts. I wrapped my arms around his neck and stood on the tips of my toes to kiss him. I loved Darius's full lips. I playfully nibbled his bottom lip before letting go to dance my tongue around his. I felt his hands move up under the back of my dress, his fingertips at my hips pushing the weight of my soaking panties until they were halfway down. Darius pulled away from my searching kisses and began his southern trek.

That's what I called Darius's slow, lazy trail to my pleasure spot. The first time he made the trek, I thought that he was taking so long because he didn't know what he was doing. But he quickly showed me I was wrong. Now I know what he knows—the slower he goes, the more excited I am when he makes it to what he calls my "honeypot." He was on his way there now, his big hands kneading the flesh of my behind. Darius started by kissing my neck as if it were an old lover with whom he'd just reunited. He moved farther down, kissing each nipple through the light cotton fabric. At the same time, he swept over my clit with his thumb, still kneading my ass. I inhaled sharply, "Ooh, Darius. Too much..." escaping my lips before I knew what I'd said.

"You want me to stop?" He paused, searching my eyes.

"No." He walked me back toward the couch as my legs began to shake. He knew what I knew—that I wouldn't be able to stand much longer with his mouth and hands working all over me. I felt the leather couch against the back of my legs and I sank down onto it, grabbing his shoulders as he pushed my dress up and began to lick my belly button. His tongue was a dizzying swirl and his hands were covered in my wet appreciation for their expertise. I stroked the muscles that lined his back as he pulled my soaking panties over one ankle, then the other. Darius kissed the soft stretch of skin between my belly button and my honeypot, his full lips stamping approval on every bulge, every stretch mark I'd ever complained about way back when we were "just friends." He'd listened, I was learning.

Darius lapped at my clit for a split second before he moved a little lower to kiss each lip, then lick the inside of each thigh. I could feel myself pulsing in excitement, my lower lips engorged. "Darius, please!" I practically yelled, one hand playing in Darius's hair while the other was covering my own mouth so I wouldn't scream. I moaned into that hand as Darius buried his face in my honeypot, licking and sucking until my legs shook uncontrollably. He held the hood down with his finger and thumb as he went back and forth between sucking and licking my little button. I felt my body climbing to the peak to which Darius had taken me time and time again, and I made the mistake of announcing it.

I call it a mistake because as soon as he heard the words, "Dee, I'm gonna cum," he pulled away abruptly and began to adjust my dress.

"What the?"

"Chill out, babe. I just want to try something new I read in this book called *The All-Day Orgasm*." He picked his hat up from the table behind him and stood up, heading down the hall.

"Darius, I ain't trying to be mean, but I could give a fuck about a book right now." I followed him to the bathroom, where he stood at the mirror rinsing my juices from his goatee.

"I know, Janae." Darius laughed. "You know I'mma take care of you." He turned around and pulled me close, kissing first my mouth then both sides of my neck. I kissed his neck too, pulling the skin between my teeth and sucking. I felt him stiffen against my wetness and I wanted to feel him inside me now more than ever. I reached for the elastic band of his gym shorts.

"Yeah, Darius. I know. Just let me..." Darius moved my hand away, standing back to kiss me at the top of my forehead.

"We'll be late."

"Dee, what is this?" I began to straighten myself out, annoyed with the game. As I fluffed out my afro where I'd flattened it against the sofa, I found Darius's eyes in the mirror. He was standing behind me and putting on his cap. "Is this some more allusive stuff that you were doing earlier today?"

"I want to see if I can extend your orgasm over hours. You know I'mma take care of you one way or the other, right?" He was behind me now, kissing my neck and rubbing my shoulders. I couldn't help but shudder; my body was so tense that the slightest touch from Darius sent me climbing back up to that peak that he was hell-bent on keeping me away from.

"And I'm just supposed to be frustrated all day?"

"Don't think frustrated; think excited. It's about perspective.

"I can't think at all when you touch me like that, Darius." I moved his hand away.

"So do you want to try it? 'Cuz if you're gonna be mad, we don't even have to go to Alicia's house. We can do it right here. I don't mind." His hands were on my hips and he pulled me back against him so that I felt his hardness against the small of my back. He moved his hands up and down my sides as he kissed the back of my neck.

"Okay. If you can be that controlled, then so can I." I laughed, turning around to kiss his lips. "I'll see it as a challenge." I was dizzy with anticipation, but I wanted to try this "new thing" that Darius had read about, so I walked toward the door.

Once we were inside his car, he reached across me to buckle me. He was close enough for me to smell his cologne, which I hadn't noticed before. I loved when his cologne mixed with the smell of his perspiration; the sweet stickiness of it made me lightheaded. "You smell so good," I said as I kissed him behind his ear.

"As do you," he said, bending down to sniff my honeypot, which grew wet just because of his proximity to it.

"Darius, you're gonna make me walk into this barbecue with cum running down both legs."

"Don't worry. We'll clean you up." He winked, starting the car. Darius drove with his left hand, his right hand playing beneath my dress. He held my pussy in the palm of his hand, squeezing every other moment until I began to move against it. I reached over and began to stroke his dick through his shorts. He was stiff as stone—so hard that I began to get frustrated with this game all over again. His pointer and middle fingers were working my G-spot now while his thumb massaged my clit. I pressed my foot against the dashboard, bracing myself as Darius began to stroke faster and faster. I closed my eyes against the blinding light that made it feel like my head would explode. I came hard, my wetness covering Darius's right hand, body shaking, eyes rolled back in my head. I didn't say a word, though, because I'd decided that the start and stop was annoying.

"You cheated," Darius smiled, still cupping my spasming pussy.

"I couldn't help it, Darius. You know what you do to me."

"What do I do? Tell me," he said, stroking my clit until it hardened again.

"I can't say it."

"Tell me," he said, pleading like a child, his finger moving in faster circles around my clit.

"You make me... You make me... Ooh, Darius, you make me..."

"We're here." Darius pulled his hand away and put the car in PARK. When I opened my eyes, we had arrived at his cousin, Alicia's house.

"No, Dee. Are you serious?"

"As a heart attack," he said, sounding like his father. "Here. I got napkins."

Darius opened his glove compartment and began to clean up the mess we'd made. But I didn't want all this wetness to go to waste.

"But Darius, can't we do it right here—just real quick? Everybody's in the house. Your windows are tinted. I know I said I would play your game, but now I'm frustrated."

"Frustrated?" Darius laughed. "You already broke the rules and came. So technically, we're not playing my game no more."

"I know. But women are equipped to have multiple orgasms, so we can always start all over. Like after this next one," I said, climbing across the divider into Darius's lap. I reached for his dick, which was hard in my hand, and I began to stroke it until I felt it grow even stiffer.

"Self-control," Darius reminded me, his rough hands playing with my booty through my skirt. "Now you said you didn't want anybody to know anything. What would happen if Alicia came out here to find you riding me? The whole world would know in minutes."

"True," I said, collapsing onto his chest in surrender. Darius and I hadn't told anyone about our new arrangement; as far as our families were concerned, we were still just platonic friends. When Darius moved to my city for work, things had started to grow past platonic friendship and near the point of confusion. I'd learned in the last few months that men operate by contract; I couldn't assume that we were together—no matter how much time I spent in his lap. Besides, I wasn't even sure that I wanted more from Darius. Sex and relationships had always been complicated for me. I wanted Darius to be in my life for the rest of it; I didn't want to jeopardize that by trying to make him my man.

"And you still don't want people to know?" Darius's voice was a whisper as he played with my hair, my head resting on his chest.

"No."

"Okay, then you might want to get up because here comes Alicia." I jumped up so fast that my head hit the roof of Darius's car. I was trying to untangle my legs from Darius's, but it's really hard to get out of a straddle position with grace. Darius grabbed me before I impaled myself on the gearshift between us. "I was just playing. Calm down!"

"Boy!" I screamed, giggling and air-boxing with him. "You play too much!"

"Don't hurt yourself now," Darius laughed, helping me out of my door and rubbing my head.

Alicia's barbecue was a blur of frus—excitement. I was glad that his parents didn't choose this weekend to visit—they know me too well and would have been able to read my face. It was hard to act normal when Darius brushed against me every time he could. When the food was ready, he pretended to drop his napkin beneath the table. On his knees, he hiked my skirt up and began to nibble and suck on my clit. I didn't know whether to scoot away or stay where I was when I felt his warm tongue lapping at my slit. I felt every second pass as I struggled to keep my face normal, belying all that was going on down there. Darius stopped—as was the norm today—and got back in his seat, waving his napkin like a flag. "Found it!" I blushed.

When I was finished eating, I decided to play with Alicia's kids. I knew Darius wouldn't mess with me around the little ones. Alicia's daughters were teaching me how to keep my hula hoop from falling when I caught Darius's eye from across the yard. His gaze narrowed as if the weight of wanting me was resting on top of his eyelids. When he licked first his top lip, then his bottom lip, I lost concentration and dropped the hoop, to the little one's dismay.

"That wasn't no long time at all!" Tadra said.

"I know. Let me try one more time," I said, turning away from Darius's distracting eyes.

But Darius wouldn't be put off. I heard him yell to Alicia, "We'll wash the dishes!"

Alicia got up from the patio chair and put her hands on her hips, yelling across the yard. "Uh-uh, Dee! Don't be dragging that girl in the kitchen like this is Atlanta Housewives or some shit. You see she's doing something! Those dishes will get washed in the morning."

But Darius was already stacking all the serving platters and bowls. I loved the serious look that seemed to take over his whole face when he was in the middle of some project. He looked calculating and focused, his thick brows furrowed, his bottom lip tucked in. "It's okay, Alicia!" I yelled back. "Dee knows I'm nobody's housewife. Besides, Tadra's about to beat me up if I drop this hula hoop one more time."

I followed Darius to the kitchen where he was running water in the sink. When he heard the side door creak open, he turned off the water and dried his hands on his shirt. He was on me in seconds, his hands buried in my hair, his mouth searching out my own.

"Janae, I've been wanting you all day. I can't keep this up."

I put my hands inside his shirt, feeling the expanse of his back before I moved around to the front to rub all over his abs and chest. I put my hand over his heart and felt the quickening thud. "Umm, Darius. What about self-control?" I giggled as his hands found their way to my ass. He was cupping me and squeezing me just the way I liked and I reached inside his shorts to grab a feel for myself. Darius had a beautiful dick. I stroked the length of it, feeling its girth fill up my hand. I brushed my thumb over the tip, where his wetness told me that self-control was out the window.

"I used all my self-control at your house." Darius whispered in my ear. "Do you know how bad I wanted to lay you across that couch? You do something to me, Nae."

"What do I do?" I said, playing the game he'd played with me earlier in the car. "Tell me."

"If you wash the dishes, I'll show you." Darius pulled himself away from me and turned my body toward the sink.

"Wait a minute. You said *we* would wash the dishes."

"We will," Darius said, sliding down the front of the sink so that he was sitting and facing my dripping honeypot. "Now you're the lookout. If you see anybody coming our way, you gotta let me know so I can get up."

"Okay," I huffed, catching my breath as I felt his tongue move up and down the line of my slit. I was trying to keep my eyes on the window above the sink, which looked out over the whole yard. Alicia's girls were still hula hooping; Alicia was in the middle of some story; her husband and his friends were playing spades; and Darius was making my love run down my legs. I didn't know if I could stand any more and I almost fainted when I heard Darius's gruff voice commanding me to wash the dishes as he gave my ass a quick, hard slap.

I knew I'd get him back, and began to wash the dishes quickly, eyes on the yard. With his quick, darting tongue and his thick lips, Darius sent shivers from my toes to the nape of my neck. I broke his rule twice before I said, "I can't take it, Darius. Not standing." My legs felt like rubber as Darius pulled his head from under my skirt, face glistening with my cream.

"You sure, babe?" He kissed my clit once through my dress for good measure.

"I'm sure. Besides, the dishes are done. It's time for you to dry them." I winked, reaching out to help Darius to his feet.

"Oh, word?" he asked, pretending nonchalance badly.

I pushed his shorts past his hips, held his hardness in my hand and sank to my knees. "Word. Now dry the dishes." My command wasn't as believable as Darius's, but it did the job. I flicked my tongue over the tip of Darius's dick, holding the base tightly in my hand. When I eased the length of it down my throat, I heard a dish clatter above my head. I smiled. "You okay?"

"Janae." I continued to deep-throat Darius, making sure I wet his dick from base to tip. Then I pulled away and began to stroke it, slick as it now was with my own spit. I was stroking Darius and sucking the head of his penis, my mouth meeting my hands so that no part of Darius was untouched. More dishes clanked and fell, and Darius's hips were bucking with every movement of my tongue. With my other hand, I cupped Darius's balls, pulling and releasing the tender flesh. Darius's moans were becoming deeper and longer and precum was seeping from the head of his penis. I lapped at it and swallowed before I pulled away, devilishly plotting to get him back for what he'd been doing all day.

"You done with the dishes, Dee?" I said, standing up and smiling sweetly. Darius's pants were still around his hips where I'd left them when I freed his dick from them. I reached around him and pulled them all the way up, giving his ass a squeeze for good measure.

Darius laughed. "Touché. Well played." His hands, smelling like Joy dishwashing liquid, were on the sides of my face as he leaned in and began to kiss me—slowly at first and then with all the passion that we had built throughout the day. I was sucking and biting on his bottom and top lip and he was doing the same to me. His hands moved down my body, massaging every part of me until I thought I would scream. When I felt his hands cup my ass, I buried my face in his neck, where his cologne had mixed with the day's sweat.

"I can't take it!" I raked my nails up and down his back. "Darius, I want you so bad right now. Let's quit playing."

"What you want me to do?" Darius asked, his hands still kneading my behind, his stiffness pressed against my pulsing clit.

"Quit playing."

"Am I playing?" He bent down and began to suck my nipple through the thin fabric of my dress. I heard the sounds of the barbecue behind me and I began to get nervous because we'd both stopped keeping watch.

"Yes!" I hissed. Darius was starting his happy trail again, and he'd reached my belly button. "You know we can't do it here."

Darius stood up and began to look around. "Follow me." I wasn't sure that I could walk on my trembling legs, but I held on to Darius's hand and let him lead me into the basement.

"Won't they come looking for us?"

"They're drunk." Darius laughed. "They ain't looking for nobody."

It took a minute for my eyes to adjust to the dark room, but when they did, I saw boxes stacked against the wall. We were in Alicia's storage closet, and Darius's hands were under my dress again. I lifted Darius's T-shirt over his head and began my own happy trail down to my prize. I held the weight of him in my hand while I sucked and licked the tip of his dick, drawing circles with my tongue. I put its full, salty length in my mouth, bracing myself against the boxes. Darius tilted his head toward the ceiling, groaning. I pulled away so that I could push his shorts down over his ankles. Darius lifted my chin with his fingers and began to kiss me, talking between kisses.

"Now what did you say you wanted me to do?" He'd unzipped my dress and was pulling the straps off my shoulders.

"I want you to quit playing with me." I moaned as he massaged my breast and began to suck my nipple. His left hand found my wetness and he began to stroke my clit.

"Am I playing now?" Darius entered one, then two fingers inside my wet hole, stroking upward until he felt the ridged flesh that was my G-spot.

"No, baby." My head was spinning; I closed my eyes and continued to stroke Darius with my hand.

"And now?" He'd cocked one leg back and was hitting my spot with more speed and force, bending to lick and suck my clit intermittently.

"No, but Darius…"

"Yeah, babe?"

"I want to feel you now." My head was about to explode. I'd already cum once and Darius was working on the second wave. "Now, Darius. Please." I backed up against the boxes, trying to escape the heat of his mouth, the strength of his fingers. I reached for his dick that was standing at attention.

"You sure?"

"Positive." Darius always waited until I asked for it. He rifled through his shorts looking for his condom. I held my breath in anticipation until I saw the gold pack. We locked eyes as he rolled the Magnum down until it rested at the base of his beautiful dick. He slid to his knees and began to suck my clit again, dipping lower to lap at the juices, then coming back up to suck some more.

"Please, Darius," I whined, reaching for his ass and spreading my legs. I wanted him inside me.

"I just want to taste you."

"I want to feel you, Dee."

"You sure?"

"Now."

I was standing against the boxes, legs spread and ready for Darius. He paused for a moment that felt like an hour, then pressed the head of his dick into my dripping slit. I thought I would pass out as I felt him stretching me, easing into my wetness. I pulled at his hips, but he wouldn't go deeper.

"Please, Dee." But he kept pulling out and pushing in, stopping at a shallow depth.

"Can I go deeper?" he growled.

"God, yes."

Darius pushed himself deeper inside me, brushing against my spot so that I covered my own mouth to keep from screaming with pleasure. I wrapped my legs around Darius's waist, determined to hold him there. He began to stroke me slowly, and I felt every hard inch of him bathed in my wetness.

"Janae, you feel so good." He kept his strokes slow and even, then gradually picked up speed. "So good."

I leaned forward to kiss him, tightening my legs for balance. We danced tongues as he stroked me and massaged my ass. Still hard inside me, Darius carried me to the other side of the storage room where a table stood in the corner. With one arm, Darius swept the boxes off the table, laying me down gently onto it. I thought I would cum then, but I was afraid to tell him, lest he pull out. I bit my lip, which was always my giveaway to Darius, who watched my every movement.

"Don't worry, Nae. I ain't playing this time." Darius picked up speed and began to stroke upward, hitting all the right spots. His left arm was beneath my head and he began to rub my clit with his right hand. "I'm not going to stop until you cum."

"Darius!" I was rising, almost at the point of no return. "Ooh, Dee...I'm gonna cum!" He continued to hit my spot and I felt myself stretching to accommodate his thick dick while his hand made magic on my clit. He was stroking and rubbing, stroking and rubbing until I burst, legs shaking, hips jerking uncontrollably. I closed my eyes tight to ride out the wave while Darius kept stroking, slower now. When I opened my eyes, he was still staring at me with the same intensity, still hard inside me.

"Again?" he asked, thumb pressed against my clit. I nodded, all words lost with the last orgasm. "Can I put you on your belly?" I nodded again as Darius eased himself out of me. My pussy began to spasm as if protesting the void he'd left. I rolled over on the table, facedown, ready for round two.

I felt Darius's hand beneath my chin. "I want to see you, Nae. Your eyes make me cum." I was growing wetter with every word. I strained my neck to look at Darius as he entered me from behind, sliding easily into my dripping pussy.

"Umm, Janae, umm," Darius moaned over and over, and I could tell he was near his own orgasm. I tilted my hips up so that Darius's stroke hit me in the right spot. I began to shake as I rode out my third or fourth orgasm of the day—I'd stopped counting.

"I'm coming, Darius."

"Me too, love." I came and I froze, Darius's last word resounding in my mind. Love? I felt Darius's hips shake and his strokes became erratic, losing all their rhythm. He collapsed against me, stroking slower now and holding both my breasts in his hand. Love? After a moment, Darius pulled out and turned me over, kissing the space between my breasts before he laid his head there. Love? I played with his hair with one hand, stroked his back with the other. I didn't know what to say. Maybe it was a nickname with the same power as "baby" or "honey." I didn't know. What I did know was that I was suddenly afraid, the weight of what we'd been doing the past week as heavy as Darius was, collapsed onto my small frame.

"They'll be looking for us," I whispered, stirring beneath him. Darius got up, interrogating me with his eyes.

"Something's wrong."

"No, it's not. You were good, baby. I like your all-day game."
I tried to smile and hide my fear.

"Something's wrong and I know it." Darius was stepping
into his shorts, pulling his shirt down over his head. "Did I do
something to make you uncomfortable?"

"No, Darius. I would tell you." I stepped into my white dress,
pulled the straps onto my shoulders. Darius came behind me to
zip up my dress, then kissed me at the nape of my neck.

"You promise?" He kissed both my shoulders. I nodded,
unable to lie to my friend. Friend?

When we got upstairs, the sun had left the sky, leaving pink
footprints in its wake. Alicia and her friends were still in the
same place, her husband and his still playing cards. The girls
were on to some other game, the hula hoops discarded in the
yard. Alicia walked us to the door as we said our good-byes to
the others. She was standing on her porch as Darius opened first
my door, then his. He started the car.

"Y'all nasty!" Alicia laughed, waving as we pulled away. I
laughed too, embarrassed and feeling dangerous. Darius's hand
found my own as we drove toward my place.

WHEN
THE RIVER

Leone Ross

Once upon a time Rosemarie met a man of integrity. He was six foot two inches of gentle, with warm blue eyes and a fiancée.

They met in a hotel in an old European country, he on business, she on business and neither intending anything more carnal than the breeze tickling the edges of the grand, oily building. Her room was bigger than her apartment back home—the management had converted ancient stables—and sometimes she thought she could hear the grunting of horses in the walls and their stamping feet at night waking her up.

She found the country an odd place, not green or red or orange like Trinidad, where all things, especially secrets, were Technicolor, but instead full of rare moments of light: a brilliant flower in amongst the shadowy walls, a flag on a car whizzing past, or the calm eyes of this man of integrity whose room faced hers on the other side of the hotel courtyard. They met in the middle, laughing at the queer accoutrements on show: a game of bowls set out for visitors; a giant chess set with figures as big as a small child and a brilliant blue and purple peacock stalking around a cage in the background.

She had a habit of fixing men she desired with her large brown eyes, and he had the same habit. They began an eleven-day staring match in which he taught her bits of his language in the courtyard below the other guests' bedrooms every night, and they laughed until 1:00 a.m. At no point was there any sugges-tion of impropriety; he told her on the first night that he loved his woman, and she understood.

Rosemarie tried to stop looking into his eyes because the water there was so very tempting, but she was drawn in again and again. It didn't help that he was awkward during the day: when he entered a room he checked to see where she was, fidg-eting, biting his fingernails, looking at her when he thought nobody was watching. He stuttered over her name when he said it in public. Some days he loitered around the edges of groups she was in; other days he ignored her. She was in a constant pit of emotions—triumphant, happy, relaxed, terrified, self-conscious. But regardless of how they were during the day, he would find her in the night: to talk politics, religion, film, and always to laugh. She was worried that he could smell her, soaking through her thin cotton trousers, and she found herself stroking things as he spoke—the tabletop between them, a pebble on her palms, her own cheek—yet each always holding the other's gaze so very deeply. He began to mirror her body language, to lean forward seconds after she did, cupping his hands to his face the way she did, his pupils dilating. He touched her three times: to flick an earwig from her shoulder, to pick something off the back of her sweater, and another time when their knees touched, like a baby's kiss, when he left his knee there for screaming seconds.

Goodnights between them lingered, and they were painful and

warm. He reached out for her, or was happy for her to hug him or kiss his cheeks, but it was all so wooden and difficult! Never had she seen two such worried people. It was because they could both feel the bedrooms around them, leaning in on them.

Why you keep finding me every night, she thought, wanting him to, but proud of his restraint, this good man. *What you want from me?*

She sought respite in another friendship: an elderly, married man called Leo, who sometimes joined them outside in the evenings to smoke. Leo laughed when she told him how much she liked the man of integrity. "I understand," he said, and patted her hand.

"But you know that he will never betray his fiancée."

She felt sick. Leo and the man were friends, and part of her had hoped that he would tell her something she didn't know, like fighting or disagreements or that the fiancée had no integrity. But she knew it wouldn't be so: every night, when the staring began to waver, to splinter at the edges, she could feel him leaving her. It was as if water began to seep through the cracks in their speech, and as time trickled by, his new reluctance became a river, unending and unquestionable. It was as if his woman was swimming toward them, whispering. At these times, his smiles didn't matter, the hours they spent together didn't matter; she was a mere puddle of rainwater when compared to the inevitability of his impending marriage.

"I will be your *butlava vrba*, your hollow willow tree," Leo said. It meant confidante in their language, somebody to fill up with words, to stop herself from saying them out loud in the courtyard. She was grateful for his affection—she could call him over and lean against him, and their easy hugs soothed her.

On the ninth night Rosemarie told the man of integrity that it had been good to get to know him. He changed the subject and began to explain theories of relativity, looking up into the sky, saying how far away the stars were, when compared to the sun, and that it took seven years for their light to reach us. She was hurt that he'd changed the subject, but then realized he hadn't; clumsily, he'd brought it back to them, saying that wherever they were in the world they would be close, certainly in comparison with the stars, that they could reach out anytime, that they looked at the same sky.

Such a sweet-mouth boy, she thought.

She could only keep her sanity by sitting in the watery sunshine, writing very bad poetry that she feared someone finding. She remembered every hair on her body, was reminded that she naturally walked to sway her hips; at night she wouldn't even masturbate, in case orgasm should, for one second, compromise the ache on her. The muscles inside her flexed, as if considering some delicious labor. She puzzled herself, drifting off to sleep, thinking of the horses in the old stable walls, splashing through rivers to mount her. She'd never seen a horse in Grenada; only rich people had them. Her girlfriends would laaaaugh, you see! To see her helpless thinking about this blue-eyed man, with her pussy open so, and calling.

On the last night they laughed and stared until 3:00 a.m., with the peacock squawking behind them and her running out of cigarettes to suck. She swore his hands were shaking. She complained she'd left her dreams back home, because she hadn't had any since arriving.

"I had a dream last night," he blurted.

"Yes?"

"You were in it."

Her stomach contracted.

"Yes?"

He looked down at the table where her hands lay, pulsing.

"I'm tired." He rose to his feet.

She wanted to die. She tried to laugh.

"So you're not going to tell me about the dream?"

He stood by the hotel doors and shook them. She wished he didn't have to go. Below her navel, her hips twitched.

He frowned. "The door's locked."

Again, her stomach.

He laughed. "They've locked me out!" There was something inside the laugh, a tremble, a change in his breathing. They stared at each other.

"I'll go and see if the door at the back is open," he said, and disappeared around the side of the building.

She sat on her hands. She thought of her huge double room, on the other side of the courtyard. If he couldn't get in, that was the only place to sleep. That, or the peacock pen. She looked at the peacock. All week the peacock had been singing to them. Leo explained that peacocks don't sing. He explained that peacocks make very little noise, except for the squawking of loneliness. This peacock has been looking at her with big bright eyes and blue feathers for eleven days. She didn't know whether the peacock reminded her of the man of integrity or of herself.

He was back, panting. There was fuzz on his broad chest that she wanted to smell. She looked at him. "Well?"

"I can't get in. Everything's locked, everyone's sleeping or gone home."

She wondered if all hotels in this country abandoned their guests at night.

Kiss me, oh, she thought. The peacock sang, even though peacocks do not sing.

"I'll just go and try something else," he said. She watched his mouth as he said it, then strode away.

She closed her eyes. God was a sadist. She'd been so good,

but she couldn't hold on any longer. This moment couldn't be any more insane or perfect or booklike or movielike. She opened her eyes. He'd come back around the hotel and was pacing in front of the door, muttering. He was so well fashioned, so tall and tight and beautiful. She could ride him like a horse. He looked desperate, and for any other friend, she would have said it already: plenty of room with me, come.

But she would hold him down if he came to her room. Doesn't matter how big and broad he is, she would hold down the boy and kill him with her love, like Trini women at carnival.

He shook the heavy doors and looked back at her. She spread her hands, questioning, tried to smile. He shrugged and rubbed his brow. "Can't get in," he said.

Please please please God, she thought. *Let him come sleep with me tonight. I won't hold him down. I swear I won't. I just want to lie with him, and have that intimacy, and maybe he could want me, just for a minute, and maybe a kiss, no more, I just want to know that he wants me, that's all. Please God, amen.*

Is those things you praying to God for, girl? She could hear her Auntie Pearl's voice in her head.

His hand was warm on her shoulder. She looked up at him. *Oh, please oh, please.* She took a deep breath, and let it out.

He was so worried.

"Tell me about your dream," she said. "Since"—her voice faltered—"since you're locked out and we have time?"

He hesitated, then moved closer toward her, intending to sit down. She shifted backward a few inches to accommodate him on the bench, which she was straddling, but he put one hand between her shoulder blades, holding her still as he swung a leg over the bench to straddle it himself. Then they were riding it like children on a seesaw, facing each other, and for one silly, sweet moment their noses nearly touched.

His breath smelled of peppermint and good wine. He rearranged himself; they were no longer as close, but their knees touched and the pressure of his on hers was firm and unyielding, like he'd made a decision.

"I fucked you," he said, almost conversationally.

She liked swearwords. She especially liked the word *fuck*.

"What?"

"In the dream," he said.

She nearly wept in relief. "Tell me."

"I fucked you in the dream and I do want to tell you about it. But I won't ever fuck you," he said. "That will never happen. But I want to tell you how it would be, so you know I know, that I've thought about you."

"A gift," she suggested.

"Yes." He hesitated. His lips were suddenly very wet. "Does that sound stupid? Ah. I want to know if what I'm dreaming about is...what you..."

"As I like it?"

"Yes."

She smiled and rocked from side to side to calm the spasms.

"For example. Do you like...me saying that I want to fuck you?"

"Oh, god"—her breath hitches in her throat and she pushes her vagina into the bench—"yes."

"Is it the word, the word *fuck?*"

"Mmm-*hm*."

He smiled, like ticking off a list. "Okay. So the dream said..."

He told her about the way it would be. That her skin would smell of cigarettes and apricots. In the dream he took her throat in his hands and ran whispers up and down it and took handfuls of her wetness and rubbed it into his skin.

She told him how sticky she gets inside, that lovers have complimented her, and that she liked the idea of him smelling like pussy for an hour afterward.

He said that all the time she was groaning and he bit down on three of her fingers. She was so aroused by the idea he had to pause so she could bite a finger to show him in real life.

He said that they touched each other with concentration and that he was making sounds he'd never heard before. They spent long moments holding, no movement, he said, just heart sounds between them as she dripped down her thighs and he tried not to come. He could tell where her erogenous zones were without touching—cells and nerve endings in the palms, fingertips, up the wrist; avoid the breasts, not because he discounted their roundness, but because he knew what she needed: mouth, hands, clit, he kept saying, that's what I'd do to you, mouth, hands, suck your clit, in his clear, sweet voice: that's who we'd be together, I think. There'll be no sex, never. No kiss, no touch. This is a gift, his voice almost pleading: I want to share with you, I want to show you, do you understand how much I want to fuck you?

He said that when he pushed inside, her vagina was interwoven with delicate grooves like some kind of sentient marble, sucking him.

Rosemarie felt as if she were rain and glass, used her index finger to stroke the bench between them, then simply put her hands on her hips and spread her legs and rubbed herself against the wood.

He leaned back and watched her, still talking.

He said that he had to keep wiping his hand on the sheets because she was too wet to orgasm; that it took some coaxing, but he made her sit on his face until her thighs gave way.

Panting, she wound her hips in slow figure-eights, jerking herself along the wood. Rarely had she felt so exposed and brave. It was like losing your virginity, a genuine waiting for something new, a revelation. She made her hands tight fists so she wouldn't touch him, because although he was smiling, and she could see his penis straining against his jeans, his eyes were so full of no.

When she finally moaned, she had to grab the bench to steady herself, head swimming, hips bucking, eyes closed. When she opened them, the man with integrity had taken himself away, and all she could hear was the stars and the creak of the oily building.

The next morning he and Leo came over to say good-bye; he opened his arms for her and they hugged and Leo looked away politely as she put her head on his shoulder and he stroked her hair, and they stood for a while, as guests streamed past. She didn't want to cry, so she didn't.

When he finally let her go, she looked up and his eyes were the Caribbean Sea.

SEX AND CHOCOLATE

Garnell Wallace

I fully understand why someone would write a song about the moon over New York City. Even after five years of living in the Big Apple, I was still spellbound by its cold, luminous beauty. But looks can be deceiving, and I soon learned why the city also had a reputation as one of the toughest in the world, especially for a small-town dreamer like me.

The day I finally closed my restaurant and sat in the window seat of my small apartment staring up at that deceiving moon was the worse day of my life. Admitting defeat had been tough for me, but night after night of nearly empty tables would make a believer out of anyone. I took what I saw as their rejection of me personally and hard. I'd never wanted anything but to become a celebrated chef.

I grew up on a small island in the Bahamas, raised by my grandmother from whom I inherited a love of food and a deep appreciation for my African heritage. Her dream was that I would someday take over the small but thriving down home–style restaurant she owned.

But a little island in the Bahamas hadn't been big enough to contain my dreams. I'd studied in Paris and spent a year roaming the Tuscan hills in search of amazing ingredients I could incorporate into my grandmother's recipes. I thought I had to adapt their simplicity to appeal to a more sophisticated palate. I'd altered them so much that even my grandmother wouldn't have recognized half of them as her own. I'd destroyed their soul to appeal to the masses and in the process changed myself until I was nothing more than a watered-down version of the person I was meant to be.

I was still trying to figure out exactly who I was as I stared at the last ten years of my life and dreams all crammed into the space I'd once called home but which now felt like a museum of my failures. There were pieces from the restaurant I just couldn't bear to part with, things I hadn't been able to donate or sell; the artwork from my last trip to Africa still in boxes, never having made it onto the shelf it'd taken me an entire weekend to set up. The restaurant had consumed my life, as had the city. It'd taken everything I had to offer and left a hollow shell I now had to fill with a personality and a purpose.

The phone rang and I allowed the machine to take care of whoever was invading my wine-infused pity party.

"Hey Mia, Miss Busy Bee."

I groaned at the cheeriness in my best friend Zoë's voice. It irritated my last nerve. "God, it should be illegal for anyone to be so happy," I said as I listened to her babble.

"How 'bout picking up the phone and calling once in a while? Now that you're a big city chef you don't have time for the little people?" She laughed, assuring me there were no ill feelings behind her words.

Zoë was important to me. She'd supported me fully in my dreams, had listened while I rattled on about the amazing life

I would have. Even when we were young Zoë knew she would spend her life on Harbour Island. She'd married her high school sweetheart and now spent her days running after adorable four-year-old twin girls and filling her art gallery with beautiful paintings for natives and tourists alike. She didn't dream of becoming the next Picasso or Basquiat. She was content just being Zoë.

I'd never found that kind of contentment, maybe because I was always changing myself into what I thought someone else wanted me to be. Maybe I needed to go back home and start all over again.

From the moment I stepped off the plane in the Bahamian capital of Nassau, I knew I'd made the right decision. I saw going back home as my failure and my saving grace. This was where I needed to be and the cloying heat welcomed me home like the prodigal daughter returning to the fold.

I loved coming home to the romance of a Bahamian summer. There's nothing quite like it. She announces her presence with cloying heat that's slightly unbearable and yet somehow sexy. She's never far from your mind and clings to everything like a jealous lover desperate to be unforgettable. She slips boldly into cleavages, slides down backs, teasing you with a whisper of cool air. She switches from seductive to moody in seconds with sudden spurts of rain and more wet heat.

The most pleasant way to get to my oasis of Harbour Island from Nassau was by the boat that left the Potter's Cay dock twice a week in the evenings just before the setting sun. As I waited to board the boat, I enjoyed a bowl of conch salad and chatted with the local fishermen. The air was alive with treasures of the sea, brought in earlier in the day and wonderfully fresh.

I'd missed the openness of my Bahamian people, their still trusting nature even in the crowded metropolis of Nassau. I listened to their voices flowing seamlessly through strains of reggae music and felt a measure of peace. This was where I belonged. I was connected to the dreadlocked rasta selling savory peanuts on the street. He gave me a big smile when I purchased a bag. The women selling their wares against the backdrop of the ocean enticed me to their tables with smiles and simple hellos. Their singsong accents flowed over me like my grandmother's caress. This was my island in the sun, my Nirvana, my little piece of heaven on earth.

Surprisingly, I wanted to be an island girl again, running along the beach with sweet, sticky cane juice running down my face and drying as I gazed up at the sun, then down, transforming the world before me with a thousand prisms of light.

My heart ached for my grandmother's house, for soft white sand and the sway of the ocean. My life in New York was over. A large part of me had died there. It wasn't home anymore; it hadn't been for a long time. Home was Zoë and finding the girl I'd lost, getting wrapped up in the ins and outs of small-town life. I boarded the boat with a sense of anticipation.

I was enjoying a local Kalik beer and watching the sunset when I heard a familiar voice calling my name. I turned and smiled in surprise and pleasure. "Brian!"

Brian smiled. "I knew I'd recognize that amazing booty anywhere."

I waved away his compliment. "Just come on over here and give me a hug!"

Brian cleared the distance between us in two steps and swept me up in his strong arms.

I sighed. "God, you feel like home."

"And you look like heaven though the thoughts I'm having about you right now are anything but godly."

I'm thirty-four, five foot eight, most of which is leg. I've got curves in all the right places with smooth medium almond skin, dark chocolate eyes and a mass of kinky curls framing a round, beautiful face. I'm well aware of the stares I get from men.

Brian placed me back on the ground and stared into my eyes. My expression told him I wasn't having the same kind of thoughts. We hadn't seen each other in years. He obviously didn't see us as childhood friends anymore.

The look in his brown eyes told me he wanted to take our friendship to another level. We'd flirted with the idea of dating in high school, but it'd never really happened. More than likely the fault was mine more than his. He seemed more determined now. The way he was devouring me with his eyes made me squirm a little.

I inhaled his musky cologne. How many women would love to be in this position? Brian had paid his way through college by modeling. His tall frame was perfectly chiseled, and that mouth of his with those sensual lips was so close to my own.

It would've been so easy to fall for his charm if I could forget the image of him crying over a skinned knee when we were ten or any number of embarrassing childhood memories. The last thing I needed was a complicated relationship. All in all, I had enough reasons tumbling inside me to resist the lure of Brian's lips.

I pulled away from him. "I bet you're getting that reaction from a host of willing women," I said playfully.

Brian remained serious. He closed the small gap I'd created between us. "I'd give up every woman in the world to have you in my arms forever. You know that, you've always known that."

With a little more force, I managed to pull away from him. "Look Brian, yes, I know how you feel about me. But do you think you could wait awhile before trying to get into my pants?"

Brian smiled that devilish smile I'm sure made a lot of women cream. "I'm sorry, you just look so damn good I couldn't help myself. How long are you planning on sticking around town? I'm here for a month then I'm off to China." He sighed. "The life of an investment banker is not an easy one."

I laughed. "Did you throw out that little bit of information to impress me?"

"Did it?" he asked hopefully.

"It impressed me enough for you to buy me another beer." I took his hand and led him over to the outdoor bar. "It's going to take a lot more for you to get into the thong though."

As Brian and I played catch-up on the four-hour boat ride, a plan started forming in the back of my mind. I needed to explore my sexual hang-ups and I felt I could trust Brian. He was warm and familiar and sexy and best of all, he had the hots for me. Maybe if I opened myself to what he was offering it could be beneficial to both of us.

But screwing Brian and working on my issues would have to take a back seat to getting my grandmother's house into some semblance of order, I decided, immediately after entering the old place.

"What the hell have I gotten myself into?" I asked the cracking walls as I stood in the middle of the vast living room in the midst of a minor panic attack. Some type of trash covered every inch of floor space. The early-1800s British Colonial three-story house looked to have been a squatter's paradise. I hadn't been home since opening my restaurant. My poor excuse for a father was supposed to be living there and renting out the bedrooms to make some extra money.

"I should've known I couldn't depend on that son-of-a-bitch," I muttered angrily. I should never have allowed him into my grandmother's house.

I forced my eyes and thoughts away from the massive clean up ahead of me and gazed out the expansive windows to the spectacular view of the morning sun seemingly ascending out of the ocean. It was breathtaking but I couldn't bypass the terribly overgrown garden, old furniture and god knows what else, cluttering the view.

Half an hour later, Xavier, the contractor I'd found after calling around, walked into the room, noted my look of mild terror, and smiled. "Don't worry, by the end of the day this place will be almost livable."

I smiled brightly. I believed him. Xavier possessed a quiet strength that said he delivered on all his promises.

I would be staying with Zoë for the time being, but I didn't want to intrude for too long. I wasn't able to give up my dream of owning a restaurant so I added renovating and opening my grandmother's restaurant to my hefty to-do list. I couldn't afford to get overwhelmed at a little trash and a man who'd been disappointing me my entire life.

Hours later I stood in the same spot facing the opposite direction from that morning and watched the sun say goodnight. This time I was able to enjoy the show. Though the real work had yet to begin, most of the trash had been hauled away. I could actually see that the beautiful wooden floors wouldn't need as much work as I'd feared.

I'd never worked so hard in my life. Every inch of my body hurt, but at the end of the first week I had a scrubbed-down bathroom, an outdated but working kitchen and a beautiful antique bed I couldn't wait to fall into at night.

It was also at the end of the first week that the dreams started again. For most of my life I'd had a recurring dream of drowning in a bathtub. As always, I awoke in the midst of a scream, bolting straight up as I cried out. It took a few minutes for my brain to register where I was and that my underwear and tank top were plastered to my skin with sweat. I got out of bed and stripped out of my clothes. The humid tropical air immediately embraced me like some prudish grandmother trying to cover my nakedness.

I left my bedroom and headed downstairs to the vintage fifties fridge whose normally tepid air felt arctic good against my hot skin. I pulled out a bottle of water and carried it to the living room where I curled up in a chair and stared out into the night.

A small island night was quite different from one in a big city. There was little to fill the silence, which left me alone with my thoughts. I got up and retrieved the photo album I'd found in one of the many boxes my grandmother had stored in the attic.

I wanted to take my time going through her memories. I knew buried amongst the things she'd collected over ninety-five years were pictures and belongings of my mother. My mother had died in a plane crash when I was only five. I had little memory of her, but my grandmother had made sure I understood what an amazing woman she'd been. I'd taken some pictures when I'd left for the States, but I knew most of her things would've been difficult for Grandma to part with. Her only child had been taken from her far too soon.

This was a happy album. I flipped it open and laughed at the first photo; me just a few days old in a pink dress with a bow that was bigger than me. The album was all about me, from infancy through high school. In each photo I looked happy, though as I flipped through I remembered how painful my childhood had been.

I'd spent too much of it trying to get my father to love me. My parents had never married and after only a year together, my mother had finally had enough of my dad's jealousy and moved back in with Grandma right after she became pregnant with me.

After she died, he'd promised I could live with him, and I believed him for the next twelve years of my life. He broke every promise he ever made to me, missed almost every important event and made me question my own validity as a human being. I always thought, maybe if I were smarter or prettier or funnier, he would love me. I'd spent my childhood trying to be what I thought he wanted me to be. It had become so ingrained in me it was now a part of who I'd become.

I closed the album. It wasn't so happy after all. The truth was painful but it needed to be faced. I needed to prove to myself that I wasn't still a scared little girl longing for Daddy's approval.

The following morning I drove to the farmers' market. It was time to begin testing recipes. I wanted a clear vision for my restaurant long before it opened. Thinking about food always made me happy, and I was happily concocting different flavor parings in my head when I bumped into Brian.

"I just dialed your number," he said after hugging me.

"Well, here I am saving you a call."

"Well, actually you're ruining my little surprise. I just wanted to make sure you were home. I was going to surprise you with a picnic brunch on the beach." He held up the picnic basket. "Just need some fresh fruits."

"Oh, how sweet. I can still go home and act surprised."

"You silly girl." He pulled me against him and this time I didn't resist. When his mouth descended I accepted his kiss. It felt a little strange, but I reminded myself that I needed to change. Eventually, the sexual feelings would come. We brought fruits then headed for the beach.

The food, sun and company were just what I needed to take my mind off my father. We tried to top each other with embarrassing stories from our childhoods. Brian had always been able to make me laugh, and I hadn't realized until right then how attractive a sense of humor really was. When he leaned in to kiss me, I wrapped my hands around his neck and kissed him with all the fervor I could muster. I felt butterflies in my stomach and wanted to cry out in pure joy.

"I want to make love to you right here, right now," Brian whispered.

"Can we just take this one step at a time?" I asked. "Even getting this far was a big step for me."

He kissed the tip of my nose. "Of course. I've waited for you for years. A little more time won't hurt, well, actually blue balls does hurt."

I slapped his hand playfully. "You will not get blue balls." I stood up and the ocean breeze blew my dress up exposing my lacy thong. I looked down at Brian and his eyes had darkened with desire.

"Some things are worth the wait." I walked back to his car, feeling his eyes on me. I was beginning to feel like a natural woman and it was wonderful.

I drove home in a state of bliss singing along with the radio at the top of my lungs. I was in the middle of Bon Jovi's "Living on a Prayer" when my phone rang. I turned down the radio then picked up my phone. I said a merry hello. As I listened to the conversation on the other end my entire body went cold.

Brian must've accidentally pressed redial on his phone. I heard him telling another guy how he was finally going to get some from me. Apparently I was the only woman who'd ever refused him, and he was under the impression that no woman could resist him. I was nothing but another notch he wanted to add to his belt.

I felt angry, betrayed and sick to my stomach. The old me would've just given in to the feelings but my newfound moxie started stirring and a plan was soon devised. Hoping Brian hadn't realized what had happened, I called him a few hours later and invited him to dinner. I implied that there was more than food on the menu. He arrived almost foaming at the mouth like a rabid dog. We went through the motions of dinner then proceeded to the bedroom.

I told him I wanted to be in charge. When I ordered him to strip, he took his time prancing around the room completely taking it for granted that I was as much in love with his body as he was. He did have a beautiful body, but he could go fuck himself or find some other fool to do it.

I stared at his cock, jutting out as proudly as its owner. I reached out and touched it. It was big, beautiful and brick hard.

"He'll make you forget every other man you've been with," Brian said confidently.

"I would have to forget my last boyfriend in order to enjoy it. He was much bigger, you see, and when he stripped for me, I would come just from watching him."

He stared at me. "What the hell are you doing?"

I walked over to the bed and sat down. I crossed my legs in a manner perfected by Sharon Stone in the film, *Basic Instinct*, giving Brian a flash of my bare pussy.

His basic instinct was to twitch, his cock now dribbling for what he now realized he'd never have.

"You heard my conversation today," he surmised.

"Yeah. I guess I'll always be the one who got away."

"Well, not really. If you hadn't heard my conversation, you'd be screaming my name right now."

A little of the pain seeped through the anger. "I really thought I knew you, Brian."

With an exasperated sigh, he knelt in front of me. "Mia, I'm sorry. You can't insult a man like that and expect him not to react. And what you overheard was just me playing it up for the guys. You know how much I care about you." He placed his hand on my knee but I quickly pushed it away.

"I want you to leave," I told him coldly. "I'm trying not to be what other people want me to be, and you obviously can't help me with that or anything else."

Uttering a string of curses under his breath, Brian got dressed, then stomped out of my house. I didn't care if I never saw him again. Besides, Brian wasn't the man I dreamt about at night. Xavier was now the one I took to bed with me.

The summer heat was in full swing and it was only the end of June. All of the men had started working shirtless, and I constantly caught myself admiring Xavier from under the safety of thick, black lashes.

God, he was hot, I thought, as I watched him instruct his crew. Xavier was just the type of man people had to take a second look at. He was basketball-player tall with skin the color of dark island honey and shoulder-length silky black hair. But it was his shockingly green eyes that grabbed at you, pulling you into his magnetic personality. To top it all off, he was really good at his job. I found myself constantly singing Xavier's praises to Zoë.

"Do you realize how much you talk about him?" she asked slyly about six weeks into the renovations, as we enjoyed tea on my porch. "If I didn't know better I'd think you were sweet on him."

I scoffed. "You should know better. I have to like a man who's trying to save me money. We have nothing but a professional relationship."

"When was the last time you had some?" Zoë asked.

I blushed but Zoë's openness wasn't a surprise. "I've got too many things to think about right now to worry about sex," I stated emphatically instead of answering her question.

Zoë's smile turned into a devious grin. "You know you want him. You're both single; you don't need to be in a relationship to fuck the guy, Mia."

"I tried that with Brian. It didn't work out so well, remember?"

"Brian is a dick who thinks the one God gave him is a gift to all women. Don't let him sour you toward other fine-ass men. I've known Xavier for six years, ever since he moved here from Florida. There are so many women around here vying for his attention but he's very selective. I know he'd do you in a heart-beat."

I laughed. "Thanks for the vote of confidence, but maybe I'm just looking for what I had with Jacques."

"What you had with Jacques wasn't love, darling, that was hero worship. On some level, don't you think Jacques was a replacement for your poor excuse of a father?" she asked.

I nodded. "I'm realizing now that he was. He gave me what I needed even if it was only an escape from the things I couldn't face about myself."

"And don't you think it's time you started owning up to those things, beginning with how much you really want Xavier?" Zoë prodded.

I laughed. "You won't stop until I give you all the sordid details of our night together, will you? Well, don't hold your breath, because I've decided to put all thoughts of sex out of my mind for a while. I've enough to worry about trying to open my new restaurant."

Zoë looked at me skeptically. "Let's see how long you can resist that tall, cool drink of water in this heat."

Zoë's words stayed with me as I went about my day working closely with Xavier to get the restaurant ready. Despite what I'd told her, Xavier made me think about sex. But then again, thinking about sex had never been my problem. But he stirred something deeper. I got just a little hotter whenever I was with him. I told myself I was too much of a professional to ever act on my feelings. I couldn't complicate my life. This restaurant required all my attention.

But at night in the safety of my room, I started exploring my sexual feelings and my body. I started touching myself with the lights on, standing in front of the mirror admiring my own body for the first time in my life.

As I watched Xavier work in the heat of the island summer, I committed every inch of his body to memory. I frequently took food and drinks out to the crew just for the chance to see sweat drip from his body. I felt consumed with an overwhelming desire to lick the salty drops from his skin. The idea was completely foreign to someone so anal about cleanliness, but nothing about me felt normal anymore.

I could tell he wanted me, and I knew his crew was ribbing him about when he was going to make his move on me. But unlike Brian, Xavier seemed quite comfortable taking his time. Of course I wasn't brave enough to make the first move.

One Saturday after the crew left, Xavier stayed behind to discuss the next phase of the renovations. I served lemonade and cookies out in the garden and tried to pay attention to what he was saying. But my mind kept imagining the more fun things he could be doing with those luscious lips. I could excuse my flushed complexion on the heat. Thank god, there was no evidence of the tingling between my thighs.

He looked like he was about to kiss me and in a moment of sheer stupidity, I panicked. I stood up quickly and made some lame excuse about having to prepare for a dinner party.

Looking disappointed, he got up and politely said good-bye. I wanted to kick myself as I watched him walk to his truck. Even if I'd had a dinner party, I could blow it off for an ass like his.

As soon as his truck pulled out of my driveway, I walked over to the enclosed area of the garden. It was surrounded by high walls and housed an array of lush tropical plants, a water fountain and outdoor shower, though over the years the plants and weeds had taken over most of the space. It was still far from the beauty it'd once been, but there was no better place to cool off in the heat of the evening. I glanced up at the sky. The clouds looked fat and impatient, ready to pour their fury down on the tiny island.

Quickly I stripped out of my dirty jeans, T-shirt and underwear. A rush of cool air embraced my body and I sighed in sweet relief. I turned on the old faucet then stepped under the cooling stream of water.

As the water cascaded down my generous breasts, I imagined Xavier's hands following suit, gliding around the curve of my hips, and disappearing into the dark valley between my thighs. His hands would be gentle and sure; he would know how to touch a woman. I pinched my nipples and imagined his white teeth grazing my sensitive flesh.

"Oh, Xavier," I moaned.

"I'm here, baby."

I spun around to find Xavier standing at the back gate. My first instinct was to cover myself in shame, but the look of pure hunger in his eyes kept me rooted to the sun-baked tiles.

My heart pounded as he walked over to me.

"You came back," I whispered.

"I forgot to show you the new paint samples, but I think you'd rather see my cock instead," he whispered boldly.

I gasped and lowered my eyes, but I liked that he was a take-charge sort of guy.

"Don't do that. I've been watching you send me mixed signals for weeks now while I go crazy with wanting you." He reached out and ran his hand along the side of one breast. "Let's not waste any more time being coy."

I shivered as my mind screamed in protest, but my body welcomed him. I wanted him too desperately to refuse. "How quickly can you get out of those sweaty clothes?"

Xavier shook his head. "Not so fast, baby." He spun me around to face the wall and pushed me up against it. I moaned as my naked flesh made contact with stones that had been basking in the sun all day.

"That's right, make that wall your friend 'cause you're going to be there for a while. Spread your arms and legs."

I did as he instructed. I was terrified and excited. His steely passions made me wonder what he was capable of doing to me, but not knowing made me wet. Xavier pulled down long vines on either side of me. I turned my head to one side and watched him as he selected the softest. He wound the vines around my arms before tying it securely at my wrists.

He stepped back to absorb the full image of me with my arms encased in climbing vines, the sides of my breasts tempting him to untie me and enjoy their succulent fullness. I felt the soft glow of the sun kiss my behind, giving life and color to the beads of water still clinging to my smooth skin. I heard the pull of his zipper, and the loud thud of his work boots hitting the ground as he undressed. He sighed and I envisioned him releasing his heavy cock from the confines of his faded jeans. He came up behind me and ran the tip of his index finger down my spine. I arched my back, luring him to skim the curve of my shapely bottom.

"Tell me how you imagined me in those late-night dreams I know you have," he coaxed. "Tell me how you see my cock just before your slippery pussy devours it."

I groaned. "Please don't make me do this."

"Would you prefer I left you alone with your dreams? Are you content wanting me only in your mind, or do you have the courage to release all that passion you've kept bottled inside all these years like some stale preserves?"

"This is so not me," I whimpered.

"This is the person you're afraid to be. You've always been afraid to be yourself, haven't you?"

Xavier dipped his fingers into my wet pussy, and I screamed out in surprise and pleasure.

"Okay, we can play this game your way," he said as he caressed my clit between his index and middle finger. "I want to see how hot I have to make you before you let go of that damn control."

Quickly he left me. I turned my head as best I could but couldn't get him in my limited field of vision until he came up behind me with a white hibiscus flower in his mouth. I looked down in a desperate attempt to catch a glimpse of his cock but couldn't. I felt the hibiscus on my behind, as soft as butterfly wings.

Xavier waited until I was truly enjoying the softness to introduce the stem to my backside. A sudden prick from a jagged edge made me jump. As he guided the stem down the slippery valley of my crack, I gritted my teeth and groaned.

"I wish you could see how beautiful you look holding this flower in your ass like the perfect vase," Xavier whispered. "I bet it would look even lovelier in the front."

He opened my behind with one hand and pulled the flower down to my dark center with the other. When the stem touched my hard, sensitive clit, I cried out his name.

"Are you ready to start talking?"

I wiggled my hips against the assault of the stem. "Oh, yes, just please, don't stop."

"Did you have a dream about me last night?" he prompted.

"Yes, a really dirty one. I'm lying in bed, naked, of course, 'cause it's just too hot for clothes. The French doors are open and there's just a hint of a breeze. I'm lying facedown on the bed with my ass in the air, and I'm rubbing my clit and thinking of you."

He removed the flower and replaced it with his fingers. He found my pink rosebud and rubbed it. "Like this?"

"Oh, yes baby, just like that." I raised my right leg and wedged my knee against the wall. "Yes, do it harder."

"Continue the story and I will."

"Okay, I hear you come into the room. I open my eyes and you're standing there naked. Your cock, my god, it's beautiful, like a tree trunk, proudly jutting straight out from your body. The size of it scares me a little." I stopped to catch my breath as he slipped a finger in me.

"Go on," he urged.

"You walk over to the bed and climb behind me. I feel your hands, doing just what you're doing now. I beg you for your cock, just like I'm begging now, please, please, please."

"Not yet, baby, you're not ready yet." He moved away from me and when he returned, I felt dried vines on my ass. "Did you ever dream about me spanking you? I bet you're one of those women who likes being punished for your desires."

"Yes, sometimes I have dreams of being tied up and getting spanked," I admitted.

"You mean like this?" The first swipe of the vines was amazing. It stung a little and sent little electric currents straight down to my toes.

"Oh, yes, just like that" I groaned.

He made each lick a little harder than the last until my backside was on fire. Then he soothed it with wet licks from his tongue.

"Please take me now because I don't know how much more of this I can stand."

"Oh, honey, you can take a lot more than you've ever thought was possible."

Xavier knelt down and buried a finger inside me. My lips were so thick, pouting because he wouldn't give me what I craved most. He slipped another finger into me, teasing my pussy into accepting his expert touch. Despite not getting what I really wanted, my pussy rewarded him with juices as thick as egg whites and sugar whipped up in my kitchen. Violent cries ripped through my body as he inserted another finger, exploring my cunt like no one had before. Suddenly, his fingers slipped out of me and I felt his arms move to either side of my head. I opened my eyes. I felt his warm, heavy breathing on my neck.

"I need to know that you trust me," he whispered hoarsely. "I want to know if you trust me to take you where you need to go and to do things to you you'd never dream of doing."

I didn't trust myself. I was in uncharted territory but at the point of no return. I wanted to see what would happen if I just gave myself over to the moment, trusted Xavier and whatever it was that had drawn us together.

"I trust you," I said on a rush of relief that felt almost as good as what he'd just done to me. Xavier kissed the back of my neck then slipped back down to my pussy.

Three fingers slipped in easily. The moan died halfway in my throat when I realized he wanted more. I felt the final finger. He cajoled the walls of my pussy to welcome his hand, slowly pushing and twisting, finding my G-spot, caressing and coaxing.

"Tell me the rest of that dream now. Tell me what you really wanted me to do to you."

With a loud moan of surrender, I gave into the craving I'd

buried and confessed how desperately I needed him to make love to me.

"Now you're ready for me, baby." He eased his penis into me knowing better than I did what I really needed. If he had been too rough, I would've had more pain than pleasure. I wanted to make up for all the times I'd denied myself but a frenzied fuck wasn't the best way to do it.

The slow steady sensation of him made me realize he'd made the right decision. It would've been easy for him to pound into me like there was no tomorrow but there was, and he wanted us to have more experiences like this one. I felt his teeth biting into my shoulder, his hands gripping my hips, testing and waiting until I was ready, until I was so slick he moved inside me with fluid grace. Only then did he increase the rhythm, allow the animal in him to take over.

I wasn't screaming anymore, I was growling. I wanted to get down on my hands and knees and rut in the dirt while he pumped me from behind. I'd never felt so alive. I felt myself falling and crying, crying and falling, as something broke inside. Everything I'd gone through over the last few months came rushing to the surface, the shattered dreams, and the definition of myself then and now. It came out in my tears and my juices, running down my face and thighs as I came in an explosion of pleasure and pain. I heard Xavier, grunting his way to release behind me. When his body finally stilled, I felt the warmth of his release inside me, just as the clouds climaxed and poured down on us.

Xavier released my hands and spun me around to face him. I couldn't look in his eyes but openly admired his beautiful semi-hard cock. I pushed him up against the wall and eased him into me.

The rain turned hard, matching the tempo of our frantic thrusts. It felt like tiny pieces of ice beating an island rhythm on my back and behind. My skin felt raw and alive under the onslaught of the wet spanking.

I buried my fingers in Xavier's hair and cried out as I came. The rain suddenly turned softer and heavier. I started crying as it washed over me, therapeutically washing away the self-deprecating pain I carried with me for so long.

Afterward he took me inside and we had sex again and again and heaven help me again. Even after he fell into exhaustion, I couldn't shut down. He'd just given me the most incredible experience of my life and I wanted to relive every delicious moment. I decided a soak and a glass of wine was the best way to do it.

While I lounged in warm water and spun sonnets describing Xavier's cock, sleep finally claimed me. The dream came again. Feeling Jasmine-scented water cover my face woke me up fast. I sat up sputtering and coughing.

Suddenly something flashed in my mind, a long-forgotten night a few months before my mother died. What I'd thought was a dream was actually a repressed memory. I remembered my mother lying in the same tub. I remembered my father kicking open our front door. Grandma was at church and I was in my room. I heard him shouting and cursing at my mother. I got out of bed and walked to the bathroom door just as mom threw her wineglass at him. It cut his arm, the blood quickly staining the whitewashed floorboards. He cursed and lunged at her, pushing her down into the water. I screamed and he released her.

"You better not become a whore like your mother!" he shouted at me before leaving.

I hadn't understood all of the names he'd called her but I knew what it all meant. He didn't like Mom because she had other men and the things she did with them were bad. If I wanted him to love me, I had to be a good girl. That message had been ingrained in my subconscious and it had set the tone for my life.

I wasn't frigid; being with Xavier had proven that. But knowing the source of my misconception was even more liberating.

I considered confronting my father, but I knew there would be little point. He wouldn't see how much he'd hurt me and getting him to see things my way wasn't important anymore. I had to let him and my desperate need for his approval go and move on with my life without the restrictions he'd placed on me.

Instead I cried for the little girl I used to be, the little girl I'd held on to until that very moment. I allowed her to flow down the drain. Then I got into bed and woke Xavier up by running my tongue down his back.

"Are you coming back to bed, baby?" I turned from the stove and smiled at Xavier standing naked in the doorway. It was only half past seven in the morning yet the kitchen was balmy from the heat and my cooking. I was wearing nothing but an apron and a contented smile. My torrid night spent in Xavier's arms had reawakened my creativity in other areas as well.

"Come here and taste this bread. I haven't had bread like this since my grandma made it." I held out a piece of warm coconut bread.

He took my hand by the wrist but didn't take the bread. Instead, he lowered his head and stole a kiss. "Taste like heaven."

I gave him a reproving look. "Baby, I'm serious. I finally feel like I'm making the right kind of food. I want your honest opinion because this will be my menu when I finally open." My hand swept over the kitchen. Almost every available surface held a tempting dish in various stages of completion.

Xavier took the bread and chewed on it slowly. "It is perfect. Your food will always be perfect when you allow the flavors to just be themselves."

"Yeah, I know that now," I said softly.

"It's Sunday. So why don't you come back to bed and allow me to feast on something I really feel like eating right now?" Xavier whispered.

I pushed him away playfully. "I can't. I have melted chocolate on the stove. I can't just leave it."

"I can think of a better way to use that chocolate."

Xavier pulled me into his arms and kissed me so thoroughly, all thoughts of cooking went out of my mind. He backed me up against the kitchen table and my bare behind landed on a loaf of warm bread. Surprisingly, it felt good, tactile and pure. I sighed blissfully at this new experience. Sensing it, Xavier untied my apron, spun me around, and bent me over the table. My breasts sank into the loaves.

I moaned and seconds later, I felt warm chocolate being spread with a big wooden spoon on my behind, down my legs then up my back. I felt covered in a big, warm orgasm. Xavier playfully knocked the spoon against my behind when he was done.

"Oh, do that again, that feels nice," I cooed.

"You just love a good spanking, don't you, girl?"

I smiled. "Isn't that what you do to bad girls?"

"And you've been such a bad girl, haven't you?" He hit me again, this time without mercy, and I begged for another.

"What do you feel when I hit you? What does the pain do for you?"

I thought about it for a second. "I guess it gives me power over my pain, physical and emotional. It allows me to turn it into something that's beautiful and feels so damn good. I thank you for showing me how to do that."

"I can show you because I've been there myself. But right now I just want to taste you." He cleared a path with his tongue from my cheeks to the nape of my neck. "It tastes even better paired with your skin."

He licked the spoon clean before rubbing it against the folds of my pussy. The big spoon cupped me perfectly. I reached behind, cupped my cheeks, and opened myself up to him. He ran the spoon over my clit, pressing gently into the tender nubbin. I started hissing like a feline. There were no words to let him know how exquisite it was.

He seemed to know exactly when to replace the spoon with his penis. I stretched out my hands and grabbed the other side of the table. He reached his long body over me and placed his hands on either side of mine. My body pressed into the food as we used the table to drive him deep into me.

I started humming. It was the only thing I could think of. I hummed a nonsensical song over and over until my thoughts jumbled into each other and nothing made sense except the force of his thrust, which I felt in every fiber of my being. When we came, Xavier buried his face in my neck and released a string of curses into my hair. It seemed a long time before we could move and even longer before my body wanted to be separate from his.

Finally he lifted himself from the table and pulled me up. I laughed as I gazed down at the food stuck to my body and the chocolate covering his.

"We desperately need a shower."

Xavier swung me up into his arms. "I can't think of a more perfect place for dessert."

I learned he had an insatiable appetite for food and sex, and I was like a virgin. I couldn't seem to get enough of him.

Our weekend together inspired my most popular desert at the restaurant, a decadent delight I call sex and chocolate. In the year I've been open, Xavier has inspired many of my dishes.

The island people have embraced my food, and I finally feel like I'm living my dream. The weekends are for adults only, and we feature the pairing of sensuality with food. Now that I know it's okay for me to be a sexual being, I've had so many amazing sexual experiences.

I'm not afraid of life anymore, and I don't spend much time stressing over what other people think of me. It's not my job to make everyone like me. It's my right to be true to myself and trust that the universe will bring people into my life who will love me just the way I am. I know it sounds like something a therapist would say. Maybe I've just done enough work on myself to sound like one.

A TASTE
OF TYRELL

Jolene Hui

It was one of those weekends I wanted to stay in bed and enjoy the feel of my soft sheets and blankets on my face and legs. A weekend where I could possibly relax, take in a few movies, eat only when I absolutely needed to, and sleep whenever I felt the need. I had no idea it would be so drastically different until Friday night when Denise roused me off my couch to try out some film festival with her.

"It's called Horrorfest, but don't get all anti until you hear me out," she said.

I had her on speakerphone while I looked through my closet, not even wanting to brush my hair. It'd been a long week at work and I just wanted to relax at home alone. Even my roommate was gone for the weekend.

"So," she continued, "my friend directed a movie in the festival and he's bringing along some of his friends."

"Male?" I was starting to warm up to the idea of an outing.

"Very," she said. "I think they're young and single, too."

I pulled out a formfitting black shirt and some designer jeans. My straight dark hair looked limp in the mirror. Why couldn't I have gotten my mother's light brown curls? Instead I was stuck with my Chinese father's straight and unmanageable hair.

"My hair looks horrible!" I shrieked.

"I'm sure it looks fine." She sounded distracted, like she was putting on her makeup. But what would she know about my straight hair? She had hair like my mother's. *At least I have a booty and boobs,* my inner critic said. I got dressed. *At least I didn't get the flat-chested and flat-butted gene from my dad's side.*

I put some shimmery lipstick on my lips, ran a comb through my hair. My slightly almond-shaped eyes looked back at me mischievously.

Nerves settled in my stomach on the drive to the theater. For some reason, this night felt more intense than others. Maybe it was because I was getting out of the house, but maybe it was something else. My jeans felt like they were fitting perfectly and my smile felt just right. It could be my lucky night.

Denise's friend Greg met us outside in front of the box office.

"Hey, sweetie," he said, encircling us both in a hug. I almost teetered off my high-heeled boots, he pulled us in with such force.

"So you directed this movie, huh?" I was impressed. Call it silly for me to be impressed by such a thing when I lived in L.A., but I couldn't help it.

"I certainly did. Thanks for coming out tonight," he said.

I laughed at his enthusiasm. "No problem. I was just going to stay at home on my couch anyway," I admitted, a slight blush creeping up my cheeks.

"Well, come on in. There's a big group of us in the last few rows."

I followed after Denise. I wasn't exactly a horror fan, and I felt a little anxious that I'd have to pretend to act normal and nonscared in a theater full of boys. And wow, what a crowd of boys it was. When we entered the auditorium, the smell of men flocked to my nose. That sweet smell of shower and aftershave stuck to my skin. And to think, I was going to stay home. The smell of men quickly grabbed my attention and made me anxious.

"Everyone, this is Denise and Lizzy," Greg said to the crowd.

The testosterone-heavy crowd looked our way and waved. They all shouted, "Hi, Denise and Lizzy!"

I couldn't help but giggle at all of their grinning faces. My eyes scanned the crowd of men and immediately settled on one. Right away I noticed the quiet guy at the other end of the row in front of me, checking his phone and not really looking around much. He was in jeans and a buttondown shirt. His head was shaved and his dark skin looked smooth, like it would be soft to touch.

"Let's go sit at the other end," Denise said, pointing to the seats in front of my sexy target.

I knew exactly what she wanted to do. She wanted to squeeze by the entire row of men. If only I could be as bold as her. I grabbed her arm and she led us to the other end, where, of course, I tripped and fell backward onto the sexy Adonis I'd been eyeing.

"Oh, I'm so sorry." I attempted to scramble back up, only to be accidentally knocked down by Denise, right back into his lap.

"Hey, I'm Tyrell," he said. I sat in his lap, my face red. He smelled amazing.

"Lizzy," I said. I was stunned and couldn't move off his lap.

My fingers grazed his arms and stopped at his thick wrists.

Meeting his eyes was a mistake. I nearly turned into a puddle when we locked gazes. His eyes were a gorgeous shade of green. He smiled, his white teeth sending me into a deeper hypnotic state. By this time, Denise had given up on me and was talking to a guy a few seats away. I couldn't seem to move. I was stunned. I kept my hands locked on his wrist, my butt comfortably seated in his lap.

"This is kind of an awkward way to meet, huh?" I tried to lighten the mood, still seated right near his crotch.

"I don't mind it," he said.

"So, um…" I couldn't even think straight. "Are you typically a horror fan?"

"Nah, I work with Greg, so I wanted to come out to support him," he said.

"Oh, what do you do?"

"The techie stuff," he said. "I don't get out much. I'm always working." His bright eyes darkened a bit. "I think I need to get out more. Especially if lovely ladies like you fall into my lap."

"Yeah, sorry about that." I smiled and started to stand up. I figured I should relieve him of my weight. But before I could get up, Tyrell pulled me back down again. "I can't stay on your lap through the entire movie!"

"Well, then I guess we'll have to save that for later." He released me to stand up but was sure to smack my welcoming round booty as I made my way to the row in front of him. Denise had left me the seat in front of him and was talking with a guy on the other side of her.

Throughout the movie, I had no idea what was going on up on the screen. Some people screeched, some people clapped, some people hollered, but I was still and only pretending to watch. I could feel Tyrell's eyes on my neck. At the end, everyone clapped and Greg went to the stage for a Q & A with a couple of the actors and a producer. I could still feel Tyrell's eyes on my neck.

Had I dated any Black guys before? Much to my traditional Asian-American father's dismay, my first boyfriend in college, Mike, had been Black. The first time I brought him home for dinner, my dad almost choked when we got to the door. He softened up easily after spending a couple of hours with his chest puffed out. It was always funny to me that my dad grew up a minority but still didn't have an easy time accepting other minorities. Luckily, my mom encouraged in me the belief that all people were alike. She had fought the controversy and married my father, so she knew that it was important for me to see people as people and not a color. For me, it was rare that I liked anything but men of color. My dating career was mostly Latino, Asian, and Black. I had dated one white guy.

Sorry Dad, I thought, when I turned to meet those stunning eyes behind me.

After the Q & A, there was a wrap party at a restaurant nearby. Denise and I headed over. I was giddy to see Tyrell.

"Wow, I don't think I've ever seen you like this!" Denise had a smile on her face the whole way.

I fidgeted with my purse. "He *did* say he was going to be there, right?"

"Yes, girl, you are being way too insane over this." She laughed and pulled into the parking lot.

My fears were quieted when I saw him standing slightly outside of the crowd at the corner, playing on his phone. I shook my head at him when he met my eye. He smiled and shrugged. "I told you I work too much!"

We grabbed a seat and proceeded to be in our own world the rest of the night. As the movie party went on around us, we laughed, smiled, and even ate. I watched him eat his potatoes. "It's only meat and potatoes for me," he said.

"I'm a vegetarian," I said. We both laughed. I learned that he had moved to L.A. with his ex-wife. She was a lawyer and he was working in business development. Neither of them had time for each other. She ended up leaving him for a female porn star.

"At least it wasn't one of my friends," he said. "I always try to look at the bright side of things."

"You're crazy!" I said. "My last boyfriend was flat-out seeing another woman behind my back. She was five years younger and a whole lot blonder." I explained that it had made me really reevaluate my relationships and my trust in people.

"Well, I hope you realize that not all men are cheaters." He sliced through his steak.

The world around was just a buzz. We laughed as we sat across from each other. I could feel the sexual tension start to build. When he was done he put his fingers on mine to gauge my interest. My hand warmed to his touch. I'd already sat on his lap tonight but hand touching seemed way more intimate.

When the group decided to leave, Denise and I lingered in the parking lot.

"So am I taking you home or is Tyrell?" Denise asked me.

I glanced over to see him talking to a couple of the guys. I knew I wanted to experience his lips on mine and his hands on my body, but I wasn't sure how to ask.

"Hey, let me give you a ride home!" he shouted before I even had to mention it.

Always a good cheerleader, Denise gave a little clap and left Tyrell and me to walk to his truck. It was a sleek SUV and when I got in I saw that it was perfectly clean. That added to his attractiveness. I always loved a clean car.

"Wow, your car is amazingly clean." It may have seemed like

a weird thing to say, but his car got me hot. Before I could look around and smell the clean scent anymore, Tyrell leaned into me and put his mouth on mine. My first reaction was to gasp but my kissing instinct took over. My lips met his with a warm greeting. He slipped his left hand behind my neck and tenderly rested it there. My entire body warmed up considerably.

The kiss deepened. I leaned into him. I wanted my breasts to rub against his chest so I moved even closer, stretching across the center console. My hands went to his shoulders. Our lips stretched open until our tongues were able to introduce themselves. I could feel the heat radiating off of his body.

It didn't occur to me that we were still in the parking lot till we heard horns honking and flashes of light blinded us. We pulled away to see Greg and Denise in her car.

"Hey, get a room! Jesus!" Greg stuck his head out the window and shook it at us.

I embarrassedly slouched into my seat. Tyrell laughed and then asked, "So where do you live, my dear?"

I didn't want to get out of his car so I invited him up to my place.

"How about I pick you up for dinner tomorrow instead?"

He leaned in to me to give me another kiss. I couldn't believe he wasn't going to come in with me. But I didn't argue. Instead I tried to persuade him by aggressively kissing him. My skills were good but not good enough to convince him.

"Girl, I am so hot right now, but I want to treat you right first," he said.

My eyes, glazed over, stared at his emerald ones. "You make me melt," I admitted.

"I'll see you tomorrow at seven," he said.

I was wobbly as I walked to my door. The sound of his SUV hummed on the street. I turned around and gave him a wave once I got my door open. He smiled, gave me a little salute, and drove off. There was no way I could wait until tomorrow night.

I couldn't help but put my fingers in my pussy when I got in bed, thinking about Tyrell's lips licking mine.

The next night Tyrell showed up with a bouquet of flowers. No man had ever given me flowers before a date.

"Impressive," I said.

"A beautiful woman needs beautiful flowers." He leaned in and kissed me. And as cheesy as the whole scene could have been—it wasn't. It made me want to jump him right there outside his truck.

We pulled into the valet lot of an Italian restaurant. I wasn't really thinking about food at this point. His cologne was making its way into my brain as a memory that triggered my pussy. I'd never gotten so hot from the smell of a person. His skin and the smell of his cologne nearly drove me wild. He led me into the restaurant to check in with the host, but I couldn't bring myself to sit down just yet.

"Will you come with me for a sec?" I asked him when we approached the host.

"Um, sure," he said to me. "We'll be right back," he told the host.

I pulled him along behind me to the women's restroom. Luckily, it was a one-person restroom instead of a larger one with stalls. I wouldn't have been able to be that quiet.

I shut the door quietly and made sure the two doors were locked. My heels gave me enough height to gently shove him against the door, tilt my face up to his and give me a kiss. I pressed my body against his and put my hands on either side of his body. His body tensed up. I could feel his cock swelling against my stomach. He kissed me more furiously and took the lead, spinning me around against the door. His fingers moved over my breasts and grazed my nipples, beyond hard and aching. He moved his hands down my waist and pulled my cunt to his leg. As he kissed me, he reached his right hand under my skirt and plunged his fingers inside my already wet pussy. I let him work the folds over and massage my clit for a little while before I unzipped his pants to feel his thick cock against my fingers. He was so ready for me it felt like he was going to burst. I stared into his eyes and stroked him a little bit. I didn't realize his strength until he lifted my body up against the door.

"Wrap your legs around me," he told me.

Before he was done with his command I had already wrapped my muscular legs around him. His pants and boxers had fallen around his ankles. I pulled the condom out of my jacket pocket as we were kissing and slid it on his large erect dick. I hadn't had sex in a while, so I was tight. And that sweet moment before he shoved his covered cock into me was almost too much. I almost blew before he entered me.

My hand reached between our bodies and positioned him right outside me. When he lowered my weight slowly onto his stick, I moaned loudly.

"You feel so fucking good," I said.

His response was fucking me against the wall next to the door. We didn't want to unhinge and break the door. The smell of his cologne invaded my senses and all my pores. My clit rubbed along the top of his cock as it moved in and out of me. He put his mouth on mine when I exploded to keep me from screaming.

He came deep inside me. I tightened my legs around him.

We left the restroom like nothing had just happened. The host was happy to seat us at a corner table with a fireplace.

I felt like a high-schooler that had just gotten away with something naughty. I couldn't help laughing.

"Why you laughing?" He joined me in my post-fucking laugh.

"I had no idea when I first fell on your crotch that I'd be falling on your crotch like that!"

"I knew that I wanted you to fall on my crouch when I first felt your weight on me in that movie theater!"

We both laughed. Instead of wine we ordered beer. Our dinner was great. I knew he couldn't turn me down when I invited him in later that night. We didn't have to worry about any doors coming unhinged and could actually feel our smooth skin rub together.

But before my place, I knew we had to get down to dessert. Our mouths made short work of the triple-decker chocolate cake and ice cream.

Back at my place, Tyrell said, "I'm ready for my second dessert." He took my clothes off slowly and took his time kissing my body parts. When I slipped his shirt over his head, I nearly shrieked at his hot pecs and abs. The dark skin of his washboard stomach met my lips with electricity. He lightly pushed me down onto my back and spread my legs with his strong hands. His eyes were the last sane thought I had that night. The rest of the night was light, stars, sweat, and sweet, hot, insane sex.

WELCOME HOME

Shakir Rashaan

Yes, my Master, you want me to wear the heels and the black lingerie and you want Roni to wear the corset and heels. I should make sure that we both have our collars on." My Layla repeated the instructions that I had given to her over the phone. "You want us on our knees, in our kneeling positions, in the dungeon area."

"Yes, darling, that is correct. I should be home within the hour," I told her, as I was waiting for my plane to begin its final descent. It had been a week while I was out of town on business, and I missed both my beloved, Layla, and our submissive, Roni, terribly.

Once the plane landed, I made my way to pick up my luggage. I began to allow my mind to wander over the possibilities that the night would hold.

Layla, my beloved, is about five eight and full figured, with a beautiful light caramel skin tone and long brown hair. She isn't top heavy, but what gets attention is her hips and ass, which can fill out a pair of jeans like nobody's business. Her ass is the type that, as a friend of mine put it, "you can sit a drink on and not worry about it spilling."

Roni, our submissive, is no real slouch herself, either. At five five, her legs and ass are her best features, and I take pleasure in showing them off to whoever wants to see them at any time and any place. She's caramel skinned, her hair cropped and styled, with big brown eyes and a little smaller than Layla. But then again, I'm a big man myself, so there's not much that a petite girl can do for me but introduce me to her thicker girlfriend. I'm sorry, but bones *do* hurt.

On the drive home from the airport, I reminisced about the last time we'd had the chance to have a night like this. We all acted as if sex was nothing more than a reckless activity, using every room in the house (and even a few discreet and not so discreet areas outside the house as well) before we were done for the evening. But this time I had planned for a more sensual, more erotic evening, especially since I hadn't really had the chance to use my floggers and pinwheels on my girls in a while. Damn, I was getting hard just thinking about it.

I tried not to make much noise once I got through the front door, but the chirp of the alarm system that signaled my entry into the house betrayed me. "I'm home, girls," I called out.

"We're in the basement, Master," I heard Roni reply.

I went into the office to put my cases on the desk, taking a moment to realize that I was actually home, and then went to check on the girls to see what they were up to.

I found them on the air mattress in the middle of the basement floor, both in their kneeling positions, eyes closed and heads bowed down, as if they were both in trances. They both had their hands clasped behind their backs, and wore the outfits I had requested they wear for me tonight.

Needless to say, it was a beautiful sight to behold.

"Come to me," I commanded.

"Yes, Master," they both replied, crawling off the bed and repositioning themselves at my feet.

I immediately brought my beloved to her feet, so that I could give her an "I missed you" welcome-home kiss.

"Were you a good girl while Daddy was away?" I playfully asked Layla.

"Yes, Daddy," she replied. "Roni did as she was told as well, and was here with me when we needed some attention, just as you specified."

I looked down at Roni, who by now had begun to untie and remove my shoes and was proceeding to unbuckle my belt to remove my pants.

"I see you missed me as well, little one?" I asked Roni as I lifted her chin up so she could look at me.

Roni nodded, never even slowing down at her task. Layla began removing my shirt and tie, in hopes that, at least my guess was, I wouldn't stop them from getting the night started earlier than I wanted to.

My body began to betray me. Hell, it had been a week since I'd had sex with either of them. I don't engage in any sexual play unless my girls are with me when I'm on business, even if it is a Dominant's prerogative to do so if he chooses. No matter what my plans were, they were about to be altered just a little bit.

They both had me completely naked in no time, as Roni began to nuzzle her lips against my shaft. Layla did not disappoint either, gently biting and sucking on my nipples, while coaxing Roni to begin performing her expert deep-throat skills on me.

Roni had me coming in her mouth before I knew what hit me, and she made sure that she swallowed every drop I had to give her. I let out a loud primal growl as I was coming, which alerted Layla that I was about to take over the whole situation.

I forced Layla to her knees, and ordered Roni into action with the single command, "Spread," at which she quickly lay on her back on the mattress and spread her legs.

I next issued the command, "Sixty-nine," and Layla straddled Roni's face with her pussy lips, sitting on the submissive's tongue before she dropped her own mouth down over Roni's pussy.

While they were busy bringing each other exquisite pleasure, I had time to compose myself and focus on what I had originally planned to do. I looked around the basement, checking one wall that housed the glass cases of weaponry that I used for knife play: knives, swords, smaller switchblades and the like. On the opposite wall were the St. Andrew's cross, floggers, bullwhips and electro-stimulation equipment. I made sure that the wax was in its place, still heating on the bar countertop, before I figured out what I wanted to do first.

I moved to the wall of floggers and picked out my leather floggers to use on them while they were engaged with each other.

I began to slap the flogger against Layla's ass first, since she was the one on top, increasing the intensity with each stroke across her skin. I heard her moaning while she lapped away at Roni's juices, which only inspired me to flog her harder to elicit a more audible response. To add to that, I alternated the slaps of the flogger with gentle rakes across her skin with my nails, concentrating on the same area that I'd just struck, knowing that it would give Layla the tingling sensation that would have her coming in no time.

Seeing her ass swaying with the sensations that she was experiencing from both my flogging and Roni's oral skills, I felt that it wouldn't take long to stroke her into an intense orgasm. I quickly mounted her while Roni was still eating her, and within a few minutes, everything culminated in the first orgasmic wave that Layla would experience that night.

"Oh, god, I'm coming, I'm coming!" Layla yelled out. "Fuck me harder, please!"

I kept stroking her, feeling Roni's fingers massaging my balls while I was pumping away at Layla's swollen pussy. Every so often, I pulled out of Layla's pussy and slid it into Roni's mouth, allowing her to taste us both before penetrating Layla again. I finally pulled out a final time so that Roni could work Layla's clit and cause her to come again.

Surprisingly, I was still hard; not as hard as I was when we first got started, but hard enough for one final climax.

I whispered the command "Sit," into Layla's ear, which meant for her to face-sit over Roni, leaving Roni's pussy and ass exposed. I then took the wax from the countertop and began to drip small trails of it onto her exposed clit.

I heard small muffled moans coming from Roni, but she did not lose her concentration. I asked Layla, "Does she want more? Her body says yes, but I want her to say it."

Layla was still grinding her juices on Roni's face when she replied breathlessly, "Yes, Master, she wants more. I feel her nodding her head. Give her more, Master."

I increased the amount of wax, but kept the same cadence as Roni wiggled and ground her pussy and hips to alert me that she was enjoying every minute of the torture that I was giving her. I used a warm, damp cloth to wipe away the wax that had hardened, but seeing her pussy begging to be fucked, my body finally heeded the call to duty.

Roni was so wet from the wax torture that it was as easy to enter her pussy as it had been to penetrate Layla. I didn't stay in her pussy too long, however, because I had something special in mind to bring her to climax.

I commanded Layla to crawl over and retrieve the dildo that

she uses with her strap-on harness, and to get it lubed up.

"Beg me to fuck your ass, Roni," I ordered her. "Tell me how bad you want it in your ass, slut."

"Please, Master, fuck my ass!" Roni screamed. "It's yours, Master, it's all yours!"

While Layla lubed the dildo, I slid a pillow under Roni's ass and slowly penetrated her anally. I managed to get my entire length inside her, and knowing how much she loves anal sex with either of us, I was certain it would be just the thing to send her over the edge. I began rhythmically stroking her, allowing her to adjust to my girth, until she received the surprise that I had in waiting for her in the form of the dildo that Layla was lubing.

Layla began teasing Roni's clit with the head of the dildo before inserting it deep into her pussy. Roni's eyes widened at the unexpected double penetration euphoria that we don't do very often because it puts her into subspace very quickly.

I adjusted Roni's hips so that both Layla and I could stroke her without getting in each other's way. With one hand, Layla was feverishly stroking away at her pussy, and with the other, she was pinching Roni's nipples hard, causing Roni to scream out loudly for her to do it harder. I kept fucking Roni's ass, which was so slick it felt like I was fucking her pussy.

"You're making me come! Oh, god, yes, I'm coming!" Roni screamed out, grabbing Layla's arm to brace against the intensity of the waves that she was feeling ripple through her body.

I pumped even harder after hearing her coming, feeling my own climax building with each stroke. I pulled out before Roni passed out and took the condom off so that I could come in Layla's mouth. The feeling was delicious, as I felt her tongue massaging my shaft to prolong the orgasm just that much longer before I pulled out of her mouth.

We all lay on the mattress completely spent, while Layla took some ice for Roni to suck on to help her transition back from her subspace experience. It was definitely a welcome-home night that I wouldn't soon forget.

LIGHTS ON
A CAVE WALL

Zaji

Kira felt the heat. It rose like a thin fog off the Cuban sand. It was the kind of heat she'd only felt in private places, places only he touched. As she sat on the fine gray sand near the mouth of the cave, she could feel the sun awakening her to memories that made her body ache. She touched her bottom lip, rubbed it gently, closed her eyes, and allowed a past moment to rise to the surface, just above the clouds that slowly inched across the sky. Each movement gave way to the shape of bodies intertwined, reaching and touching every inch of flesh. She exhaled. A single cloud moved quickly as though blown by her breath, rushing aside to let the sun share in the moment. She opened her eyes and caught Imbe watching her as she watched the sun.

The Cuban sun was unlike the sun that touched other places in the world. The Cuban sun was only for Cuba. Its heat felt like that of two suns, twins suspended on nothing, each competing for the attention of the small island. It radiated its essence like a song permeating the heart.

Kira didn't live in Cuba, Cuba lived in her. It lived as deep within her as Imbe. He lived in her soul. Cuba was like Imbe, deep, dark and sensual, ready to give everything. That was Cuba, and that was Imbe.

"Let me read to you," he said in a baritone hum that floated on the air.

Kira didn't answer. She smiled and continued watching the candles in the cave flicker, the light dancing on the walls with the same quick excited motions as the sounds of the Tumba. She wondered when they would go inside.

"Let me make love to you," he said, as he leaned into her.

"What did you say?" She blushed, feigning innocence.

"Let me make love to you with words. Let me read to you."

She lowered her head.

He tossed back his locs that were a touch beyond his shoulders. They were dark, filled with the vibrations of night. They told the story of his life over the past six years. Every experience was interwoven between every strand of hair that wrapped itself around his spirit. Each strand spoke to her, whispered his secrets to her. A loc brushed her cheek. It left her with a moment of his life she could feel but not express. It threatened to steal her away, add her to an inch of memories, maybe two or three inches of life that grew as he grew. His thin orange linen shirt, open in the front, blew in the wind. His bare chest glistened under the sun that had begun its journey into dusk. She lay back.

"Make love to me then," she said.

"Where did we leave off?" His sly grin sent a rush of warmth through her body.

"Page sixty-two." She turned toward him and propped her head on her arms.

"Are you comfortable?" He looked at her, almost gauging whether he was reaching her soul.

"Yes. It is always comfortable with you."

He began to read.

The words moved about the air like black butterflies. They flew high. They seemed to create new stories in the sky. Their wings and bodies formed words, then sentences. Before Kira knew it, a world imagined unfolded on the wings of tiny life forces that were the epitome of metamorphosis. Imbe's voice transformed her, morphing her into the woman she needed to be. The black wings of the butterflies beat with her heart. They flew around Kira, landed on every part of her, and moved inside her. They were Imbe in flight. The words and the butterflies. As the image faded, the ocean waves crashed against rocks that watched over the vast landscape. They'd been there for many millennia, guarding the secrets of the shores. They'd seen intimate moments filled with passion to move mountains and stop time. They waited for yet another moment to unfold as Kira and Imbe grew through love.

"Are you listening?" Imbe asked.

"Yes, I am."

"Then what was the last thing I read?"

"Huh?"

"You heard me."

Kira looked down at the sand, then over at the water, then at Imbe. Her eyes shined like onyx on snow as she stared into Imbe's eyes, hoping he would let her off the hook. But he wouldn't.

"I'm sorry. I was just thinking about something. But I remember some of the story, just not the last part you read."

"What do you remember?"

He was relentless.

She sighed. "Armah was unfolding the many seasons of our existence. Throughout, he's been showing us that we are going through a two thousand season period of hardship. The strongest point that he unfolds is his opening. That we are not a people of yesterday is a strong theme."

"We are not. We have been here many seasons."

"Yes, we are a people who are virtually timeless in our existence."

"That is sensual."

Kira laughed. She sometimes couldn't understand Imbe. But she knew that his ways moved her to imagine.

"Sensual?"

"Yes, sensual. The way of our people is so rooted in spirit, it becomes sensual in a way that is not perverted."

"I've never thought of it that way."

"Yes, you have, you just don't let it surface. Take you for example." Imbe turned the book over and placed it on the sand, next to a group of pink seashells. "You are a woman of yesterday, a force that stretches across the expanse of time. The way you move is filled with history. The way you talk is laced with knowledge of the past. When you look at me, I feel my loins tense in a way that makes me want to moan. You are a sister of a different season in our lives, even as you are here in this season, moving me, making me feel like a man, giving me the opportunity to love you with a depth you could never imagine. You are history, history is sensual, you are sensual."

Kira sat up and shifted uneasily. She placed her hands on each side of her and let her fingers shape the sand. A flicker of light from the cave caught her eye. The sky continued to dim, leaving streaks of orange, red and indigo across the horizon. She looked at the sky, then looked at the cave and knew she wanted to go inside with Imbe. But he would not be rushed. He wanted to savor her essence. He wanted the tantric moment to last for as long as possible. He wanted to make love to Kira through words, slight touches, glances and conversation. He wanted to know her from a place of spirit...that place that allowed for sexual pleasure without intercourse. Yes, he wanted that too. But he wanted to feel the intensity of her pure love. He wanted to build to a point of inescapable intensity.

"The sun is going down. Are we going inside for dinner?" Kira was ready to be touched. She wanted Imbe's touch.

"Sure. We can light a few more candles and prepare for the night. I do hope you brought something delicious. I don't want to have to go fishing for our dinner tonight," he chuckled.

"No. You won't have to do that," she smiled. "I made a great meal. Fresh salmon with a vegetable medley. I placed a tea light under it to keep it warm."

"Are you always this prepared?"

"Always."

"I like that. Let's go inside."

Imbe gently took her hand and led her toward the cave. They stopped for a moment to watch the sun lead the procession of light to the other side of the world. Kira, Imbe and the sun walked together into another time. Imbe cradled Kira into his shoulder. They allowed the evening to come, at its own pace, in its own time and watched as the sun winked its final wink for the day. They walked on toward the cave. The tide moved away, heading off to its slumber. It bid them goodnight as the last splash of the ocean touched their feet. It was wet.

The cave was warm and bright with candles of every color and scent along every ledge and in every corner of the floor. Shadows danced about threatening to possess Kira and Imbe, wanting to rouse them to dance, to feel the heat as they felt it...to live in a world untouched but touched by everything. The shadows wanted to play, but it was not their evening. It was Kira and Imbe's time. Their moment. The shadows danced on, unrelenting, untouched but touched by the presence of the two.

"Would you like some wine?" Imbe asked.

"I don't drink."

"No, no, my dear, wine is not drink. Wine is the blood of the land, the essence of nature. It is the grape transformed. Wine should never be thought of as drink. Only those who bastardize it call it drink. But those of us who make it with our hands, and nurture it in the coolness of time, know it is life."

Kira looked at Imbe intensely.

"Wine," he continued, "is pure soul. It is the embodiment of everything earth and ether. Untainted wine does not make you drunk. It raises your level of awareness and opens your spiritual center. It allows you to fly free. Wine is sex without boundaries in its purest form."

Kira continued to stare at Imbe. His broad shoulders began to undulate, seemingly without his permission. Her body began to soften, in preparation for what she felt should come. Imbe was unmoved by her eyes almost closing, as though she felt him entering her with a warmth that set her flesh on fire. He could not deny it. He did enter her. As he sat across from her, pouring a glass of wine for her, he entered her. He entered her deep and long, through the dancing lights, through the hot air, through the echoes from his voice that bounced off the cave walls. He entered her across oceans of time, into the place she was before Cuba, into that place she was before her birth. She sighed a hot sigh.

"Take this wine into you, Kira. I made it with my hands."

He handed her a glass. She reached for it. As she took it, she felt his fingers lightly touch her hand. She backed away slightly, feeling the charge from his body.

"What's wrong?" he asked.

"Nothing, it's just..."

"It's just what?"

"There is such a strong energy in you. I felt it in your hands.

You would think I've never touched you before."

Imbe let out a hearty laugh that journeyed through the cave, bouncing about on every wall within.

"We've never touched in this way before, with patience."

"What do you mean?"

"We've kissed. But always with a wanton passion that was impatient and all too ready to jump into sex. "

"What's wrong with sex?" she giggled.

"Nothing. Taste the wine."

Kira put the glass to her lips and let the smooth taste wash over her tongue. She bit her bottom lip, realizing how glorious wine was, when done right...no preservatives and filled with love.

"How is it?"

"Delicious. It is potent. It reaches inside and warms me, without intruding."

"Yes. You just made love."

Imbe leaned forward to kiss her. He gently tasted the remnants of the wine she'd drank. He then leaned back.

"And now, we've made love."

Kira took another sip of the wine, then kissed Imbe. The kisses were different. There was a deep wanting that awakened her imagination. She wanted to make love to Imbe, but she also wanted their intimate moment, wrapped around the essence of the wine, to last. She was experiencing a new level of sexuality and eroticism that was bordering on explosive. She sipped more wine.

"Are we ready?"

Kira blushed not knowing what to expect. Imbe knew what she was thinking and decided to rescue her from her uncertainty.

"The fish? Are you ready to eat now?"

Her eyes widened and she began to fumble around for the

plates. After preparing the food, she placed the plates in front of them and refilled their glasses with wine.

"Where are the forks and knives?" Imbe asked curiously.

"Today, we eat in the old way. With our hands. I will feed you."

Imbe was surprised, but up for the challenge. He'd never been fed by a woman before, except as a child by his mother. And certainly not by her hands.

"Touching your food connects you with the energy within."

Imbe felt the tables turn.

Kira picked a piece of the fish from the bone and lifted it slowly to Imbe's mouth. He opened to take in the food and felt as Kira gently placed the fish in his mouth and her warm fingers pulled out from between his lips. Electricity ran through his body. He was tempted to hold her fingers in place by gently sucking them. But he let her go. She reached for a piece of spinach. Before he could finish chewing the fish, she was placing the spinach in his mouth. Her fingers had a life of their own. They spoke to him. He could feel that they too wanted him, in their own way. Kira felt his tongue twirl around her fingers as he licked every trace of seasoned moisture from her fingers.

She ate a few bites of food and sipped some wine. A bird flew inside and perched on a high wall. Its wings were blue and green; its underbody was a golden brown. It was a tiny thing, little larger than a finch. They each admired the bird as it admired their food. Kira reached up to share some fish with it. Unafraid, it jumped down and took the fish from her hands, then flew away.

"You are good with animals. Have you always been that way?"

"Actually no. Never. That was strangely the first time anything like that has ever happened to me."

"You are the first time anything like this has happened to me," he responded.

Kira smiled and picked up a piece of mango.

"Tell me what you were like when you were a boy," Kira asked inquisitively as she munched on the mango slice.

"Why do you want to know that?"

"I want to know everything about you."

Imbe curiously looked at Kira, one eyebrow raised. A heavy sigh emanated from him.

"I was a boy who dreamed he was a man. And that man dreamed he would someday have a boy like me."

"I don't understand," she asked.

"I saw myself in every aspect of my future. I saw me in the child I believe I will some day have. Strange, I know. But I saw myself as a man. I'm sure it is not the kind of thing most boys dream about. It wasn't a dream I wanted to have. It just came to me nightly. In the dream, I dreamt. Odd, huh?"

"Yes, very odd. So you dreamt you were a man, who dreamt he had a son?"

"Yes, crazy, I know."

"Odd, but not crazy. It's an interesting dream for a child."

"There is more. In my dreams, I saw the woman I would have my son with."

The silence between them filled the air. Sounds of the ocean interrupted the silence. Water beat against rocks. Kira's heart beat, but not in her chest. It beat in that place where life was born. She wanted to be reborn through Imbe. She wanted him to plant within her the seed of a life she'd never forget. She wanted the magic that lived inside him.

"Would you like more wine?" Kira asked uneasily.

"I want more you," Imbe said as he lay back on the sand in the cave.

Kira's hair fell forward as she crawled closer to Imbe. She straddled him as he watched her every move. He never took his eyes off her. She bent down close to him, but did not kiss him. His breath smelled like mangos, fresh and sweet. He touched her raven black hair and twirled her curls around and between his fingers. Her brown skin became deeper brown in the candlelit space. She heard him moan as he closed his eyes for a moment. He touched her face then looked at her.

"You are the most beautiful woman I've ever seen."

"Oh, stop it. I'm sure you've seen many beautiful women in your day."

"Yes, beautiful on the outside. But your beauty is complete. Your outer beauty is astounding. Your inner peace and kindness is amazing. And your mind," he sighed. "Your mind has made love to me a thousand times over."

She felt him moving beneath her. But not his hips, just where she sat, on his manhood. What was once at ease, was now paying closer attention to her presence.

"I feel you."

"You made it happen," he responded.

"How do I know I made it happen? Maybe you just…"

He took her by the shoulders, pulled her to him and began to kiss her in a way that stopped her heart. There was no more sound. The wind stopped, the shadows froze, the water was silent and the floor was no longer beneath them. Everything disappeared and it was just them. Kira felt his hardness throbbing between her legs, rubbing against her panties that were now moist. Imbe wanted the cotton to dissolve from between them. But it didn't. It kept their passions at bay. Her sweet scent began to fill the cave.

"You smell sweet," he said.

Kira kissed his neck and slowly moved down to his chest. She hunched her shoulders, unwilling to move for fear of no longer feeling his throb beneath her. She lifted her dress higher to feel more of his flesh against her skin.

"Take off your shirt." Imbe obeyed.

His body was entrancing. He rippled as he moved beneath her, pulling each arm out of his shirt. He tossed it aside, causing the candles to move with the light breeze from his shirt being thrown.

"Do you want to read to me now?" Kira asked.

"I want to read you," he said. "I want to begin with each letter on your body. Your nipples are *L*. Your navel is *O*. Your lips are *V*. And your sensual glory that throbs in time with me is *E*. Every inch of you is *L-O-V-E*. Love. Your movements are the words I read. And us, together, is the story I want to tell you. Yes, Kira, I want to read to you. I want to read you our life together. It is a timeless tale of two people, in love. I want to tell you of their adventures together. I want you to hear the action and suspense of places they've been and the things they've seen, together."

Imbe squeezed her hips into him. His hardness pressed against her firmly.

"Yes, Imbe. Read me our story," she moaned.

"Once upon a time, in a land far far away, and long long ago, there was a couple. They met each other in a past life, but centuries later, didn't recognize each other when they returned."

Kira lifted her tank top over her head and pulled it off.

"They met in a small village one day," he continued. "They felt something familiar, but because they were trained in the ways of their new world, they had forgotten the ways of their old world, and about the power of spirit connection. They'd forgotten how to connect through mind. They continued through their lives, always eyeing each other askance, but never speaking beyond hello. The attraction was a fierce one. It overpowered them, but they were afraid."

She placed her top across his nose. He inhaled the scent of her, mixed with gardenias and lavender...and a touch of verbena. He grabbed the top and pulled it closer, to inhale deeper. He placed it next to her glass of wine which was nearby.

"Why were they afraid?"

"Because they were not one with that which created them... the All. So they could not remember who they were and why the connection was so strong. So they tried to avoid it."

"So what happened?" She picked up her wine and took a sip. Imbe lightly thrust his hips up beneath her, reminding her of his desires.

"They grew."

"They grew? What do you mean?"

"They began to grow in ways they couldn't imagine. As the years went by, they began to see the truth. Memories of experiences they never had came to them in dreams. They both began to feel a past that felt familiar but was still unfamiliar in many ways."

"Did they ever realize what the connection was?" Kira asked while tracing her name in Imbe's chest.

"Yes, but very late in their lives. It was as though they were lost in the sea of stars, flying to and fro, unable to find what they didn't know they were looking for."

Kira looked at him quizzically.

"Let me explain. Haven't you ever had a feeling you were looking for something vastly important, but you didn't know what it was? Like you knew there was something great for your life, waiting off in the horizon, but you just didn't know exactly what it was?"

Kira's eyes lit up. "Yes, that has happened to me. And

somehow, even though you don't know what it is, you distinctly know when you don't have it."

"Exactly!" he responded excitedly.

"Please, continue."

"Well, one day, it happened. And even when it happened, they still didn't really know that that was it. They had found each other. But they still played the silly courting games of the world, not giving in fully to what they both knew."

"Which was what?"

"They were made for each other and had promised themselves to each other for thousands of years. They knew long ago that they would spend many incarnations together, and vowed always to find each other, no matter how difficult the journey."

Kira outlined his eyebrows with her finger. They were the most incredible eyebrows she'd ever seen on a man. They were majestic and strong. They regally accented his face. She ran her finger down between his eyebrows to his nose and then across his lips. He opened his mouth to suck her finger. She pulled back swiftly. He grabbed her and placed her finger in his mouth. Then he quickly sat up and took one of her breasts into his mouth.

"How long have they been searching and finding each other?" she asked in pleasured gasps.

He sucked gently, one, then the other, watching her head fall back and her mouth open. "I don't know. But as the story goes, they hope to always find each other, no matter how many ages go by."

Imbe turned her onto her back, onto the waiting blanket, and cradled himself between her legs. He moved his tongue around her nipples and down to her stomach. As he moved closer to her life force, to the place where villages and worlds were created, her scent became stronger. It made Imbe melt away into a world where they were one. She smelled like coconut water. It was the strangest thing to him. But it was the distinct smell of coconut water. His desire to drink her essence was overwhelming. He placed his nose on her bright yellow panties. The cotton was sheer. She was ripe and ready to be taken to the moon and beyond. He wanted to go slow, but it had been too long. It had been easily over a thousand years since he'd been with her. He remembered what she couldn't. The memories flooded in one night as the cool breeze from the ocean blew through his home on the beach. On the wind traveled his lifetimes. They were many, all filled with adventure and wonder...all filled with Kira. He saw her just as clearly as he saw the full moon that night. He knew he would not let her get away. There was no denying it any longer. She was the one he had been searching for. She was the one he had lost over the vast expanse of time. He would not let her go. He would hold on to her until their current journey was over and he had to search again. He would never stop searching. Until then, he would not leave her. He belonged to her and he knew it. He liked it that way. She rubbed her hands across his chest and again kissed his neck.

"Kira, do you believe that two people can be made for each other?"

"Yes. " She closed her eyes and lay back.

He looked at her breasts as the many shadows played across her body. They too wanted to touch her. They knew what he knew. Her soul was beautiful.

"I want to be with you, Imbe."

He took her skirt between his fingers and pulled it down, brushing her legs as he went. Her body was a work of art. An image of it was not worthy to touch the tainted walls of even the most famous museum. She was filled with the most exquisite flaws that made her all the more flawless. A cut on her right leg. It looked as though something had gone through it and it was never stitched. Maybe a stick or piece of glass. He kissed it. A scrape on her left shin. Maybe running through the woods as a child she scratched herself on a twig. Or her pet cat, Night, who thought he was only playing with her, took a swing at her. A deep scar next to her navel. A fall maybe. He kissed each one. She was filled with the most beautiful flaws. Each one was a piece of her life. The ones invisible to him, he knew, were the deepest scars. Those were the ones that traversed time and followed her to Cuba. He wanted to know her stories and life while she was away from him.

"You're amazing," he said as he bent low over her, touching his cheek to her cheek. He touched his lips to her lips. He hovered, his mouth over hers, unmoved. He wanted to breathe with her, breathe for her, let her breathe for him. He wanted her breath of life to move through him and transform him, make him reborn. She exhaled into him, he inhaled her. It was all he could take.

Their bodies intertwined. Their shadows intertwined. They began to move about the walls in syncopated strokes. The bird flew back in. It watched the shadows on the wall move in heat. The walls began to sweat. The shadows moaned and scratched and cried out with joy. Echoes filled the space. The bird chirped. But the shadows did not hear. The echoes threatened to extinguish the candles. The candles threatened to go supernova.

The air was hotter. The shadows began to steam. With each stroke, the shadows echoed a love to stop time. Kira and Imbe were in love. And everything around them knew it. The walls would carry their story for all time.

Their climaxes permeated the air, out through to the beach, into the ocean and across the sea. In a thousand years, they would hear their own voices crying out to them to remember. It would traverse the universe, and at the right moment, they would each hear their echoes of love. They would stop to listen, think it was a couple down by the beach, but it would be them, reminding each other to wake up, meet again.

Tears ran down Kira's cheeks. She looked at Imbe. Sweat lightly moistened his face. His breathing was heavy. He looked happy.

"Nice to meet you again," Kira said.

Imbe pulled her close.

"Glad to have finally found you," he said.

VELVET

Fiona Zedde

This place was nothing like high school. The people were different. They had sex, they drank; some, Sara heard, even had HIV. She walked around in a daze, soaking it all in, looking, she knew, as naïve as she felt with her big eyes and exclamations of "Really?" or "No way." Her roommate, Raven, sat with her in the cafeteria, elbow pressed to Sara's at the long table in the high-ceilinged room ripe with the smell of D-grade meatloaf, watery mashed potatoes, and the strangely colored peach cobbler.

Most of the older students walked in then out of the cafeteria, carrying away plastic-wrapped sandwiches and small containers of juice, while the newest ones sat captive to their meal plans and limited social opportunities, staring down at the brown and white mess on the chipped canvas of their dinner plates. To Sara's inexperienced eyes, the older students all looked so sophisticated. Never mind that most wore ragged jeans and oversized flannel shirts, with their hair long and stringy to their waists or blooming around their heads in intimidating Afros.

And that was just the boys. The girls, or women, held Sara in thrall. She couldn't quite look at them, they all seemed too bright, too beautiful, too confident. There was one girl who she did look at, though. Raven said that the girl's name was Merille Thompson. She was a fourth-year physics major with glass green eyes glowing against her cocoa-bean skin and a head full of dark blonde curls.

Now, when Merille caught her staring, Sara quickly looked away but not before she saw the smile and quick wink. She blushed, glad that the girl wouldn't see the color through her teak skin, and looked down at her dinner tray. Beyond the glass doors of the cafeteria, the sun slowly sank behind the trees. From the corner of her eye, Sara could see how the falling sun haloed Merille, making her appear angelic and unattainable.

"Stop being so obvious," Raven said, looking down at her own tray. Today, her chemically straightened hair was braided back over her scalp like tiny fields of grain. Small wooden beads clacked quietly at the end of each braid just above her shoulders.

She was straight, but fancied herself able to give advice because of the nearly six-month gap in their ages—and the fact that she had a boyfriend in Tampa only fifty miles away who made her the happiest freshman Sara had ever seen.

"Shut up," Sara said, a helpless whine in her voice. "I'm not being obvious."

"Then why did she just wink at you?"

"She just had something in her eye."

Raven snorted then choked on the toxic meatloaf. A piece of it flew out of her nose and bounced off the tray. With a faint coating of slime on it, the meat actually looked more appetizing than the original version on her plate. Sara said as much and they both looked at the piece of meat.

"Gross."

The girls looked at each other and laughed. They already loved their new school, but not because of the food.

"We'll have more interesting things to eat at the party this weekend."

Sara looked up at the low, resonant words and almost died. Merille stood quietly next to their table, her long brown hand extended. A piece of paper, bright pink with black ink scrawled across it, dangled from her hand announcing a party later that week. When Sara didn't lift her hand to take the flyer, the older girl slid it onto the table next to her tray. Sara blinked when the clear gaze caught hers. There was destruction in those eyes, she thought stupidly. And a chance to be reborn.

"Hi, I'm Rille," she said. "Both of you are invited to come."

Her voice was a husky rasp. Somehow Sara hadn't thought anything else could possibly make the girl more appealing. Obviously, she was wrong. Sara swallowed.

"Thank you," she mumbled.

Rille smiled. "You're welcome. I hope to see you there."

"Are you going?" Raven asked after Rille went back to her table of friends and out of earshot.

Sara swallowed again, still staring at the paper.

"Of course you're going." Raven rolled her eyes, realizing she'd just asked the most ridiculous question on earth. "Be careful."

The party was in three days in a part of the campus where Sara hadn't been, Third Court, ruling place of third and fourth years and a few giddy second years. Would she be the only first year at this party? Sara didn't know what she wanted to do first—hyperventilate at her ridiculous luck, or back out, not bothering to show up at that party with Rille and her friends. She wasn't quite sure if she was ready to play with the big girls.

"I don't think there's anything to be careful of," she said, trying to convince herself.

Already she'd heard the fantastical rumors about all sorts of things that the upperclassmen indulged in on the campus. Vreeland College was what many called a "hippie school," a place of free love, drug experimentation, and a reckless disregard for consequences. Sara, fresh from her parents' house and a high school she gleefully abandoned with her virginity intact, wasn't sure if she was ready for any of this freedom. She folded up the neon invitation and dropped it in her pocket.

The days between the issued invitation and the party crawled slowly past. Sara sat in her philosophy class—the first one she'd ever taken in her life—and thought about the abstraction of Rille, the certainty of her presence at that party on Friday night, and the shiver down her spine at the thought of what would happen there.

All five windows of the room were open to let in the fresh burn of the early morning Florida sunshine. Light reflected off the bald head of Professor D. J. Holloran as he perched on the desk in front of the room, looking more like a TV version of an Irish thug than a philosopher.

"If you can't think logically, this isn't the class for you." His mouth twisted into a charming smile that invited the class to share some conspiracy. "I see nineteen people in here. No offense taken if some of you walk out of here right now. I don't mind you wasting my time today, it's the first week of classes, but don't come here next week if you don't want to be challenged." He waited to see if anyone would leave. When the entire class seemed bent on staying put, he hopped off the desk and went to the chalkboard. "Great, now let's take a look at our reading list."

Sara studied the syllabus and the list of unfamiliar names—Voltaire, Kant, De Beauvoir, Fanon—and wondered dimly how they would prepare her for the world here at Vreeland College, for the world beyond its terra-cotta walls, or even for Rille. But maybe she was asking too much of one class.

"So what are you going to wear?"

Despite her boyfriend's eagerness to see her, Raven stayed in school past her last class on Thursday morning to prep Sara for her first college party.

"I don't know," Sara said. "Jeans. Nothing serious."

"What do you mean? You need to wear something fun and sexy so she can't miss you."

"I thought you wanted her to miss me, pass me altogether in favor of other young virgins to debauch?"

"Don't be a smartass." Raven propped an elbow on her duffle bag—already packed for her weekly booty call to Tampa—and looked Sara over carefully. "You should wear something pretty. Maybe some velvet?"

"What?"

But in the end, Sara took Raven's advice and wore red velvet, a quintessential party dress, with spaghetti straps and a bodice fitted over her breasts and belly then flared out in an A-line to make the most of her thick hips and thighs. Sara arranged her straight-permed hair into a French twist, fastening it with red-beaded crystal clips and slipped on black high-heeled pumps she'd had for years but never had an occasion to wear.

Her feet felt strange in the shoes, squeezed tight but sexy in a way she'd never known before.

"You look hot. Very fresh meat." Raven's smile slowly faded until she watched Sara with grave eyes. Finally, she turned away and grabbed her bag. "My work here is done. See you Monday. And take care of yourself."

"That's it?" Sara turned to her new friend, hyperconscious

of the way the stilettos elongated her legs under the silk-lined velvet while propping her bottom up and out.

"Sure. What else do you want me to say?"

The truth was that Sara wanted company at the party. Raven was the only person she knew on the Vreeland campus, and she often felt out of place among these people who were largely the opposite of chic, but still possessed their own sophisticated mystique.

"Nothing," Sara finally said with the tiniest pout. "Tell Kevin I said hello."

Even though she had never met Raven's boyfriend, the two strangers had often ended up talking to each other on the phone while Raven dashed out of the shower or ran up the stairs to their dorm from a late class.

"Definitely." Raven quickly hugged her and breezed out of their shared room.

It was after ten, too late for anything good to be on TV, but far too early to go to a party that started at nine. Or at least that's what Raven said. Sara waited until eleven o'clock on the dot to leave her room and walk to the other set of dorms across the courtyard. A cool Florida breeze off the nearby ocean brushed against her cheeks and stirred tendrils of her hair.

Was she really going to do this?

Sara's footsteps slowed, but they didn't stop.

Her parents wouldn't approve. Definitely not her homophobic friends from high school who she'd abandoned after making the decision to come to Vreeland. Yes, the school was a place to indulge in all the excesses she'd heard about but felt too afraid to try—mushrooms, weed, alcohol, sex, skinny-dipping in the ocean under indifferent stars. But the campus also had one of the largest percentages of gay students of all the schools she'd been interested in. When Vreeland had said yes to her applica-

tion, Sara dismissed all the other universities and their acceptance letters, even Columbia, where her father had hoped she
would enroll.

She wanted to be in a place where she could be herself.

She wanted to be in a place where it was okay to have crushes
on other girls.

Sara drew a deep breath. Finally she had arrived at that
place.

Third Court was one big party. Loud voices raised in laughter,
philosophical disagreement, and general raucousness immediately greeted Sara as she crossed its invisible threshold. Bright
blue Christmas lights decorated the trees in their small courtyard
and twined around the cement-work balconies. Large Japanese
lanterns decorated with flitting dragonflies and cherry blossoms
bobbed gracefully in the breeze while marijuana smoke wove
its way through the air, coming from all sides and slipping into
Sara's hair, dress and nose.

Boys, and girls, watched her walk by, sliding their inquisi-
tive gazes over her body, up her newly long legs and the shifting
heat of her bottom under the dress. She smiled nervously but
kept going. With the neon invitation clutched in her hand, Sara
walked past each glass door on the bottom floor until she realized that 318 meant the top floor, not just the court number.

Before she could knock on the door, it opened, releasing the
scent of more marijuana, and something else, something sweeter
that she'd ever smelled before. The person at the door—it was
hard to tell if she was a he or vice versa—smiled gently at Sara
and tugged her into the room.

If the atmosphere outside was a party, this was a dream.
D'Angelo's "Brown Sugar" wove its smooth, jazzy funk through
the room, rocking into the bodies gathered there; the sleepy eyed
women in flowing skirts; the liquid-limbed boys lying across the

queen-sized bed, passing a pipe back and forth between them; the girls who stood talking around a table filled to overflowing with food. They all seemed to rock gently to the song's beat, mellow and loose.

"Come on in." The stranger's voice was warm and feminine.

"Hey," Sara murmured, shyness suddenly overwhelming her.

Short spiked hair, dark eyes under slashing brows, nutmeg skin: the woman gently rubbed her palms up and down Sara's arms, smiling. "Where did you come from?"

"Um...First Court. I got an invitation." She nervously waved the pink flyer.

"You must be a first year. Are you?"

"Yes." Sara cleared her throat of its squeak. "Yes, I am."

"I thought you were leaving, Devi." An unmistakable, throaty murmur emerged from deep inside the room.

Devi, who still had her hands lightly grasping Sara's arms, didn't look toward the voice.

"I was, and now I'm not," she said.

Looking past Devi, Sara saw Rille in the bed. She wondered how she'd missed her presence before. She sat at the head of the bed, leaning back against a wall draped with a plum purple Om tapestry. A woman smoking her own pipe, a bone-colored antique with silver accents gleaming in the low light, lay across Rille's lap. Thick white smoke hovered over them, growing thinner as it swam toward the rest of the room. The fourth year caught Sara's eye and winked again just like she'd done in the cafeteria that Monday afternoon.

Rille nudged away her girl to slide across the bed and emerge from the slow-moving wave of bodies in the room, a compelling vision in low-rider jeans and a tiny tank top advertising shucked and raw oysters. "I was the one who invited her, not you," she said to Devi.

Sara shifted in Devi's arms, suddenly uncomfortable. Everyone at the party, at least those she could see, was casually dressed in jeans, shorts, or vintage frocks. Nothing approaching the formality of Sara's dress.

"I like your outfit," Rille said. "Red velvet. How appropriate."

"Does that mean we'll get the chance to eat you up, too?" Devi asked.

"If we're lucky," Rille answered for Sara.

Sara blinked at the two girls, watching the game between them like the spectator she was.

"You have to learn to share," Devi said.

"I always share with you, all of a sudden you're complaining?"

Rille linked her fingers with Sara's, while on the other side of her Devi gently held her hand. "You're just in time for spin-the-bottle," Rille said.

The two women guided Sara to the food table with everything sweet her heart could desire—devil's food cake, chocolate-covered strawberries, baklava, and sparkling plum wine. Devi briefly relinquished her hold on Sara to cut herself a slice of cake. Looking at Sara suggestively, she sank her finger deep into the cake and then, after it emerged coated in velvet brown crumbs and sticky chocolate frosting, sucked it clean. Rille watched her antics with a cool smile.

"Don't try so hard, baby. It makes you look the opposite of fuckable."

Soft color washed beneath Devi's cheeks and Sara reached out to squeeze her hand. She glanced at Rille, surprised by her casual cruelty.

"What?" Rille asked as if she'd done nothing more innocuous than blow her nose. "It's true." She turned back toward the other partygoers.

Everyone seemed to be doing his or her own thing, smoking, talking, lingering over the table of edibles. That was until Rille made an announcement, tapping a spoon that had traces of sugar on it against a gigantic glass bong.

"Gather round, one and all. It's time for more festivities to begin." Her gaze swept the room. "Those who want to watch, can. Those who prefer to play, let's play."

A few of the two dozen or so people gathered in the room and arranged themselves in a circle on the floor. At least five chose to stay out of the game, including the girl who had been lying in Rille's lap. She sat back in the bed, still puffing on the pipe with its sticky-sweet smelling smoke, making herself comfortable against the pillows to get a good view of the show. A girl on the floor nearest Sara, with her hair cut close to her pretty head and a wealth of dark skin exposed in very short shorts, sucked her teeth.

"I wish Thalia would take her damn opium pipe somewhere else. She can be such a poser."

But the words tumbled past her lips without any real heat. A few people laughed, but the girl on the bed paid them no attention. As Devi drifted away from them, Rille tugged Sara down on the floor next to her.

"I'm not sure if I'm ready to play this game." Sara had heard of this on television and even whispered about in middle school, but she thought that people in college, especially those at the party, were way past such childish games. Apparently not.

"You have to play." Rille's eyes were heavy-lidded. "I promise you'll have fun."

Devi dropped an empty beer bottle in the center of the circle and dropped herself between a soft-looking boy with pretty, full lips and another butch girl directly opposite Rille and Sara. A boy with a thick Afro leaned over to start the game.

"By the way," Rille said, leaning close. "Gender doesn't matter. Whoever the bottle lands on, that's who you have to kiss." Sara had already figured that part out on her own. "You can decide to kiss here in the circle, or in the semiprivacy of another space in the room, balcony included." Rille grinned, the perfect picture of a charming fourth-year lecher.

Sara sat at Rille's side watching the game, mesmerized. This was what college people did? They spun and kissed, leaning toward each other in the circle, bottoms high in the air, wriggling with pleasure if their kisser was doing it right. No one took the activities away from the circle. When it was Devi's turn to kiss, the boy with long dreads down to the middle of his back and the scent of sandalwood on his skin, neatly cupped Devi's head, sliding his fingers through her short hair and down to the back of her neck. She shuddered when he touched her and they drew back, finally, to catcalls and whistles.

"Very nice."

The D'Angelo CD segued to Johnny Hartman, sinking the room deeper into sensuality with his strong rich voice and words of yearning. When someone lit a joint and passed it around, the game got even slower, with couples taking up the circle to form their own make-out area. The girl next to Rille passed the joint and she took it, holding it between her index finger and thumb like it was something surprising she'd just found. Sara watched her take a hit, drag the smoke slowly into her lungs, her eyes squinting against the sting of smoke. Rille leaned close to Sara, to tell her a secret maybe, pressed her lips to hers, and probed with the quick flick of her tongue, until Sara, caught off guard and still amazed that people did such things in public, opened her mouth.

She coughed and sputtered, the smoke burning behind her face and in her lungs.

"Open. Suck it deep inside," the gravelly voice licked at her ear.

Sara blushed, still coughing, still reeling from the sound of those words so close, and at the feeling they sparked in her body, the electric shock under velvet, the startling zing in her lap.

The people who saw what happened laughed. But the couple in the circle, bored with waiting for their turn at the spinning bottle, earnestly made out, reaching tongues and hands in places where Sara could not see. She blushed again. And this time, Rille laughed. She put the joint to her lips again, inhaled deeply before holding it to Sara's mouth.

"Just one," Rille said, smoke trailing from her nostrils.

Sara inhaled, coughed, pushed the joint away.

"Good girl." Rille kissed her quickly as a reward then passed the weed down the line. "Come on," she said and stood up to lead Sara away from the circle toward something Sara wasn't sure she was ready for but wanted to taste anyway.

"Are you a virgin?" Rille asked with her lips a whisper from hers.

They were out on the balcony now, squeezed in next to another couple already half undressed and moaning into the warm Florida night. The lanterns dipped in the air near them, providing a pseudo light. Light to seduce and smoke by, to say and believe anything by. Sara closed her eyes, convinced suddenly of the magic in the night and in this girl by her side.

"Yes." She felt rather than saw the older girl's smile.

"We can take care of that for you tonight, if you like." Rille's breath teased her lips and Sara felt herself leaning closer to initiate contact.

"I'd like," she murmured.

Sex was a surprise for Sara, but no miracle. Even with the hazy high blown into her by Rille's careless mouth, the promise of fulfillment turned out to be just that. The older girl tried everything on her—tongue, fingers, the firm pressure of her thigh, until finally she found an old dildo with a condom already on it from previous use. Rille stripped it off, looking only half apologetically at Sara as she went quickly inside to rinse the dildo in the sink before putting a fresh rubber on it.

"This will be better," Rille said.

With her jeans discarded and wearing only her skin and the dildo harness, she pulled Sara down on top of her in the couch. Hot delirium of her mouth, hair exhaling the scent of marijuana smoke as she nuzzled Sara's throat, encouraged her to touch, whispered sweet filth in her ear. Rille seized the new territory of Sara's flesh. Opened her for intrusion.

She bled and called out in pain, straddling the green-eyed dream in the semiprivacy of the balcony sofa. The couple next to them came and went. Rille soothed her until she almost forgot that pain, until she found some sort of rhythm with the red velvet shoved up around her waist and down below her breasts and Rille sighing how beautiful she was. On the inside, Sara felt battered.

"That was really nice," Rille said when they were finished.

Sara's thighs quivered from the ache between them. "Nice" wasn't quite the word. Her cheeks warmed with embarrassment as she moved against the sofa to pull down her dress. She bit her lip. But the older girl's eyes glowed in the dark as if she still wanted to devour her. Sara blushed then, feeling somehow special.

"You can stay with me tonight, if you want."

But Sara heard the token offer for what it was. Smoke. She shook her head and adjusted her legs next to Rille on the sofa, trying to take up less space. The older girl patted Sara's still smoothly French-twisted hair and peered around the balcony door to see what was going on inside.

"Go inside," Sara said. "I'll be fine out here."

Rille smiled, gratefully, Sara thought, and left her outside with the lanterns and the faint strains of music and the laughter floating up from the courtyard. Sara didn't know how long she stayed, but the sky was lightening and the party was at its lowest with almost everyone on the bed or on the floor or in the bathroom. She didn't see Rille's bright head anywhere.

So this was college, Sara thought, looking around. The beginning of everything. More laughter rose up and died from people in the courtyard below. No one noticed when she left the party, passing slowly out the door in her crushed red-velvet dress.

Sara's room was silent and dim. After the abundance of the party, it seemed especially lovely now where before she'd only found comfort in it. The display on the answering machine flashed. A message waited. She sat on her bed, carefully arranging the soreness between her legs. Her thighs felt sticky. She was sure there would be more blood. That was what all the books said.

Sara ran a hot bath and sat in the water with her head resting against the tiled wall. Rille's shadow rose up, kneeling again between her thighs, her mouth on Sara's, her body vibrating with want. Sara closed her eyes.

When she opened them again it was fully light and Raven was shaking her shoulder. A shiver raced through her as she shifted in the water. It was cold.

"You need to get out of there."

Raven brought a towel and spread it wide for her to step into. Disoriented, Sara stood and stepped out of the tub. Her roommate dried her unresisting body.

"What time is it?" Her mouth felt sticky as if something old had finally died in it. She shivered again.

"After nine, I think. I called, but you didn't answer the phone."

"I didn't get back from the party until late." Sara registered, dimly, that her roommate should've still been in Tampa over fifty miles away with her boyfriend, not crouched over the tub, worry carved into her forehead.

Raven's touch through the towel was clinical but concerned. She only lightly skimmed over Sara's thighs with the cotton, not drying between them. Sara looked down at her body. The glaring red towel looked too familiar against her skin. She wanted to rip it away from her body. But that wasn't a normal thing to do.

"I think I stayed in the water too long." She cleared her throat to get rid of its croak.

"Yeah, a little."

They both looked at Sara's skin, wrinkled and gray from the soak.

"At least you weren't under it."

"The party wasn't that traumatic," she said, stirring finally. Sara gently pulled away from Raven and from the towel, reaching over the toilet to her small stack of clean towels to get another, a green one this time, and securing it like a sarong around her body.

Raven looked away from Sara to the discarded velvet dress on the floor, the balled up panties. "What did she do to you?"

"Nothing I didn't want."

"Is that really true?"

Was it true? Had she wanted Rille to feast on her like a snack, to peel away her wrapping, gorge herself and leave Sara vulnerable and empty, on the balcony?

"I swear. Yes."

Raven sighed, but said nothing else. Sara looked away from the concern in her friend's face. She was all right. And even if that wasn't completely true, she would be soon. Sara left the bathroom and Raven followed.

"Are you going to see her again?"

The question echoed in Sara's head as, "After tonight, do you think she's interested in you anymore?"

"Yeah, why not?" she murmured. "I think we had a connection. Something."

Raven opened her mouth, dark eyes flashing a familiar fire, but whatever she saw in Sara's face made her sigh instead. Then: "Okay."

ABOUT THE AUTHORS

PRESTON ALLEN is the author of the novel, *All or Nothing,* and the short fiction collection, *Churchboys and Other Sinners.* A recipient of a State of Florida Individual Artist Fellowship in Fiction and the winner of the Sonia H. Stone Prize in Literature, he has published stories in numerous anthologies such as *Miami Noir, Las Vegas Noir, Wanderlust* and *Brown Sugar.* His new novel, *Jesus Boy* (Akashic Books) is due out early in 2010. He teaches writing at Miami-Dade College.

SHANE ALLISON's poems have appeared in *Mississippi Review, Oyster Boy Review, Chiron Review, Absinthe Literary Review* and others. His chapbooks, *Black Fag* and *Cock and Balls,* continue to wreak havoc.

TENILLE BROWN is a Southern writer whose erotica can be found online and in more than twenty anthologies including *Dirty Girls, Rubber Sex, Iridescence, Sex and Candy, J Is for*

Jealousy, *Spanked: Red-Cheeked Erotica*, *Tasting Him* and *The Greenwood Encyclopedia of African American Women Writers*. She keeps a blog at myspace.com/tenillebrown.

ZETTA BROWN is editor in chief of LL Publications. She is the author of *Messalina—Devourer of Men* and several short stories. In 1998, her short story "Black Water" was a regional first-place winner for the National Society of Arts & Letters (NSAL) Award for Short Fiction. She lives in Scotland with her husband.

DEEPBRONZE, whose work has been previously featured in classic anthologies by Zane and Carol Taylor, writes erotic tales of adventure, sexuality and excitement. A Chicago native, she holds advanced degrees in speech and is a college lecturer. She is a mother of two.

JOLIE DU PRE is a full-time article writer, a ghost writer, and an author and editor of erotica. Her erotica has appeared online, in e-book, and in print. She is the editor of *Iridescence: Sensuous Shades of Lesbian Erotica* and *Swing!: Adventures in Swinging by Today's Top Erotica Writers*. She is working on an erotic horror novel and the anthology, *The Cougar Book*. Visit her site at joliedupre.com.

MONICA ELAINE loves a good naughty story. This is a pen name for a well-established novelist with a major fan base. She lives in the Midwest with her daughter.

ASHA FRENCH is a writer and a doctoral student at one of the leading Southern universities. She wants to build a readership for her stories of love and lust.

R. GAY is the editor of *Girl Crush* (Cleis Press).

REGINALD HARRIS is an acclaimed poet and writer, who is the recipient of the Individual Artist Awards for both poetry and fiction from the Maryland State Arts Council. He is responsible for IT Support and public computer training for the Enoch Pratt Free Library. His work has been published in numerous literary magazines and anthologies.

JOLENE HUI's literary fiction has been published in *Tonto Short Stories, Tonto Christmas Stories* and *More Tonto Short Stories*. She's been published by a variety of newspapers, magazines, websites, Cleis Press, Pretty Things Press, Logical-Lust and Alyson Books. She is based in Los Angeles.

SHAKIR RASHAAN broke into the BDSM erotica genre with his debut series, *The Awakening, Book One of The Chronicles of the Nubian Underworld* in March 2009. He is also the author of the novel *Obsession*. He founded Kemi-Ka Publishing to promote African American writers in this genre. He lives in Atlanta, Georgia with his family.

LEONE ROSS, a writer of Jamaican-British heritage, has published two novels, *All the Blood Is Red* and *Orange Laughter*, and her many stories have appeared in the United States, England and Canada. She is working on her third novel.

KWELI WALKER has been a journeywoman electrician for the last twenty-five years. She simply loves to read and write. Also, an artist and designer, she created the cover of *Chocolate Fetish*, a popular Black erotic collection. She lives in Long Beach, California.

GARNELL WALLACE is a freelance writer and native Bahamian who loves using her beautiful and exotic country as the backdrop for her stories. Her writing credits include everything from poetry to romantic erotica. She has written for American and British publications. Visit her at myspace.com/garnellwallace.

ZAJI is a writer and webmaster who lives on the East Coast, but her heart and bloodline belong to the tropics.

FIONA ZEDDE is a transplanted Jamaican currently living and working in Atlanta, Georgia. She is the author of four novels, the Lambda Literary Award finalists *Bliss* and *Every Dark Desire*, as well as *A Taste of Sin* and *Hungry For It,* and the novellas, "Pure Pleasure," "Going Wild," and "Sexual Attraction." Readers and voyeurs can find out more at www.fionazedde.com.

ABOUT
THE EDITOR

COLE RILEY is the writer of several street classics: *Hot Snake Nights, Rough Trade, The Devil to Pay, The Killing Kind, Dark Blood Moon,* and recently, *Harlem Confidential* and *Guilty As Sin.* His erotica and reviews have been featured on several websites and anthologies including *Intimacy* and Maxim Jakubowski's *The Mammoth Book of Best New Erotica.* He lives in New York.